Dark Overlord New Horizon

THE CHILDREN OF THE GODS
BOOK THIRTY-EIGHT

I. T. LUCAS

Dark Overlord New Horizon is a work of fiction! Names, characters, places and incidents are products of the author's imagination or are used fictitiously and are not to be construed as real. Any similarity to actual persons, organizations and/or events is purely coincidental.

Copyright © 2020 by I. T. Lucas

All rights reserved.

No part of this book may be reproduced in any form or by any electronic or mechanical means, including information storage and retrieval systems, without written permission from the author, except for the use of brief quotations in a book review.

Published by Evening Star Press

Jacki

As Jacki escorted Jin to Kalugal's front door, she had a sinking feeling that she was never going to see her bestie or her other new friends again. In the short time that she'd spent with the bunch, they'd become like a family to her, and finding out that most of them were immortal hadn't changed the way she felt about them. They were her teammates, and she was going to miss them.

Thankfully, a feeling wasn't a vision, so it might not come true. Jacki's gut had been wrong about things before. Besides, being left alone with Kalugal was reason enough for the churning in her stomach. The rest was just panic induced, and Jacki refused to let it bring her down.

She'd survived worse, and she was going to survive this as well.

"I hope that Arwel isn't still mad at me." Jin took a deep breath before walking out the door.

"He loves you too much to stay mad."

"I know that he loves me. But that doesn't mean that he's not angry."

During their imprisonment in Kalugal's bunker, Arwel and Jacki had become good friends, and at the beginning, they had even pretended to be a couple. The thing was, Jin must have witnessed some of their pretend flirting through the mental link she'd had to Jacki, and she must have also heard Arwel ranting about her decision to surrender herself to Kalugal.

Perhaps that had created doubts in Jin's mind?

Jacki wrapped her arm around her friend's shoulders. "I won't lie to you. When Rufsur told us that you were going to be traded for Arwel, your guy was majorly pissed, but that was because he was terrified of what Kalugal might do to you. Since nothing bad happened, and you are going back to him unharmed, all is good in Arwel's world."

Jin nodded. "I was scared too. Thank God that Kalugal turned out to be a decent guy. But while that might be true for me, I'm not sure about his intentions for you." She eyed Jacki with concern. "I hate leaving you behind. Without the tether, I can't check up on you." Glancing at Kalugal and Julian, who were standing further down the driveway, Jin leaned to whisper in Jacki's ear. "I don't like it that he demanded that I remove the tether from you. It should have been enough that I removed it from him, and it was also what he and Kian had agreed on."

"I think that it makes perfect sense for Kalugal to ask that," Jacki whispered back. "If you'd kept the tether to me, you could've spied on him through my eyes. If I were in his shoes, I would have done the same." She gave Jin a slight push. "Get out of here and go to your boyfriend. Everything is going to be okay."

Jin pulled her into a tight embrace. "See you soon."

"I hope so. Give Arwel a kiss for me. On the cheek, of course." Jacki winked. "The other kind of kisses are all yours."

"I can't wait."

"Then go." She pushed Jin away. "I'll be fine."

Thankfully, empathy wasn't one of Jin's paranormal talents, so she bought the lie and the fake smile that Jacki had plastered on her face.

Watching her friend walk down Kalugal's driveway, Jacki didn't feel fine.

She was scared.

When Jin reached Kalugal, she pointed a finger at him. "Be good to her."

"Don't worry. I'll treat her like a visiting dignitary."

Taking a last glance at her friend, Jacki turned around and walked back in. With a sigh, she sat at the dining room table and reached for a piece of toast. Perhaps chewing on it would relieve the churning in her stomach.

So much for thinking of herself as tough, resourceful, and fearless. Except, there was a limit to how much she could take in such a short time.

Jacki felt as if she was staring down a tunnel, and it seemed that with each step she was tumbling deeper into an alternate reality.

The thing was, she knew precisely what had gotten her to where she was now. She'd been having visions her entire life, but the first tumble down the rabbit hole had started with one particular vision, which in hindsight, she regretted not keeping to herself.

As soon as she'd seen the old clunker that her friend Allison had gotten, the vision had hit Jacki hard. The car was going to break down, and Allison was going to end up in a ditch with multiple fractures and spend the next six months in rehabilitation.

Naturally, Allison had dismissed Jacki's vision as nonsense and had taken the clunker on a road trip to California. Jacki's prediction had come true, and a week after Allison's accident, she'd been contacted by Marisol, who had offered her a job in the paranormal talents' division.

Apparently, during her phone calls to Allison, Jacki had mentioned the words visions and predictions, and the bots had picked up on the trigger words, flagging her as a potential paranormal talent. When her prediction about Allison's accident had come true, her talent had been confirmed.

Still, all of that had been small potatoes compared to what happened next.

Meeting Jin in the program and foreseeing her rescue was the reason Jacki was sitting in the dining room of the fanciest house she'd ever seen, and until a few minutes ago, staring at the face of the most gorgeous, arrogant, sexy man ever born.

Correction.

Not a man, an immortal.

And not just any immortal, one of the two most powerful immortals on the planet.

Damn.

Up until three days ago, she hadn't known that immortals even existed, or that the people who'd helped her escape from the program weren't human.

Her biggest fear was that the knowledge could mean the end of her.

Humans were not supposed to know that immortals had been living among them since the beginning of civilization. If not for her immunity to mind manipulation, they could've erased the memory from her head like they did with all the other humans who had the misfortune of finding out about them. But there was no way to erase Jacki's memories, and she was stuck with what she'd learned.

Even if Kalugal released her in exchange for what Kian had promised him, she would never be free again. The way Jacki saw it, there were three possible outcomes.

One was being Kalugal's prisoner for the rest of her natural life, the other was the same fate at Kian's hands, and the third one was her death.

Was she being overly dramatic? Fatalistic?

Probably.

Jacki doubted that Kian and her new friends would kill her, but she was quite certain that she would never be allowed to go back to her old life.

There was also a fourth possibility.

Kalugal could fall in love with her, and they could live happily ever after.

Right. Talk about fairytales and fantasies.

A man like him might want her in his bed for a night or two, but no more than that.

Except, Jacki was not going to be his or anyone else's plaything, not even to save her life.

For her, it always had been and always would be all or nothing.

Kalugal

"Welcome back, my friend." Kalugal pulled Rufsur into a one-armed embrace and clapped him on the back. "How was your stay with my cousin's people?"

"For the most part, uneventful." Rufsur dug a key out of his pocket and leaned down to open the lock on his leg restraints.

"They gave you the key?" As Kalugal looked down at the chain connecting Rufsur's ankle cuffs, he wondered whether they were the same ones that Phinas had put on Arwel.

"The only reason they did that was so I couldn't run. If I had stopped to open the lock, that would have achieved the same result. They wanted Jin to reach their side before I reached ours." Rufsur tossed the chain aside and straightened up.

"Come, Jacki is waiting for us in the dining room." Kalugal turned and started walking.

Rufsur followed. "She is still here?"

Kalugal arched a brow. "Where else would she be?"

"I thought that you'd already talked to your mother and released Jacki."

He stopped and turned to his lieutenant. "Didn't they tell you about what happened with Jin?"

"Only that the exchange was delayed because she didn't feel well." Rufsur cast Kalugal a regretful look. "You must have been disappointed to find out that she was not an immortal and therefore not a clanswoman. That ruined your plans to forge an alliance with the clan by marrying the spy."

It had been a contingency Kalugal had come up with in case Jin couldn't remove the damn tether she'd attached to him. If that had been the case, he would have needed to keep her by his side, and the only way he could have done so without starting a war with the clan was a political marriage. The alliance with Kian had been a secondary consideration. Luckily for them both, Jin was able to demonstrate that the tether was gone.

The problem was that he wasn't a hundred percent sure that it was.

"Those plans were irrelevant anyway. Jin is in love with Arwel."

"So I heard. Is she all better now? She looked fine to me when I passed by her and that guy. Who was he?"

"That was one of the clan's doctors. Jin got sick all over the gazebo floor before she could demonstrate the tether's removal, and then she passed out. I couldn't let her go, so they sent the doctor. After he gave her an antibiotic shot, she recovered almost immediately."

"And then she proved to you that the tether was gone?"

Kalugal shrugged and resumed walking. "I'm still not convinced that it is."

"So why did you let her go?" Rufsur followed.

"I didn't have a choice. It was either that or start a war with the clan."

"But you felt something, right?"

Kalugal nodded. "I did. But it might have been a placebo effect. I might have felt it because I expected to feel it. I compelled Jin to tell me the truth, but that's not foolproof either. She might have believed that the tether was gone while some of it still remained, or she might be able to re-establish the connection remotely. I've just realized that I didn't ask her about that."

"Do you mean that you forgot to compel her to answer that truthfully?"

"It didn't occur to me to ask about it at all. I've made a mistake, and it might cost me dearly."

"What are you going to do?"

"I don't know. I guess I'll have to trust her that it's gone."

Rufsur arched a brow. "That's not like you."

His friend knew him well. Kalugal had an idea of how to prove the tether's removal, but he couldn't tell Rufsur about it because it would defeat the purpose.

His plan was to pretend that he believed the tether wasn't there, do something that would provoke Kian, and then wait for his cousin to react.

As they entered the dining room, Jacki smiled at Rufsur. "We meet again after all."

He grinned and walked up to her. "You are a sight for sore eyes, Miss Jacqueline the Fair." He took her hand and kissed the back of it.

"I like it. You make me sound like a fairytale princess."

Kalugal didn't like it at all, barely stifling the impulse to grab his lieutenant by the throat and toss him across the room.

Fortunately, Jacki pulled her hand out of Rufsur's. "Are you hungry? There is plenty left over, but it's cold. I can take it to the kitchen and warm it up for you." She started to rise.

Kalugal put a hand on her shoulder. "Sit down, Jacki. Shamash can do it. You are my guest." He put a slight emphasis on the *my*.

But Rufsur hadn't been paying attention and pulled out a chair next to Jacki. "I don't mind that it's cold. I'm not a finicky eater like my boss."

Taking his seat at the head of the table, Kalugal glared at Rufsur. "Tell me your impressions from the time you spent with Kian's men."

Rufsur lifted the coffee carafe and poured the cold brew into a cup. "There was a female there as well."

"A female warrior?" Kalugal asked.

"I don't think so. Vivian is the commander's wife, and she's a very pleasant woman. She made sure that the warriors treated me well and that I was made as comfortable as possible given the circumstances. They had me chained to a chair."

Kalugal looked at Jacki. "Do you know her?"

"Vivian is Magnus's wife, and she is not a soldier."

"Is she an immortal?"

Jacki shrugged. "Did you forget that I didn't know anything about immortals until you captured Arwel and me and informed me about Arwel being one? They told me that they were a group of paranormally talented people."

"Point taken." Kalugal turned to Rufsur. "Is Vivian an immortal?"

"I didn't think it was polite to ask, but I assume that she is. Otherwise, what's the point of marrying her? It's just asking for heartache when she gets old and dies."

Kalugal turned back to Jacki. "Does the clan have female warriors?"

She shrugged again. "How the hell would I know? They didn't tell me anything."

Rufsur loaded his plate with eggs. "Before taking me to where I met Vivian, they took me someplace else to search me thoroughly. There was a female there, who I'm sure was a warrior." He lifted his hands and spread them wide. "She had shoulders nearly as broad as mine, but she was still fine to look at, and so was Vivian. If all the clan females are that pretty, then we should start negotiating with your cousin for visitation rights." He glanced at Jacki. "Not for me, but for the others." He winked at her.

She shook her head. "The reasons why I can't date you haven't changed since yesterday. And as you have mentioned earlier, getting involved with a human is asking for heartache." She leaned toward him. "After all, I'm going to get old and die."

Rufsur reached for her hand, but she snatched it away. Undeterred, he smiled suggestively. "I'll take whatever time you're willing to give me."

She let out a breath. "When you stop goofing around and give it some serious thought, I'm sure you'll arrive at the same conclusion I did."

Kalugal really needed to have a talk with the guy and make it clear that Jacki was his. Otherwise, the moment Rufsur discovered that Jacki was a possible Dormant, he would redouble his crude flirting efforts and get twice as bold.

The thing was, Jacki seemed to respond to his lieutenant's unsophisticated approach.

Kalugal had a feeling that Jacki simply didn't know any better because she hadn't met any high-caliber men like him before. All she was familiar with were the clumsy flirtation attempts of uneducated young men, who shared her lowly socioeconomic background.

He hadn't missed her comment about growing up in foster homes. She was a poor girl, with no family and no higher education, and the only things she had going for her were her beauty and her immunity to mind manipulation.

Except, that same ability was an indicator of a strong mind. Perhaps Jacki's lack of education was the result of lack of opportunity, and not the lack of intelligence or the drive to acquire knowledge. If that was the case, he could teach her all she needed to know.

It reminded Kalugal of an old musical he had once seen. *My Fair lady* was a story about a stuck-up professor trying to teach a poor girl to talk and act like a lady.

Had the musical prompted Rufsur to address Jacki as Miss Jacqueline the Fair?

Or was it the other way around, and Rufsur's remark had planted the idea in Kalugal's mind?

Since his lieutenant had probably never watched a musical in his entire immortal life, the second assumption was more likely.

Rufsur had just wanted to impress Jacki with his good manners and fancy talk.

Nevertheless, the idea was sound. Jacki wasn't the perfect companion Kalugal would have wished for, but he might turn her into one yet.

The question was whether she would let him.

Once he executed his plan to verify that the tether was gone, Jacki might never forgive him or allow him anywhere near her, and regrettably, he would not be able to erase the nasty memory from her head either.

Director Simmons

Director Simmons opened the door to his office and motioned for his top recruiter to come in. "Good morning, Marisol."

"Good morning, sir." She walked over to his desk, took a seat in one of the leather chairs facing it, and put her hands on her knees.

"You look lovely."

"Thank you, sir."

"Please call me Edgar. You make me feel like an old man when you address me as sir."

"How about Doctor Simmons? Or Director Simmons?"

"We are friends, Marisol, and we are alone here. Save the titles for when we are in front of the recruits."

"Yes, sir. I mean, Edgar."

"That's better." He smiled and patted her bony back.

He wasn't flirting with the woman, but one of the things he had learned early on in his career was that personal touch always made his subordinates work harder for him.

Maybe if she were better looking and was a little more charming, he would have considered it, but Marisol had the sex appeal of a dull knife, and her personality bordered on sociopathic. Still, the new blonde hair softened her harsh features and made her look a little more feminine, which might help her with luring male talents into joining the program.

Sitting on the chair across from his recruiter, Edgar leaned toward her and steepled his fingers. "Wendy left a very interesting message on my voicemail."

Marisol's eyes widened. "She contacted you? Where is she? Are the others with her?"

He lifted a hand. "Slow down. When she left the message, they were in Big Bear, California, but Wendy must have gotten caught making the call because less than an hour later, there was no one at the address she provided. There was a for rent sign outside the cabin, and the guy that I'd sent to investigate found a cleaning crew preparing it for the next renters. They didn't know who stayed in it before."

"That should be easy to find out."

"Not really. Someone infected the rental records with a computer bug and turned everything into a jumbled mess. Not only that, the recording that Wendy left on my voice mail got erased. I tried to listen to it again, but it was no longer there. We are dealing with professionals, Eleanor."

He rarely called the recruiter by her real name, using it only when they were conspiring to do things that were not approved by the higher-ups.

"Did Wendy say anything else?"

"Yes, and it's more important than the location she provided. Apparently, an organization of paranormally talented people is collecting new members. Somehow, they knew about Jin and came for her. Jacki and Richard jumped on the opportunity to escape, and Wendy joined them so she could report to me and tell me where they were taken. She had to steal someone's phone to do so. Evidently, the organization that took them is not allowing them any more freedoms than we had."

Marisol snorted. "Fools. What did they expect? Some shady paranormal organization that is competing with us is not going to give them better terms or treat them better than we do. We need to stop the weekly leave until we figure out who we are dealing with, or at least beef up security."

Despite her abrasive and mistrustful nature, Eleanor was naive. But she wasn't entirely wrong.

Even though not everything was aboveboard, and not everything that the recruits had been told or promised was the truth, no one could compete with the US government's resources. He had no doubt that the program was leagues better than anything they could expect on the outside.

"We can't stop the outings. Not only are they good for morale, but they are also important for keeping up appearances. Trainees in other programs using this facility get to have days off. We can't treat ours differently. I can, however, increase security. We are already driving them to a different town every week, so the outings are not as predictable as they used to be before the escape."

Marisol's fingers drummed a nervous beat on her knees. "I don't remember much of what happened to me during the time I was gone, but I know that they got the information from me. That whole hotel room with drug paraphernalia was a setup. I've never used drugs, and I would have never gone to a hotel room with some guy I'd just met."

"I know, Marisol. We've been over that, and I don't blame you. It could have happened to anyone."

She looked down at her hands. "I don't know how they found out about me."

"You must have said something to Jin, and she told it to someone. She must have been resistant to compulsion."

Marisol shook her head. "She was so convincing. I can't believe that the girl managed to fool me."

Getting played bugged the hell out of Marisol, but what bugged her even more was that she'd had to change her name and her appearance once again. Her new name was Gina Voldachevsky, and she wasn't happy with it.

"I should start calling you Gina."

"It's confusing to the recruits who know me as Marisol." She touched her blonde curls. "This hair was adjustment enough."

"It looks good on you."

She smiled. "You are a bad liar, Edgar."

He laughed.

She couldn't have been more wrong. There were so many things he was keeping from her while pretending that she was his friend and confidant.

Eleanor, aka Marisol, aka Gina, had no idea that Wendy was his niece.

In fact, Wendy was his grandniece, but the distinction was not important. His sister's daughter was gone, most likely dead from a drug overdose, and his sister had passed away decades ago. He and Wendy were the only family members left.

The other thing Eleanor, aka Marisol, didn't know was that no matter where the missing trainees were hiding, he could find them quite easily. The only reason he hadn't done so already was that finding out who had taken them was more important than finding the trainees themselves.

Unlike Marisol, he was a patient man, and he was waiting for the dust to settle and for everyone to get comfortable and complacent. Not having a large force at his disposal, Edgar needed the recruits as well as those helping them to stop looking over their shoulders before he made his move.

Kian

Eleven in the morning was too early for a drink, but Kian felt like celebrating.

The crisis was over.

Jin and Arwel were on their way to the clan's jet, and they were due to arrive back in Los Angeles in a couple of hours. The village and the keep were no longer in danger, and Turner could go back to the rescue missions that he'd had to postpone while helping Kian manage the near catastrophe.

Kalugal was still a danger to the clan, and he still had Jacki, but by tomorrow morning, that would get resolved as well. Kian was going to put his cousin on the line with his mother, and in return, Kalugal would release Jacki.

The question was how to proceed from there.

The best thing would be to meet face to face and start negotiating a long-term coexistence agreement, but first, he needed to figure a way to protect himself from Kalugal's compulsion.

Dragging Turner with him to every meeting was a possibility, but it was unfair to the guy. Turner was a busy man, with his own hostage rescue operation to run. He helped the clan whenever he could, but there was a limit to how much Kian could ask of him.

"Who wants to join me in a toast?" Kian lifted a bottle of a twenty-one-year-old Suntory Hibiki.

Syssi grimaced. "Shouldn't we do it with champagne? I can have a tiny sip of that."

"You are right." Kian put the bottle down. "I'll have Okidu bring it."

Turner got up and walked over to the cart. "It's too early to celebrate, but I'll have some while we wait for your butler to get the champagne." He took the bottle and examined the label. "I've heard it's excellent."

Kian cast Syssi a sidelong glance. "Do you mind if I have some too?"

"Not at all. Perhaps we should save the champagne for later. Isn't it time we got out of the war room? We can go home and celebrate there."

"I'm expecting a phone call from Kalugal. We can leave after that." Kian turned to Onegus. "How about you? Too early for a drink?"

Leaning back in his chair, the chief had his arms crossed over his chest and a frown furrowing his forehead. He didn't look ready to celebrate just yet. "I'm always game for good whiskey."

"You look worried."

Onegus shrugged. "We are not home free yet. Kalugal is a sneaky bastard, and I wonder what his next move will be. This is not over by a long shot."

"What are you going to do about the Guardians posted around his mansion?" Syssi asked. "He will probably demand that you lift the blockade."

"Not until he releases Jacki. After that, I will no longer have an excuse for it. I will, however, keep tabs on him, just more covertly."

When his phone rang, Kian expected to see Kalugal's contact on the screen, but it was Julian's.

After spending part of the night at Kalugal's home, the doctor had probably picked up a few tidbits of information that he wished to share.

"Hello, Julian. How was your stay at Kalugal's?"

Kian put the phone on the conference table and switched the speaker on.

"Interesting, troubling, disconcerting. He compelled me to tell him about immortal females and how similar or different they are from immortal males. He also got me to reveal that Jacki was a possible Dormant."

"Fuck!" Kian emptied the shot down his throat. "I didn't expect him to do that, but I should have. The bastard took advantage of the situation."

"I didn't tell him anything he could use against the clan."

"I know that. You and Jin couldn't reveal things you didn't know, which was why I didn't stipulate what he was allowed or not allowed to compel you to answer."

Kalugal had told him that he was going to compel Jin because he needed to verify that she hadn't been lying about the tether's removal. He'd also said that he was going to compel Julian to verify that the doctor hadn't been sent to do him and his men harm.

It had occurred to Kian that Kalugal might use the loophole to ask things that were unrelated to those two conditions, but it would have been difficult to start making lists of questions he was allowed to ask and those he wasn't. Given that Jin and Julian couldn't reveal any strategic secrets, Kian had figured there was no need for that.

The one thing he hadn't wanted Kalugal to find out was that Jacki was a possible Dormant, but then he couldn't have stipulated that without giving it away.

"He also compelled Jin to answer his questions," Julian said. "They were mostly about how you found her and how many other Dormants the clan has discovered so far. Jin told him that you found her sister by chance, and that was how you got to her. Luckily, she didn't know the answer to his other questions. She did, however, tell him about the government program we freed her from."

Damn. It wasn't a big deal unless Kalugal figured out the connection between paranormal talents and Dormants. If he did, he might go after the remaining females in the program. Maybe the males as well.

"I need to talk to her and find out exactly what she told him about that. What else did he ask you?"

"How to find Dormants, and how I knew that Ella was my fated mate." Julian let out a breath. "You can't blame him for asking that. Every immortal wants answers to those questions."

"That's true. But now that Kalugal knows Jacki is a possible Dormant, he is not likely to trade her for communication privileges with his mother."

"He might," Syssi said. "Isn't that what we were banking on when Alena posed as Areana for those cosmetics ads? You believed that he would get sentimental and look for her."

Kian shook his head. "My mother believed that, and I humored her. Annani is a romantic and thinks that everyone is motivated by the same things that motivate her. I'm more pragmatic than that. Given a choice, most adult males would choose a chance of having an immortal mate over contact with their mothers."

She arched a brow. "Would you?"

"I would have done anything for you. Even that."

"Kalugal is not in love with Jacki," Turner said. "He might choose Areana."

"Or not," Julian said. "When Jacki hugged me, Kalugal got upset, practically growling at me, but he tried to hide it."

"Maybe he's just easily irritated" Syssi smiled at Kian. "Like someone else I know. After all, you are cousins, and you might share similar traits."

"I don't think so," Julian said. "Kalugal seems much mellower than Kian, and he has better control over his emotions."

The unfavorable comparison grated on Kian's nerves. "He is also more devious, and his morals are questionable. Kalugal might try to come up with a way to have both." He poured himself another shot of whiskey. "I need to find something to hold over him in perpetuity."

"You already have that." Turner handed him his empty glass. "He might give up contact with his mother to keep Jacki, but he wouldn't want anything to happen to her. As far as he knows, you still hold her life in your hands."

Kalugal

"Let me show you to a guest room." Kalugal offered Jacki a hand up.

"I can do that." Rufsur jumped up from his seat.

Kalugal cast him a chilling glance. "I'm going to escort Jacki to her room and continue from there to my office."

Rufsur looked unhappy, but he knew better than to argue when Kalugal used his commander tone. "Yes, sir."

"Am I going back to the bunker?" Jacki ignored his offered hand, getting up without his help.

"Do you want to?"

She shrugged. "It's a nice room."

"The one up here is nicer."

For the past hour, his men had been busy converting the small office adjacent to the master bedroom into a cozy space for Jacki. Hopefully, they were done, but perhaps it was better to inspect the room before bringing her up there.

He put his hand on the small of her back to guide her. "Would you rather spend some time in the library?"

Her eyes brightened. "I would love to. What kind of books do you have in there?"

"All kinds. There is a large selection to choose from, and if none are to your liking, I also have a television in there with every subscription service available."

"Naturally." Her tone was mocking.

"Do you have a problem with that?"

"Not at all. It just makes sense for a rich guy like you to have that."

"I see." He opened the library doors and motioned for her to go ahead of him. "So, your problem is not with the subscription services but with rich people."

Jacki stood at the entrance and gaped.

The library was Kalugal's favorite room in the house. It was two stories high, with an interior staircase that led to a second-floor interior balcony spanning the perimeter of the room, a fireplace, and a wet bar. Only the finest materials had been used in its construction, from the exotic woods used for the paneling and the floors to the marble columns, the leaded-glass windows, and dozens of other small details that he had personally seen to.

"I have no problem with rich people," Jacki murmured as she turned in a circle. "You can leave me here."

Kalugal dipped his head to cover his smile. "Enjoy."

Stepping out, he closed the doors of the library behind him and motioned for Shamash to stand guard. "If Jacki needs me, I'll be in my office."

"Yes, sir." Shamash took a seat in one of the armchairs facing the doors.

Kalugal's office was adjacent to the library and had a door leading directly to it. It was camouflaged as a bookcase from both sides, but the reason for it was purely esthetic. It wasn't meant to provide a secret passage, but Jacki didn't know about it, which would play nicely into his plan.

Taking a seat behind his desk, Kalugal called Kian and swiveled the chair to look out at the garden.

"Hello, Kalugal. How is Rufsur doing?"

"He is well, thank you. And how are Jin and Arwel?"

"Excellent. But I'm not happy about you compelling information out of Jin and Julian."

"Can you blame me? You didn't forbid it, which I took to mean that neither knew anything of tactical importance. My questions were not designed to find out your weaknesses, cousin, only to satisfy my curiosity."

"That's why I'll let it go this time. However, next time you pull something like that without checking with me first, there will be consequences."

"Such as?"

"How would you like to wait another week to talk to your mother?"

Kalugal chuckled even though he wasn't amused. "Are we playing games, Kian? I think we are both too old for that. I've waited many decades to speak to my mother, and I can wait another week. But I'm sure you want your immune back sooner."

"True. But your first conversation with Areana is not going to be the last, and any that follow would depend on the level of your cooperation and show of goodwill."

Kalugal grimaced. "You keep forgetting that I wasn't the one who started this thing. You were the instigator, so stop issuing threats, and let's act like civilized men. When will the first call take place?"

"Tomorrow morning at seven. That's when Areana contacts us every day. When the call comes in, my tech guy will patch you through."

Rubbing his chest, Kalugal swiveled his chair around. "I'm looking forward to it."

"I bet. At seven sharp, have Jacki ready to leave, and the moment you verify that you are indeed talking with your mother, signal to your men to let Jacki go. If she is not out the gate five minutes after the call starts, my guy is going to cut you off."

"How long will I have with my mother?"

"Ten minutes. That's the maximum length of her daily calls. Anything longer than that might endanger her."

"I understand. What about the blockade? I've seen that most of your men are gone, but I bet they are not far away."

"Correct. Once we have Jacki back, I'll call the rest of them off. I assume that after that you plan to relocate and disappear once again."

"We should talk, Kian. Let's turn this unfortunate fiasco into an opportunity to get to know each other better. I still have many questions that you can answer for me."

Kian chuckled. "I'm not going to get anywhere near you or talk to you without my immune on standby."

"Tsk, tsk, cousin. At some point, you will need to start trusting me. As long as we suspect each other's every word, we can't make progress."

"That's true. But I'm a cautious man. As much as I'm curious about you and would like to establish some form of cooperation between us, the safety of my people comes first."

"Same here. I'm sure we will figure something out. Goodbye, cousin. We will talk again tomorrow. But if you come up with a creative idea for how we can meet while guaranteeing each other's safety, don't hesitate to call me beforehand."

"You've got it."

Ending the call, Kalugal put the phone on his desk and swiveled his chair once again to look at his beautiful garden.

It would be a shame to leave it behind, but maybe there would be no need. Kian's tone was softening, and he seemed eager to find a way for them to coexist without animosity.

The question was whether he would still feel this way after the stunt Kalugal was about to pull.

He wished there was another way to test if the tether was gone, but regrettably, there wasn't. To provoke a response from Kian, Kalugal had to step out of his comfort zone and do something that he really wasn't looking forward to.

Jin

"We are almost there." Arwel stroked Jin's hair.

Without opening her eyes, she shifted on his lap and wrapped a lazy arm around his neck. Pulling his head down, she planted a soft kiss on his lips. "Wake me up when we get there."

Ever since running into his arms at the airstrip, Jin had left their safety only to change out of her borrowed clothes and put on her own. It was a shame to leave Alena's beautiful things behind, especially the warm coat, but no one wanted to risk bringing a tracker into the village.

When that had been done, she had crawled onto Arwel's lap and finally allowed herself to sleep.

She'd slept throughout the flight, had woken up for a few minutes when they landed, and then had promptly fallen asleep again in the limo on the way to the village.

"I bet your sister is organizing a welcome party for you," Kri said, reminding Jin that they weren't alone in the limo.

Burrowing deeper into Arwel's chest, Jin tucked her hands between their bodies to keep warm. "I just want to crawl into bed and keep on sleeping."

She was no longer sick, but her body had taken a blow and was now demanding the rest it had been deprived of. Jin was cold even though the driver had turned the heat up, and being cradled in Arwel's arms helped to stave off the shivers, but nothing other than a long sleep in a comfortable bed was going to restore her depleted energy reserves.

"I should take you to Bridget when we get there," Arwel said. "You still look like a ghost."

With a pout, Jin lifted her face to him. "Thanks a lot."

He dipped his head and kissed the tip of her nose. "A most beautiful ghost."

"You're forgiven." She returned her cheek to his chest.

His strong heartbeat and even breathing soon lulled her back to sleep, but it wasn't as deep as it had been before, and thoughts of Jacki managed to filter through the barrier separating her subconscious from her conscious.

"I hope Jacki is okay," she murmured into Arwel's shirt.

"She's fine. Rufsur has a serious crush on her. He'll take care of her."

Jin lifted her head. "Really? I thought that something was kindling between her and Kalugal."

"Nah. Kalugal is too much of a snob to go for a simple girl like Jacki."

Jin felt offended on behalf of her friend. "She isn't simple."

"I didn't mean it like that. You've interacted with him and seen his place. My impression is that he wouldn't settle for any woman who isn't royalty of some sort."

"Yeah, you are probably right." She pushed up in Arwel's arms. "He behaves like he is some freaking prince, so he probably thinks that he deserves a princess."

"He is a goddess's son," Kri pointed out.

"Which he didn't know about until two days ago." Jin waved a hand. "He was a stuck-up snob even before that."

"Maybe it's in his genes?" Michael suggested.

When the limo stopped, Jin thought that they had arrived, but then it started moving again, and the sensation she got was that they were going downward. The windows were opaque, just as Kri had told her they would turn once they got close to the village, but Jin had missed the transition because she'd been asleep.

Damn. That meant that the computer was driving the limo and not the driver, and it made her nervous as hell. The others were immortal and could survive a crash, but she was still a fragile human.

"What happened?" Arwel asked. "I can sense your anxiety. You were fine up until a moment ago."

"Is the computer driving the limo?"

Kri chuckled. "You could say so. But nothing has changed. It's still Okidu who is driving the car."

"I'm confused."

"Okidu is a cyborg," Arwel said. "That's the easiest way to explain it."

"You can't be serious. I've talked with him. He is as real as you and me."

"Trust me. When you pay better attention to him, you'll notice the oddities."

Since Kri and Michael were not laughing, it meant that Arwel wasn't pulling her leg.

"Is that a clan developed technology?"

"I wish. We could use a hundred more of him, but Okidu and his brothers are ancient relics, and we don't know who made them. Your sister seemed fascinated by him, though."

"Mey didn't mention Okidu."

When the limo finally came to a full stop, Jin pushed up to get off Arwel's lap, but he held on to her.

"I'm not letting you go."

"You are not carrying me into the village."

Arwel looked at her with disappointment on his handsome face. "I get it. It's a matter of pride for you." He lifted her and put her on the seat beside him.

Leaning toward him, she whispered in his ear, "When we get home, you can carry me to bed."

Naturally, Kri and Michael had heard her, but they were doing an admirable job pretending they hadn't.

As Okidu opened her door, Jin took a really good look at him but still couldn't see anything that would indicate that he wasn't human. His skin looked real, but maybe a little too nice for a guy who seemed to be in his early fifties.

"Madam." He bowed. "Welcome to the village." He offered her his hand.

Taking it, Jin concentrated on how it felt, but it was warm and squishy like any human hand. Maybe Arwel had been pulling her leg after all?

"Jin!" Mey rushed to her and practically shoved Okidu out of the way. "God, I'm so happy that you are finally here." She crushed Jin to her chest. "I was so worried."

For a long moment, they just stood with their arms wrapped around each other, and then the waterworks started.

"Don't cry," Mey whispered in her ear. "We have an audience."

As Jin lifted her head off her sister's shoulder, the first thing she noticed was a large banner hanging between two of the parking garage's pillars, and the second thing was the group of people standing under it and clapping with happy smiles on their faces.

Callie and Brundar, Amanda and Dalhu, Wonder and Anandur, Syssi and Kian, and Ella, but no Julian because he'd stayed behind.

There were others too. Bridget, who she knew, and other people she didn't know, but they were all smiling and clapping as if she was some homecoming hero.

Wiping the tears away, she pushed out of Mey's arms. "Thank you for the wonderful welcome. I don't know what to say."

Bridget walked up to her. "Amanda wanted to throw a party for you, but I vetoed it. You need to get in bed and rest. This was the compromise." She waved at the banner and then leaned to whisper in Jin's ear. "Go home with your mate and celebrate the start of your new life together. You can thank me later." She winked.

Arwel

As they entered the elevator, Mey leaned and whispered in Arwel's ear, "Everything is ready."

"Thank you. You are the best."

She smiled. "I didn't do it alone. I had a lot of help from my friends."

"Then thank everyone for me."

"Will do."

Thankfully, Jin was busy answering Bridget's questions, so she hadn't paid attention to the whispered exchange. It would have been a shame if she had gotten a whiff of the surprise that he and Mey had worked so hard on keeping a secret from her.

As the elevator doors opened and they stepped out into the pavilion, he wrapped his arm around Jin's waist. "Welcome to the village."

"I'm so excited." She leaned her head on his arm. "I love how green it is."

As the sliding doors opened, a golf cart driven by his roommate pulled up to the entrance, stopping right in front of them. "Welcome home, Jin and Arwel." Ben grinned. A banner with the same message was attached to the golf cart's canopy.

Jumping down, Ben offered Jin his hand. "I'm Ben, Arwel's roommate."

"I hope you are okay with me moving in," Jin said as she shook it.

"Of course." Ben winked. "I'll see you later." He started walking away.

"Wait, aren't you coming with us? There is enough room."

He turned around. "I just brought the ride. I'm meeting a friend in the café." He waved.

"Your chariot, my lady." Arwel offered her a hand up.

Gripping it, she climbed with effort. Jin was still weak but trying not to show it. "I could have walked, but this is fun. We had golf carts in the program, but I only got to ride them a couple of times, and I've never gotten to drive. Is this one yours?"

Arwel sat behind the wheel. "Not mine exclusively, but we can take it out for a spin whenever you like."

"Take Jin home," Bridget commanded.

"Yes, ma'am."

"Aren't you coming?" Jin looked at the doctor and then at her sister.

"Thank you, but I'm going back to the office," Bridget said.

Mey smiled. "I'm heading to the café. Get some rest, and tomorrow, I'll give you the grand tour."

"It's a date."

As Arwel put the golf cart in gear, Jin crossed her arms over her chest. "Something is going on. Everyone wanted to get rid of us as soon as possible. Or was it just me?"

"They all know that you've been through a lot, and they don't want to keep you from resting."

"I must look awful." She ran her fingers through her hair. "I have dark circles under my eyes, and my skin looks gray."

"It's in your head. You look radiant to me."

Jin cast him a lopsided smile. "You're such a sweet liar."

"I mean it." He wrapped his arm around her shoulders. "Your eyes are glowing, your hair is shining, and you look happy."

"I'll take your word for it." She leaned her head on his arm. "This place is gorgeous, and it's so peaceful here. It really is a village."

"I'm glad you like it. But I'm afraid that a city girl like you will get bored here pretty quickly. There isn't much to do, and the only place to hang out and meet friends is in the café." He pointed as they passed by it.

Several people waved, and Jin waved back. "I think that's awesome that everyone knows each other here. I'm actually looking forward to doing nothing. I've had enough excitement to last me a decade."

As they crossed into the other side of the village, Arwel spotted the house with the white and red balloons tied to the porch railing and parked in front of it.

"Your home is lovely." Jin shifted and put her leg down. "And Ben is really sweet for putting up balloons for us."

"Wait." Arwel rushed to her side and lifted her into his arms.

"What are you doing?"

"Carrying you over the threshold."

Jin wound her arms around his neck. "We didn't get married yet, but okay."

Arwel climbed the three steps and stopped at the front door. "Look at the plaque."

Ella had crafted a beautiful one for them, and it was the first hint.

She turned her head. "Jin and Arwel? What about Ben?"

Arwel shifted her weight to free one hand and opened the door. "This is our house. Just yours and mine." He kissed her lips as he stepped over the threshold.

Jin looked at the banner hanging over the kitchen counter, the flower vases, and all the homey touches their friends had brought over.

One of Dalhu's landscapes was hanging over the couch, and a handmade throw was draped over its back. An ice bucket with champagne and two crystal glasses waited for them on the coffee table.

He walked over and sat down with Jin still cradled in his arms. "Nothing to say?"

"I'm speechless. When did all of this happen?"

"I applied for a house for us when we were still in the rental. Mey organized everything else with a lot of help from her friends."

"You mean our friends."

"Yes. Are you happy?"

"Are you kidding me? I'm just stunned. I can't believe we have a house all to ourselves. It's awesome."

Was it his imagination, or did her voice falter on the last word?

"I hope you are not angry at me for being presumptuous and asking for a house without checking whether you wanted to move in with me. I just assumed that you'd be okay with that."

Jin lifted her hand to his cheek. "Of course I am, silly. I told you that my future is with you."

Vlad

Vlad put his guitar away and took his coat off. It should have felt good to be back home in the village, but he was too empty on the inside to feel anything.

After stripping out of the clothes he had worn for the past two days, he got into the shower and turned the lever almost all the way up. The hot water couldn't wash the stain of failure from his mind, but it might help relax his knotted muscles.

The ride back to the keep had been the worst experience of his life, with Wendy's actual betrayal coming in second place.

Sitting in the back seat of the car with her and seeing her misery had been gut-wrenching, and forcing himself to do nothing about it had shredded his damn soft heart.

Bowen had blindfolded Wendy, tied her hands together, and secured the rope to the seat so she couldn't lift them to take the blindfold off. And that had been a big problem since she'd kept sobbing miserably and wetting the blindfold. Not only that, her nose had been running, and she couldn't wipe it off herself, so Vlad had been forced to do it for her. There had been no tissue in the car, so he'd used her long scarf for that. By the time they had parked across from the keep, the entire thing had been covered in snot, and he had tossed it into the trash.

Throughout the ride, Wendy had kept murmuring that she was sorry, but since he hadn't responded, she'd quit and just sobbed quietly.

If it had been possible for him to keep his anger up, the ride might have been less of a nightmare. Instead, he'd felt sorry for Wendy, and the urge to wrap his arms around her and forgive her had been nearly overpowering.

The effort it had taken to keep his distance had turned his shoulders and back into one solid mass of knotted muscles.

Thankfully, once they had reached the keep, Bowen had locked Wendy in her former room, which was now fulfilling its original purpose as a prison cell.

Vlad no longer had to look at her or hear her heart-wrenching sobbing, but after two hours of that during the ride back, her sniffles and apologetic murmurs kept playing on a loop in his head. He'd spent a sleepless night in Jacki's old room, and this morning he'd headed home together with Ingrid and Mey, while the Guardians had stayed behind to watch over Richard and Wendy.

"Vlad, lunch is ready," his mother called from the other side of the door.

"I'll be right out."

"Jackson is here. He's going to join us."

Great. So Jackson had heard already and had come to offer his sympathy. The village was like a computer network, with rumors spreading in real time. By now, everyone probably knew about Wendy's betrayal and felt sorry for him.

Evidently, the nightmare wasn't over yet.

Getting dressed in clean clothes made him feel a little better, and as Vlad brushed his hair, he didn't let his long bangs fall over his left eye as he usually did. In defiance, he slicked them back and gazed into his mismatched eyes. Wendy might have been full of shit, and every word that had left her mouth had been a lie, but she'd been right about his eyes not being so bad. He should stop hiding behind his hair.

It was difficult to live with imperfections when everyone around him had none, but Vlad was sick of hiding in the shadows because of that. He was a decent guy, he worked hard and studied hard, and that should be enough.

His less than perfect looks should not make him an outcast among his own people.

When he walked into the kitchen, his mother smiled up at him. "I'm so glad that you brushed your bangs away from your eyes. You look so handsome."

He leaned and kissed her cheek. "Thank you for making lunch. I'm starving."

"What else is new?" Jackson got up and pulled him into a bro hug. "You could always beat Gordon and me in an eating competition." He clapped him on the back.

"Except, nothing ever stuck to my bones." Vlad winked at his mother.

Jackson laughed. "I always wondered about that. Your body must burn fuel at double the normal rate for immortals."

"It would seem so. Nothing about me is normal, so why should food be any different?" Vlad pulled out a chair and sat down. "How come you can spare time for your old friend?"

"Sometimes a guy has to prioritize, and when my best friend needs me, I should be there for you." Jackson sat back down.

"I don't need you. But I'm glad that you are here."

His mother lifted the lid off the casserole. "Dig in, boys."

"Thank you, Stella." Jackson cast her one of his megawatt smiles. "I've missed eating in your kitchen."

"You can drop by anytime. I'll always have something for you."

"Thank you. I appreciate the offer, but usually I run around the city all day long. When I get home, I'm all Tessa's."

"You can bring your lovely mate as well. It was so nice when you and Gordon used to come over. Then as soon as you finished high school, the three of you moved out and went to live over Nathalie's café."

"We felt so grown up," Jackson said. "Working in the café during the days and rehearsing and performing at clubs during the nights." He sighed. "Those were good times."

Vlad chuckled. "You sound like an old man reminiscing about his youth. You have a mate, and you are running a successful business. Your good times are now."

When Jackson had moved in with Tessa and Gordon had gone to college in another state, Vlad had decided to move back with his mother. Independence had been fun, but with his friends gone, he'd preferred that to sharing a house with new roommates who were much older than him.

Jackson pushed his plate away and leaned back in his chair. "So, tell me what happened."

Vlad grimaced. "Didn't you hear already? I'm sure the entire village knows."

His mother waved a dismissive hand. "No one knows anything. The only reason Jackson heard about Wendy was that Onegus contacted Vanessa."

Jackson nodded. "That's right. Onegus wants my mother to talk to Wendy and see what's up with her. Maybe she had a good reason to do what she did."

"I'll leave you two alone." Vlad's mother got up and put a reassuring hand on his shoulder. "I've got a big order to deliver to the theater by the end of the week, and the costumes are not going to make themselves."

"Thank you for lunch, Stella," Jackson said. "Vlad and I will clear the table." He smiled. "Like old times."

"You're welcome. And thank you. I meant what I said earlier. Next time, bring Tessa along."

"I will."

When his mother left, Jackson leaned toward Vlad. "Get it off your chest, man. You will feel better."

With a sigh, Vlad leaned back in his chair and told Jackson a modified version of what had happened. The things he omitted were minor. Like the fact that Wendy was the first girl he'd kissed, or that he had believed that she was the one for him.

He'd been so naive. Such a fool.

"Maybe the director is holding something over her," Jackson said once Vlad was done. "Maybe she has a young sibling or a cousin that he will retaliate against if she doesn't spy for him."

"Wendy is an only child. Her mother left when she was young, and her father raised her alone."

"So maybe she was protecting her father?"

Vlad shrugged. "I don't know, and I don't care. Bowen is going to erase her memories, and they will drop her off somewhere. I'm never going to see her again."

"It's not going to happen before my mother makes her assessment. Kian is not in a hurry to get rid of a possible Dormant. They are too hard to come by."

"Good luck with that. I'm done with her."

Wendy

When the door to Wendy's cell started to swing open, she turned her head to see who it was, even though it could only be Bowen.

No one else had come to visit her.

"Lunch." The guardian entered with a tray.

On it was a sandwich from the vending machine, a can of coke, and a muffin, also from the vending machine.

But at least they were feeding her.

When Bowen had dumped her in the room and locked the door behind him, she had had the suffocating fear that she'd be left to die in there.

The room she'd stayed in before had been turned back into its original purpose with the simple removal of the device controlling the door. The house phone was still there, so she probably could still call the security office, but they could just ignore her call even if she was dying from hunger or thirst. Wendy remembered that there was a set of rules about how countries should treat prisoners of war, but she doubted that these people adhered to the Geneva Conventions, whatever those were. She could just be a prisoner with no rights.

Was she a POW?

Not really. War prisoners didn't get rooms with televisions, comfortable beds, and decent bathrooms. It could have been much worse.

Bowen put the tray on the coffee table and turned around.

"Wait," she called after him. "What are you going to do with me?"

"Me, personally?" He pointed at his chest. "Nothing. I'm just making sure that you don't run away or make another call."

"I meant your organization."

"I don't know. I haven't been informed. But my guess is that someone will come in to erase your memories, and then you'll be dropped off somewhere with pocket change to call your director to come to pick you up."

"That's all?"

He looked at her with unfettered disdain. "What did you expect? That we would torture you, or kill you?"

The thought had crossed her mind once or twice. "I thought that Kian would want to question me."

"He might. As I said before, no one has informed me about Kian's intentions for you."

"Okay. Thank you for lunch."

When the door locked behind Bowen with an audible click, Wendy let out a breath and turned the television on. She had no doubt that she was being watched, and she didn't want the watchers to see her cry.

Mostly, she felt like crying because she was lonely and scared, and because of the guilt that was eating her alive.

Still, what Bowen had said should have cheered her up.

No one was going to torture her, and she was going to be dropped off somewhere. She would call her uncle, who would send for her, and this whole thing would be over. She wouldn't even remember any of these people or what had happened to her in recent days. If they were good at erasing memories, the last thing she would remember would be sitting on a bench in the mall and waiting for Richard to finish buying shoes. It was like pressing rewind on a movie, only in her case, she wouldn't remember watching anything beyond that point.

She wasn't going to remember Vlad or the hurt look in his eyes when he'd discovered her betrayal, and she wouldn't remember Mey or the angry looks she'd gotten from her, Ingrid, and even Richard.

Wendy was going to miss them, but she wasn't going to miss Bowen and Leon. Those two tough guys were acting the most hostile toward her, and her tears had no effect on them.

Vlad, on the other hand, had been affected by her misery and then some, fighting the urge to put his arm around her the entire drive back to the underground. The sweet fool wanted to console her despite the way she'd treated him.

Wendy was going to miss him the most.

She had a feeling that Vlad would be the biggest regret of her life.

One stupid phone call that had achieved basically nothing had ruined everything. By the time the director could have sent people to the address she'd given him, she and the others had been long gone from there, and all traces of their stay in the cabin had been erased. He might even think that it had been a prank.

The phone call had achieved one thing, though. Wendy was going home to the program, and her life would resume as if it had never been paused.

Yay.

Wendy choked down a sob. It hurt to think that no one here was going to remember her fondly.

Especially Vlad.

But it was for the best. Regret for what could have been was not as bad as regret for what was and couldn't be undone. If she hadn't called the director and had stayed with Vlad, a relationship with him would have been inevitable, and he would have most likely disappointed her like her father had disappointed her mother.

As difficult and heart-wrenching as it was, she had done the right thing, putting an end to it before it had even begun. No matter what, Wendy wasn't going to repeat her mother's mistakes.

Kalugal

After talking with Kian, Kalugal spent the rest of the morning going over his portfolio, selling some stocks, buying others, and making phone calls to check on his numerous startups.

By lunchtime, he'd run out of excuses. It was time to implement his plan, and he dreaded it. Perhaps he could ask Rufsur to do it?

That way, he would kill two birds with one stone. He would conduct the test and at the same time ruin any hope Rufsur might have harbored of getting Jacki to respond to him.

Except, Kalugal had never asked his men to do things that he wouldn't have done himself. Well, except for cleaning toilets or scrubbing floors, but no one expected him to do that.

Regrettably, though, what he had in mind didn't fall under the category of domestic duties. It was more like running through a minefield under enemy fire. He could ask for volunteers, but he couldn't command anyone to do that.

Besides, Rufsur might refuse the order, and then Kalugal would have to throw him in the brig for insubordination.

Not only that, there was another problem with having someone other than himself implement the plan. It would only prove or disprove the existence of Jin's tether to Jacki, but not the one attached to him, which was more important.

Taking a deep breath, he rose to his feet and walked over to the bookcase that concealed the passageway between his office and the library. A slight push was all that was needed to get the thing to swing open, and the well-oiled pivot barely made a sound.

He found Jacki sleeping curled up on the couch with an open book resting face down on her ample chest. It was rising and falling with each of her deep breaths and tilting precariously on each inhale.

The situation made his task even more difficult.

Chickening out, he walked over to the bar, poured himself a drink, and then sat on the armchair across from Jacki and watched her sleep while sipping on his whiskey.

More than half an hour passed before she stirred, causing the book to slide off her chest and land with a loud thud on the floor, waking her up.

"Oh, damn." Jacki unfolded her long limbs and reached for the book, only noticing him when she lifted it onto her lap. "How long have you been sitting there?"

"Not long. I came to ask you to join me for lunch, but you were sleeping so peacefully, and I didn't want to wake you up. What were you reading that has bored you so?"

She lifted the book and turned it so he could read the embossed lettering.

"*War and Peace*." He nodded. "I can see how it could put a contemporary reader to sleep. Today's literature is more action-packed."

She glanced around his sprawling library. "Most of what you have in here is non-fiction. Do you ever just read for fun?"

He smiled. "I find learning new things enjoyable."

Jacki grimaced. "Good for you."

"What do you like reading?"

The peachy color of her cheeks reddened. "I like spy stories, romance novels, and sci-fi, but only if it has romance in it."

Kalugal lifted his hands in apology. "Regrettably, I have nothing of the sort in my library. The best I have to offer are political-intrigue novels."

"Not my idea of fun." Pushing to her feet, she stifled a yawn. "This place is so big, and you have so many books that I thought that I'd missed the section of entertaining books, but apparently there are none. Did you say something about lunch?"

Her long hair was a mess, with a big clump of tangled strands sticking out at the back, but it didn't detract even an iota from her beauty. On the contrary, the 'just got out of bed' look was most enticing, and if not for his damn dastardly plan, Kalugal would have found it arousing.

"Yes." He put his empty glass on the side table, got up, and walked up to her.

Standing very close, he was invading her personal space, but not to the extent to cause alarm.

Not yet.

"Your hair is very beautiful." He reached with his hand and combed the messy clump with his fingers.

"Ouch." She gripped his wrist and tried to push his hand away. "It hurts."

Kalugal didn't let go. Instead, he roughly grasped her hair and crushed his lips over hers.

Too stunned to respond, Jacki didn't fight him as he forced his tongue into her mouth, but when he pushed her down on the couch and got on top of her, she started to struggle.

Hating what he was doing with every fiber of his soul, Kalugal didn't enjoy the kiss, nor did he get aroused.

What surprised him, though, was that Jacki did.

Despite fighting him off with everything she had, the unmistakable scent of her arousal intensified.

Some women enjoyed rough play, but usually not without prior consent. To get aroused by what he was doing to her, Jacki must be either extremely attracted to him or starved for sex.

The thing was, he hadn't sensed it from her before.

When her struggles became frantic, he realized that she'd run out of air and let go of her mouth.

"Get off me!" She tried to buck up, but he was too strong for her.

"Why? You seem to be enjoying this."

"You're a pig!" She followed her curse with raising her knee to his groin.

For a brief moment, he contemplated letting Jacki have her revenge, but it just wasn't in his nature to seek punishment as a way to ease his guilty conscience, and he stopped her by shifting his weight.

Was this enough to enrage Kian? Or should he pretend to go for more?

Gripping both of her hands with one of his, he pulled them over her head and snaked his other one under her sweatshirt.

"Stop! Why are you doing this?"

As he caught the sheen of tears glistening in her eyes, and instead of the sweet scent of arousal, he smelled the acrid smell of fear, Kalugal stopped just short of touching her breast.

Jacki

When Kalugal had fisted Jacki's hair and kissed her, she had been surprised, but not scared. She'd encountered enough idiots to be able to spot those who wouldn't hesitate to rape a woman if they thought they could get away with it, and those who just thought that every woman they put their sights on should feel blessed and that there was no need to ask her permission before making unsolicited advances.

The best strategy to deal with the first type was to never get caught alone with them, and the best strategy to deal with the second was to make it absolutely clear in words and actions that she wasn't interested.

Kalugal wasn't a rapist, so she hadn't been afraid to be caught alone with him, but apparently he was the second type, and she hadn't made it clear enough that his advances were not welcome.

And that was because she herself wasn't convinced of that, or rather her traitorous body wasn't.

Logically, she knew that nothing good could come from letting Kalugal get close. He was immortal royalty, and she was a human nobody.

He would have his fun, discard her, and never look back, while she would never be able to forget him and move on. But that wasn't even the main issue. Jacki would never willingly get intimate with a man who didn't love her, cherish her, and vow to stick by her side for richer, for poorer, in sickness and in health.

For some people, the scarcest and most expensive commodity was time, for others it was money, and for many of her generation it was sex.

But for Jacki, it was love because she'd never had it.

There had been no parents or grandparents, no siblings, and no romantic love either. She'd had friends, and some of the foster parents had been kind to her and had cared for her, but no one had ever loved her.

Men loved her looks, though, which meant that they never bothered to get to know the person inside the pretty shell.

Except, she was a healthy young woman, and as much as she'd suppressed her sexual urges, they were still there, and Kalugal had reawakened them with gusto.

The best she could do was to pretend that the kiss was doing nothing to her and wait for him to get a clue.

But he didn't, and instead of letting go, he pushed her down on the couch and got on top of her.

Had she read him all wrong, and he intended to rape her?

Did Kalugal have an evil twin who he'd switched places with while in his office?

This was getting scary, and Jacki's fight or flight response finally kicked in. Since he was lying on top of her and pinning her down with his body, flight wasn't an option, which left only fight.

She wasn't a small woman, or weak, but pushing Kalugal off her was like trying to push on a concrete wall. He didn't budge, and she was running out of air.

The moment he let go of her mouth, the first thing she did was to suck in a big gulp of air. The next was to yell at the top of her lungs, "Get off me!" She tried to push him off, but it was just as ineffectual as her previous efforts.

'Why?" He smirked down at her. "You seem to be enjoying this."

Ugh, talk about the most conceited, arrogant, self-absorbed, egotistical jerk.

"You are a pig!"

She wanted to emphasize her words by spitting in his face but decided that a knee to the nuts would deliver a clearer message. Except, she should have known that Kalugal would anticipate her move.

As he shifted to block her knee though, she managed to free her hands, which until then had been trapped between their bodies, and reached for his face with the intention of scratching that smug smirk off.

But once again, he was too fast for her. Gripping her hands with just one of his, he pulled them over her head and pushed his other hand under her shirt.

Crap. He was going to rape her, and no one in the damn house would come to her rescue.

Tears pooling in her eyes, she resorted to pleading. "Stop! Why are you doing this?"

As a guilty look flitted across Kalugal's eyes, the library doors burst open, and Rufsur ran in.

His face a terrifying mask of rage, he bellowed, "Get off her right now!"

"Get out of here, Rufsur." Kalugal didn't even raise his voice. "Close the door behind you, go down to the bunker, and wait for me in my office."

He must have imbued his command with compulsion because Rufsur obeyed, walking out like a robot who was fighting every step.

Jacki was doomed.

No one was going to help her even if they wanted to.

But then Kalugal did the unexpected again.

He got off her and even offered her a hand up. "You need to rethink your attitude."

"Like hell!" She batted his hand away and jumped to her feet. The urge to punch him in the face was so strong that she almost succumbed to it, but that would have been stupid.

What was she going to do after that?

There was nowhere to run, and besides, he would catch her before she even made it to the door.

Where was she going to go? She didn't even have a room to lock herself in, and even if she had, no lock would keep Kalugal out if he wished to enter.

When dealing with a dangerous and much stronger predator, the best option was to play dead. Maybe she should pretend to faint?

It had worked for Jin.

He solved the dilemma for her. Walking up to the library doors, he opened them and stepped out. "Shamash, please take Jacki back to the room in the bunker."

Rufsur

Rufsur's feet obeyed his boss's command, but his mind was free to plot revenge. He was going to attack the son of a bitch in his sleep, shut his mouth with one powerful blow that would knock his teeth out so he couldn't use his damn compulsion, and then turn him into hamburger meat.

Physical strength was the one advantage Rufsur had over his boss.

Lately, Kalugal had been neglecting his training and was relying mainly on his mental tricks for defense as well as offense. Rufsur had no doubt that he could overpower his boss once the fucking compulsion ability was taken care of.

What had gotten into him, though?

He'd been with Kalugal since the very beginning, and the guy had never acted like that with a woman before. He even kept his men in check, drilling into their heads the importance of consensual sex.

So what was his deal?

Thralling a woman into having sex was not allowed, but forcing her physically was okay?

Perhaps he'd misinterpreted the situation?

Impossible.

Jacki hadn't been playing when she'd yelled for Kalugal to stop and get off her. And the scent of her fear was not an act either.

Was he raping her right at that moment?

Rufsur managed to walk up to the door, but his hand refused to obey and reach for the handle, and he was still standing there when Kalugal opened it from the other side.

Without leaving the boundary of the office, Rufsur swung his fist at Kalugal, smiling as he heard the bone crack.

"Freeze." Kalugal stopped him from swinging with his other fist.

His feet glued to the floor and his arm pulled back and ready to swing, Rufsur was at his boss's mercy, but he didn't regret what he had done.

"Did you rape her?"

"No." Kalugal rubbed his injured jaw.

"Where is she?"

"Back in her room."

"What has gotten into you?"

Kalugal tilted his head. "Can I unfreeze you now? Or are you going to swing at me again?"

"That depends on what you have done to Jacki."

His boss cast him a glare that would have frozen the blood in his veins if it hadn't been running so hot. "You'd better get your priorities straight, Rufsur. On account of our friendship, I will let this time slide, but if you swing at me again, I'm going to throw you in the brig. Are we clear?"

"Yes."

"You can move." Kalugal waved a hand. "Now get out of my face."

Rufsur didn't need to be told twice. Casting one last glare at his boss, he marched straight to Jacki's room.

He found Shamash sitting across from her door, a guilty expression spread over his face. "I didn't know what to do. I don't know why he did that, either. One moment they were talking about books, and the next she was yelling at him to get off her."

Rufsur clapped him on the back. "There was nothing you could've done. I tried to stop him, and he just compelled me out of there. Is Jacki okay?"

"She's been crying ever since she closed the door in my face. I can still hear her sniffling."

"Yeah, I can hear it too." Rufsur knocked on the door. "May I come in? It's me, Rufsur. I just want to make sure that you are okay."

"Go away! You are all perverts."

"I'm not. I swear on my honor that I will never touch you without your permission." He tried the handle, but the door barely budged.

Had she blocked it with something?

Pushing harder, he managed to open it while shoving forward the couch that Jacki had used to barricade the door.

"That's not going to stop any of us." He walked into the room.

Jacki was sitting on the floor, wedged between the nightstand and the wall, with a pile of used tissue paper in front of her.

"I see that you've erected an impromptu shield."

"Yeah. No germaphobe will dare to pass."

He was glad that she still had her sense of humor.

"Are you okay? Did he hurt you?"

Jacki shook her head. "Not physically, but he hurt my pride. Why did he do that? Have I given him any misleading signs without being aware of doing it?"

"No." Rufsur sat on the bed. "And even if you did, that didn't give him the right to force himself upon you. I don't understand what possessed him. He's never acted like that before."

She reached for another tissue and blew her nose. "It's me. I have this effect on men."

"What the hell are you talking about? It's not your fault that you are beautiful."

Jacki shook her head. "I don't think it's about my looks. I must emit some freaking pheromones or something. Shit like that keeps happening to me, no matter how careful I am or how uninterested I appear. Kalugal was not the first, but he was the hardest to fight off. If he hadn't let go..." she shook her head again. "I can't believe that he did that to me."

Jacki

It had happened so many times before.

Jacki had been lucky so far, and none of the assaults had ended in rape, but she'd been groped and fondled ever since she'd grown boobs, which had been at the very young age of twelve.

Living in the same house with a bunch of people who hadn't been her real relatives was like an open invitation for any male with predatory inclinations.

She'd had to fight off a couple of foster dads, half a dozen or so older foster brothers, and several of her employers and coworkers at the various jobs she'd worked.

What had saved her time and again was her size and her loud mouth. Jacki had never hesitated to scream murder and fight with everything she had. She also tried her best never to be left alone with the pervy types, always refusing to have a room of her own and preferring to share it with at least one more girl. But sometimes all of that hadn't been enough, and a creep had managed to corner her alone. Then she had yelled, scratched, kicked, and usually that was enough.

None of that had worked with Kalugal, though, and that had been scary. All that he'd ended up taking without permission was a kiss, but the unexpected violence and the violation of trust left behind a deep sense of disappointment and emotional pain that was not going to abate anytime soon.

"I punched Kalugal in the jaw," Rufsur admitted sheepishly. "That was the first time I ever raised a hand against him. Outside of training, that is."

Jacki gasped. "What did he do to you?"

"Nothing. He just warned me to never do it again. If I do, I'm going to be sent on a long vacation to the lovely cell you and Arwel shared before Jin insisted that we move you to a better room."

She was touched. No one had ever fought for her before or avenged her honor, so to speak.

"Thank you." She pushed away from the corner that she'd tucked herself into and moved to sit next to Rufsur. "I should tell you that you shouldn't have, but I'm glad you did. Your arrogant asshole of a boss deserved it."

He smirked. "Yeah, I'm glad too. Though to be perfectly frank, I thought that he'd raped you. That's why I punched him before he had a chance to say a single word in his defense."

"Did he?"

Stupidly, she hoped for some sort of explanation. A temporary psychosis, Kalugal's body having been overtaken by malevolent spirits, anything that would explain the sudden attack.

"No. But then Kalugal never apologizes for anything. He thinks that he is always right."

"How can you work for him?"

Rufsur sighed. "Because usually he is right, and he has never steered me or the others who followed him wrong. If not for Kalugal, I wouldn't be here. I would still be serving in the Brotherhood, a mercenary soldier going out on missions to kill humans I had no beef with, for reasons that didn't make any sense to me. I hated that life."

"This must be tough for you. But the good news is that by tomorrow I'll be gone, and things will return to normal. I hope that you and Kalugal will go back to being friends."

Rufsur shook his head. "I don't know if I can do that. I respected Kalugal. Hell, I worshiped him. But in one stupid move, he has shattered my belief in him. I can't follow a man who would force himself on a woman."

Jacki grimaced. "He didn't go through with it."

"It doesn't matter. He intended to."

"I don't think so."

"What do you mean?"

She took in a long, steadying breath. "He wasn't excited, if you know what I mean. It was as if he wanted to prove a point or something." She looked down at the tissues bunched up in her hand. "Why would he want to hurt me, though? What have I done to him?"

"I don't know, Jacki. I wish I had an explanation that made sense. Right now, I'm not sure I want to stay with Kalugal. After this is over, and you are back with your people, I think I'm going to say goodbye to him." He cast her a sidelong glance. "Do you think your boss will take me in?"

"Kian?"

He nodded.

"I don't know him well, but if I were in his shoes, I would welcome you with open arms. You are a good man, and you can provide him with insight on Kalugal, which was the purpose of this entire clusterfuck. Kian wanted to know what Kalugal was up to before approaching him."

Rufsur grinned. "If I switch sides, we could go on the date that I've asked you out on before."

She smiled and nodded. "I owe you for punching Kalugal. But it will be just one date. You are still an immortal, and I'm still a human. There is no future for us."

"Maybe not. But that doesn't mean we can't enjoy each other's company."

If he meant sex, then the answer was no. But if he wanted to be her friend, she would gladly accept his offer.

"Friends?" She extended her hand.

"Friends." He took it gently and shook it. "To start with."

Vlad

After Jackson left, Vlad had thought that he was done with well-intended but annoying relationship advice.

He was wrong.

Two hours later there was a knock on the door, and when he opened it, he found Bhathian standing on his front porch.

"Good afternoon, Vlad. Can I come in?"

"Sure." He opened the door all the way and motioned for the Guardian to come inside.

"Who is it?" his mother called out from her craft room.

"It's Bhathian, Mom. He is here to see me." He looked at the Guardian. "You are not here to commission a costume from my mother, right?"

"No. I came to talk to you. Would you like to join me on a walk?"

Vlad cringed. "I'm not in the mood for meeting anyone and seeing more pitying looks."

"No one knows anything."

"Jackson does, and apparently you do too."

"I'm a head Guardian. There isn't much I don't know. But as you wish. We can talk over a cup of coffee."

"I'll start the coffeemaker."

As Bhathian sat down, the couch sank under his bulk. The guy must weigh nearly three hundred pounds, and all of it was muscle. He was a mountain of a man, but he had a gentle soul.

Perhaps talking to him could actually help.

One thing was certain, it wouldn't be as embarrassing as talking with Jackson. His childhood friend was everything that Vlad wanted to be but could never hope to become. Jackson was strikingly handsome, outgoing, and ambitious. He'd never faced the kind of problems that Vlad had to contend with his entire life.

It wasn't that he begrudged Jackson his good fortune, but the guy could never understand how deeply Wendy's betrayal had cut him.

Still, he'd meant well, and Vlad was glad of his friendship.

"I'm sorry that I got you into that mess," the Guardian sighed. "I should have never pressured you into meeting the girl."

Vlad sat in an armchair facing Bhathian. "I could've said no. Besides, I don't regret it."

"You don't?" Bhathian arched one bushy brow.

It definitely felt easier to talk to Bhathian than it had been with Jackson. Maybe it was because Vlad regarded the Guardian as a mentor. Or maybe it was because Bhathian was a father of a grown daughter and a baby son, and despite his youthful looks, it wasn't hard to imagine him in a paternal role.

"I kissed a girl for the first time. Well, she kissed me, but then something in me snapped, and I took over. It was amazing. I don't know how I knew what to do, but I wasn't awkward, and I didn't fumble." He smiled. "Wendy said that I was a great kisser."

"Good for you." Bhathian puffed out his chest, looking like a proud dad.

Vlad lowered his head and pretended to examine his black-colored fingernails. "But it might have been an act. She had us all fooled. Even Edna."

"Some things cannot be faked," Bhathian said.

"True. But that's neither here nor there. Wendy might have been attracted to me a little bit, but the rest was an act. She pretended to like me, and I wanted to believe that it was true, so I did."

"It might not have been an act. Did you try to talk to her after the incident?"

Vlad shook his head. "The entire drive to the keep she was crying her eyes out, which was probably an act too, and I was waging war with myself not to be an idiot and forgive her. If I opened my mouth to say anything, that's what would have come out."

"What about later, when you got to the keep?"

"I stayed away from Wendy for the same reason. I didn't trust myself with her. She is too good of an actress."

"Again, it might not have been an act, and Wendy might have genuine feelings for you. Maybe she had no choice but to make that call, and she was crying because she hated hurting you."

"That's what Jackson said as well. Vanessa is going to talk to her and find out what's the deal with her. Maybe Wendy is schizophrenic, and the voices in her head told her to steal my phone and call the program's director. Or maybe she has a split personality, one who likes me, and the other who is the director's spy."

Vlad had said those things mockingly, but secretly he wished they were true. Dealing with a psychological problem was easier because that was a disease, not a malicious act against him.

"Wendy is very young. She might have done that because of misplaced feelings of loyalty. Maybe in her mind the director has become a father figure."

Vlad frowned. "Did you come up with that, or did you talk with Vanessa?"

Bhathian smiled sheepishly. "That was Eva's suggestions. But don't worry, Eva is like a vault. No one is going to hear about it from her."

"Not even Nathalie?"

"Eva would not whisper a word of it even to our daughter."

Vlad let out a breath. "I wonder who else knows."

"Don't worry about it. And if I were you, I wouldn't dismiss Eva's opinion. She has a lot of experience in dealing with humans. She was a private detective for many years, and she is one hell of a smart lady. She is very good at figuring out motives and anticipating moves, and she asked me to tell you not to give up on the girl just yet. She might still be the one for you."

It was utterly stupid to pin his hopes on Eva's insight, but Vlad couldn't help it. Eva had met Wendy and interacted with her. Maybe the former detective's well-honed intuition had picked up on something no one else had noticed.

Kalugal

An entire hour had passed with Kalugal staring at his phone and willing the call from Kian to come in. He was actually looking forward to his cousin yelling and threatening him with retribution because it would prove that he'd been right and that the tether hadn't been removed.

He hated to think that he'd attacked Jacki and alienated his best friend for no good reason.

Except, proving that the tether had been indeed removed was vital. Until he was convinced of it, Kalugal was de facto paralyzed.

Regrettably, attacking Jacki had been the fastest and surest way to verify it one way or another. If Kian didn't respond, then the tether was gone, and if he did, then the tether was still there.

Kalugal would apologize to Jacki later, explain his motives, and hope that she could find it in her heart to forgive him.

Rufsur was another story.

Was the guy in love with Jacki? Because save for that, there had been no justification for his gross insubordination.

First of all, he should know Kalugal well enough to suspect that the attack had not been a momentary act of insanity, and that Kalugal would have never done it just because he desired a woman who didn't reciprocate or who took too long to submit.

"Really, Rufsur. I'm disappointed in you," he said to the computer screen.

Kalugal didn't mind Rufsur comforting Jacki, but hearing his lieutenant talking about crossing over to the other side hurt. Rufsur was well aware that the room was bugged and that Kalugal was most likely listening in on their conversation, and the things he was telling Jacki were actually meant for Kalugal's ears.

The passive-aggressive approach was unbecoming of his second-in-command. As punishment, he should promote Phinas to the position and put Rufsur on bathroom-cleaning duty. That would teach him a lesson.

Kalugal glanced at his phone again, but the device remained stubbornly silent.

Should he initiate the call to Kian instead of waiting for it?

His cousin wasn't a good actor, so even if he tried to behave as if he knew nothing about the attack on Jacki, he wouldn't be able to hide his anger.

Except, they had already agreed on the terms for tomorrow's exchange, and Kalugal needed another excuse for calling again. Perhaps he could ask after the spy's health? Or maybe he could start negotiating for the visitations that Rufsur had suggested.

The clan had available immortal females, and he had a bunch of available immortal males. Pairing up would be beneficial for both sides.

Except for Phinas and Rufsur, the rest of his men didn't know about his grand plan for taking over the world, and even if they'd overheard him talking with his lieutenants, they'd assumed it was done jokingly. As far as they were concerned, Kalugal was busy making money and acquiring startups, which was precisely what he was doing. What they didn't know was that those were just milestones on the roadmap for his long-term plan.

So if any of his men got overly talkative with the clan females, there wasn't much they could actually tell them that concerned Kalugal.

Yeah, that was a good one. If Kian knew what had happened to Jacki, he would be opposed to arranging meetups between his females and Kalugal's males.

Placing the call, Kalugal wasn't surprised that his cousin didn't answer right away. Since he hadn't been expecting another call from him that day, he probably didn't have his immune adviser next to him.

The return call came in a full half an hour later.

"I thought that we were done for today." Kian's tone was as gruff as usual, but no more than that.

"So did I, but I forgot to ask how Jin was feeling. Is she all better?"

"She is."

"I bet she's asleep. She was exhausted when she arrived at my house, and she didn't sleep much after Julian gave her the shot. We spent a long time talking."

"So I heard. You compelled her to reveal information."

"We've already covered that. Jacki asked that I check on her friend."

"Jin is fine. I've just spoken with her before returning your call, and she asked me to do the same. How is Jacki doing?"

"She is well, enjoying the selection of books in my library."

"I hope that you are treating her well."

"Like an honored guest."

Kalugal didn't enjoy lying, but he was very good at it when he needed to.

"Good. Is that all you wanted to talk to me about?"

It seemed that both Jin and Kian were oblivious to what had happened, and it wasn't because the spy had been asleep. Apparently, she was worried about her friend, which meant that she would have checked on her if she could.

"There is one more thing. Rufsur had a great idea that I wanted to discuss with you."

"I'm listening."

"Your clan has immortal females, and I have immortal males. If we could arrange meetings, some might result in happy endings. It's a great way to solidify the ties between us."

Kian chuckled. "It's too early to discuss matchmaking. I still don't know much about you or your men. Although I have to admit that so far what I've learned gives me hope. From what I've heard, Rufsur behaved himself, but I can't say the same about you."

Kalugal tensed. "What do you mean?"

"The first opportunity you had, you compelled information out of Jin and Julian. I can't trust you around my people."

Kalugal let out a relieved breath. "My questions were harmless. I only wanted to learn more about immortal females and how to tell them apart from human women."

"It was more than that, but I'll let it go this time. In the future, though, I won't tolerate you using compulsion on my people for any reason. If you want to know something, just ask, don't force anyone to tell you more than they are comfortable revealing."

"Noted. I'll do my best to behave."

"Can I have your word?"

"As you've just said, it's too early for that. When I give my word, I don't do it lightly, and right now, I'm not comfortable making such promises."

"That's regrettable, but I understand. Your compulsion ability is your only real advantage. It's no wonder that you are not willing to give it up yet."

"I beg to differ, cousin. My real advantage is my mind, and I'm not referring to its paranormal capabilities. Do you play chess, Kian?"

"Rarely. I'm too busy to play games."

Could've fooled him. Every time the two of them engaged in conversation it was game on.

"So am I, but I find that a good game of chess against a worthy opponent sharpens my mind. Exercising my brain is no less important than training to keep my fighting skills up and my body in peak condition. We should meet up and play. It has been a long time since I've sat across from a champion player."

"I'm far from that, cousin. But my friend Turner would gladly accept your challenge."

"Ah, the brilliant strategist I've heard about. It would be my pleasure."

When the call ended, Kalugal leaned back in his chair and let out a breath.

The tether was gone. He was almost certain of that. It was possible that Jin hadn't been following it to Jacki or him during the incident, but Jacki had spent the last hour crying her heart out to Rufsur, which expanded the window of time available to Jin.

Now all that was left to do was damage control.

Kalugal had to apologize to Jacki and explain why he had acted so badly. Hopefully, she would forgive him. Maybe not right away, but with some serious groveling on his part, she eventually might.

Except, he sucked at apologizing, and he doubted there was an online crash course that he could take on the subject.

His natural charm would have to do.

Jacki

"I need to go." Rufsur returned his phone to his pocket after reading a message that she guessed was from Kalugal.

Jacki looked up at him. "Your jerk of a boss is demanding your presence?"

"I've been here for over an hour." He smiled. "It was my pleasure, but I'm getting paid to work, not to enjoy myself talking to a pretty lady." He pushed to his feet and offered her his hand.

"Thank you." She shook it.

"Anytime. If you need anything, just let Shamash know, and he'll call me. He's outside in the corridor."

Jacki grimaced. "So much for Kalugal's promise to give me a room in the house."

"I'll talk to him about that."

"Don't bother. It's only for one more night. Whoever is in charge of laundry will thank me for not having to wash two sets of bedding."

"I'll come again when I can." He opened the door.

"I'd like that."

Jacki meant it, but given the happy grin on Rufsur's face, she shouldn't have said it.

He was a nice guy, and if he were human, she might have considered dating him. Although that would have been wrong too.

The truth was that she wasn't attracted to Rufsur. She was attracted to his asshole of a boss.

Way to go, Jacki.

Talk about falling for the wrong guy.

The absolutely worst possible guy. Not only was Kalugal a quasi-rapist, but he was also arrogant, conceited, and immortal. He was at the very top of the food chain, while she was two or three levels below with the rest of the anonymous human masses.

When there was a tentative knock on the door, she assumed it was Shamash. It was lunchtime, and even though she wasn't hungry, eating would be better than staring at the walls and thinking about Kalugal.

"Come in."

Speak of the devil. Kalugal entered the room with a bottle of wine in one hand, two glasses in the other, and a sheepish smile on his face.

The nerve of the guy.

"Get out of here." She pointed at the door.

"I brought a peace offering." He lifted the bottle. "I was saving it for a special occasion, but I decided to sweeten my apology with a superb wine."

Crossing her arms over her chest, Jacki jutted her chin out. "I don't want your wine, or your apology, or your company. I have nothing to say to you, nor do I want to hear anything you have to say in your defense because there is nothing that can justify your behavior. Please get out."

Ignoring her request, he sat on the couch next to her, but not too close.

"I'll get straight to the point. I had to make sure that the tether was off." He put the wine and the glasses on the table. "And the only way to test it was to do something extreme enough to provoke a response from Kian. I didn't enjoy it. In fact, I hated every moment of it, and I'm so sorry that I had to use you in such a despicable way. I'm here to apologize and do whatever it takes to make it up to you."

Well, that explained it.

At least she hadn't been wrong in her assessment of Kalugal. After what he had done, Jacki had started to doubt her ability to tell the rapists from the garden-variety jerks.

But that didn't mean that she was going to forgive him, especially not after he'd added insult to injury with his comment about hating every moment of it. Was she so repulsive that he'd hated kissing her?

He arched a brow. "Nothing to say?"

"Oh, I have plenty to say. But I'm too much of a lady to use such language."

He smiled and beckoned with his hand. "Let me have it. And if you want, you can punch me in the face like Rufsur did. I'll turn the other cheek."

Damn him. Why did he have to be so charming?

"You are a conceited jerk, a manipulator, and a liar, and I don't trust you not to try to rape me again."

As she'd expected, her jibe worked, and Kalugal cringed.

"I swear that I will never again touch you without your permission."

After he'd admitted to hating touching her, Jacki believed him. But if he hadn't been attracted to her, then why had he decided to test the tether that way? Surely there were other ways to do it.

"How did you even come up with the idea to attack me? Couldn't you have done something else to enrage Kian?"

He pushed his hair back with his fingers. "It was Jin's comment that gave me the idea. You were both out in the corridor, and she said that she was afraid to remove the tether because my men or I might make improper advances, and without the tether, she wouldn't be able to do anything about it."

Jacki snorted. "You forgot to mention her comment about immortals being notoriously horny."

He chuckled. "That's true. At least for the males. I don't know much about immortal females."

She wondered how that was possible. Maybe Kalugal had been a virgin when he'd escaped with his men? But then he could have asked them. Some were much older than him and must have had sex with the immortal females of their community before leaving.

The other explanation could have been that they hadn't been allowed access to the immortal females. Perhaps extramarital sex wasn't allowed. That made sense. A lot of patriarchal societies had very strict rules about those things. The males were allowed to sleep around with so-called loose women, but the females were expected to be virgins on their wedding nights.

"It makes sense for the females to have a libido to match the males, but I'm just a human, so don't expect me to lust after you."

Liar.

His attack had killed her desire for him, but his apology had rekindled it. Except, Kalugal had also said that he'd hated every moment of the kiss, which meant that he wasn't even attracted to her, and it had all been an act.

He smirked. "If you change your mind, you are welcome to lust after me anytime you want. But the ball is entirely in your court. You will have to initiate because I'm not going to lay a finger on you unless you do that first, and even then, I'm going to ask your permission."

Jacki snorted. "Dream on, buddy. That's never going to happen. I wouldn't touch you even if you were the last male on earth."

"Ouch. Am I so repulsive?"

"Right now, yes. You are."

With a sigh, Kalugal uncorked the wine. "You are a tough negotiator, Jacqueline. Maybe the wine will soften you up." He poured the dark-red liquid into the two glasses.

"Not unless you plan on slipping a roofie into my drink."

"I swear that there is nothing in this glass other than the best wine you'll ever have the privilege of drinking."

With such preamble, Jacki couldn't force herself to refuse.

As she took a tentative sip, the wine's flavors exploded in her mouth. It tasted of berries and chocolate and some other flavors she couldn't name.

"How old is this wine?"

"Sixty-five years old. Only a small batch was made, and collectors around the world were going crazy trying to get their hands on it. Naturally, I outbid them all and got two bottles."

She eyed him from under her eyelashes. "You outbid them or compelled them to sell it to you?"

"No compulsion was involved. I only resort to it when everything else fails. In this case, the money was compelling enough."

She took another tiny sip, savoring the flavors for as long as she could. "It's nice to be rich and get to buy whatever you want."

He sighed dramatically. "I don't always get what I want whenever I want it. Money can't buy everything."

She rolled her eyes. "They say that it can't buy love, but that's not true, or not entirely true. Having a big house and a fancy car and dressing in the best designer clothes will get you noticed. Which is the first step. And if you have an ounce of charm, you can easily turn it into love."

Kalugal

Kalugal cast Jacki an amused sidelong glance. "I consider myself a charming fellow. Does it mean that I still have a chance of winning your heart?"

She grimaced. "When hell freezes over."

As Kalugal had expected, Jacki wasn't going to forgive him that easily.

It was understandable. He'd hurt her feelings, scared her, and had taken advantage of her. He couldn't even apologize in earnest because if he could turn back time, he would do it again.

Proving that the tether was gone was even more important than winning Jacki's affection.

He hadn't given up on that, though. He could still have both the proof and the girl. Jacki was a fine female and a possible Dormant, and she was worth the effort.

Except, to work his magic, Kalugal needed more time with her than the mere eighteen hours or so that he had until tomorrow morning's trade.

Kian expected him to deliver Jacki in exchange for communication with Areana, but Kalugal could just claim that he'd had a change of heart and was no longer interested in talking to his mother, and that he preferred to keep Jacki instead.

Would that be reason enough for Kian to start a war?

He doubted that.

Jacki was not a clan member, not yet, and she didn't know anything important. Kian might rant and rave, but he would not go to war over her.

And perhaps Kalugal didn't need to give up on talking to his mother entirely, only to postpone it until he managed to convince Jacki to stay with him of her own free will.

If Jacki agreed to stay, she would no longer be a hostage, and Kian would have no grounds for denying Kalugal communication with his mother.

Was there a way he could convince her to stay with him by tonight?

So far, there hadn't been a woman he couldn't charm, and some of them were much more sophisticated and experienced than Jacki.

How hard could it be to charm a country bumpkin like her?

Hard.

Jacki was smart, suspicious, and right now, he was at the top of her shit list.

He should start with humor, get her to lower her defenses, wine her and dine her some more, and then make her an offer she couldn't refuse.

The question was what that offer could be.

She would refuse anything monetary, but perhaps a trip to Paris would do the trick?

A poor girl like her had probably never traveled abroad. He could invent some excuse about needing a female companion for some charity function. He would dazzle her with the prospect of wearing a designer gown, real diamond jewelry to match, flying to Europe on a private jet, and being driven down the Champs-Élysées in a limousine.

Even a stubborn and prickly girl like Jacki wouldn't be able to say no to that.

Happy with his plan, Kalugal lifted the wine glass to his lips. "Who knows, maybe hell is already frozen? Maybe instead of fiery pits, it's covered in ice?" He took a small sip. "Personally, I'm not a fan of the northern lands, which is why I think that Kian shouldn't have built his sanctuary in Alaska, even if it was cheaper to do it there. Those poor kids deserve sunshine and green vistas after what they've been through. Not ice and snow."

Jacki gave her wineglass a slight spin, swishing the deep red liquid around. "I bet this one bottle of wine could provide the sanctuary with meals for a month."

"More like a year."

Her eyes widened. "How much is this thing worth?"

"I purchased it fifty years ago, and it was pricey back then. I haven't checked the auctions lately, but I guess it could fetch over three hundred thousand dollars."

Jacki put the glass on the coffee table. "I can't drink that."

"Once a bottle is open, the wine will spoil quickly. It's too precious to go to waste. We have to finish it." He refilled the glass and handed it back to her.

"You said that you had another one."

"I do."

"You should sell it and donate the proceeds to a worthy cause. It doesn't even have to be Kian's sanctuary."

"And why would I do that?"

"Because you can, and because it's the right thing to do."

That was brilliant. Jacki had just handed him the perfect bait to reel her in. One that was even better than his Paris idea. After that little speech, there was no way she could refuse to do her part to help the poor victims of trafficking.

"I'll make you an offer. If you agree to stay here of your own free will, I will donate twenty-five thousand dollars to Kian's sanctuary for every day that you do."

For a long moment, Jacki just gaped at him, and then she narrowed her eyes. "Why?"

Kalugal knew precisely what she was asking, but he played dumb. "You said it yourself. Because I can, and because it's the right thing to do."

"I mean, why do you want me to stay so badly that you are willing to spend so much money on it?"

Jacki

Jacki knew precisely where Kalugal was going with that and what he wanted in exchange for his contribution.

Should she feel flattered?

It would make her the most expensive whore in recent history, but a whore nonetheless.

She could tell him where to shove his twenty-five grand a day, but the problem was that it made her feel selfish. None of the money would go to her, so if she agreed to his proposal, she would be sleeping with him for a good cause, and it would probably not be such a terrible chore either.

Except, she couldn't do it. Not even for charity.

Jacki had vowed to never have sex with a man who didn't love her, cherish her, and was willing to spend the rest of his life with her. She'd held on to that conviction ever since men had started noticing her when she was twelve, she'd carried it into adulthood, and she wasn't about to discard it now.

She'd had to compromise on so many things in her life. Simple things that others took for granted, like having a full belly, or sleeping without a baseball bat clutched in her hand. But she wasn't going to compromise on love.

All or nothing. Now and forever.

But damn, she could be earning the charity over seven hundred thousand a month.

No, not going to happen.

Kalugal refilled his glass and motioned for her to drink some more from hers. "I want a chance to make it up to you for what I've done, and since you are not about to forgive me by tonight, I need more time to grovel properly and earn your forgiveness."

He sounded so sincere, but she knew he was full of shit.

"I'm not going to have sex with you for money. I will not prostitute myself even for a worthy charity."

Kalugal's eyes widened, and he put a hand over his heart as if she'd wounded him.

What a damn good actor he was.

"I would never propose such a thing. I've never in my entire life paid for sex, and I'm not about to start with you. What gave you that idea?"

"Don't play dumb, Kalugal. What else could you want from me? I don't know any clan secrets, and I'm a nobody from nowhere. What I don't understand is why you are even interested in me. A guy like you can have any woman he wants, with or without the use of compulsion." She took a sip of the freakishly expensive wine. "Frankly, I don't know whether I should feel flattered or offended."

With a sigh, Kalugal reached for her hand. "Please forgive me for giving you the wrong impression. Perhaps I should have explained my reasons first."

This should be interesting. "I can't wait to hear them."

"First of all, I want you to know that I would never expect sex from you or any other woman in exchange for material goods. I'm way too vain for that."

That she could believe. "Okay. So why tempt me with that obscene amount of money?"

"Because you wouldn't have agreed to stay for anything less." He sighed. "I love my men like brothers, but I'm quite tired of strictly male company. Since I never leave the house without a shroud, the women I pick up in clubs don't know who I am, or even what I really look like. I spend the night with them in a hotel or at their place, two at most, and then it's back to this sprawling bachelor pad."

"Poor baby," she mocked.

"You think that I even notice the luxury? Once you get used to it, the wow effect dissipates, and all that is left is loneliness. You know who I am, and you know what I really look like, and it would give me enormous pleasure to just interact with you as me, not one of the many faces I wear. I want to talk to you and hear your feminine perspective on things. To me, it's priceless." He chuckled. "I've just proved that not everything can be bought with money."

He was making it really hard to say no, and if he was sincere, then there was no reason for her to refuse. It wasn't like she had an important job she needed to get back to or even a place to stay.

She was a fugitive in need of a hiding place, and Kalugal's mansion was perfect for that. It was protected by a state-of-the-art security system, there were guards posted at the gate, and there was even an underground bunker. The director could send an army after her, and it would hit a brick wall.

What did she have to lose other than her freaking heart?

Damn.

It wouldn't be easy to stay indifferent to Kalugal.

Hell, who was she kidding?

She wasn't indifferent to him now, but she wasn't in love with him either. Not yet.

If what she was seeing now was the real Kalugal, though, and it wasn't an act, she was going to fall for him in no time, and he would break her heart.

Decisions. Decisions.

"I need to sleep on it."

Kalugal

It wasn't a no.

"I wish I could give you more time, but I need an answer by tonight. Kian expects me to release you tomorrow, right after he lets me talk to my mother."

"What's the story with that? Jin said something about your father keeping your mom locked up in a harem?"

Telling Jacki the truth might paint him in an even worse light, but on the other hand, he could play on her sympathy. Women were suckers for sad stories involving children who'd been taken away from their mothers.

"Regrettably, that's true. But it's even worse than that. My brother and I were taken away from her as babies and raised by caretakers. If not for my compulsion ability, I would never have met my mother. When I was five, I snuck into the harem to see her. I compelled the guards to let me through and then forget that they had seen me."

"Weren't you scared?"

He chuckled. "The first time I did that I almost peed in my pants. But then I got bolder, and my mother worried that I would get caught and asked me to stop coming."

Jacki's hand flew to her chest. "I can't imagine how hard it must have been for her to do that."

Kalugal nodded. "She told me to keep my ability secret from my father and from everyone else. As far as my father knows, he is the only one with the ability to compel other immortals. My mother believed that it was best if he didn't know that I inherited that from him."

"Did she think that he would do something to you?"

"She implied it."

"Poor woman. She is stuck living with a monster. Did you ever think about saving her?"

Kalugal smiled sadly. "Despite everything, she loves him. She doesn't want to be saved."

Jacki huffed. "She is brainwashed. After you get her out, you can get her into therapy and cure her of that."

He laughed. "Can you imagine a therapist hearing her story? He would have her committed."

"Not going to happen because you would compel him not to."

"Oh, so suddenly you approve of my use of compulsion?"

She shrugged. "When it's for a good cause, why not?"

"Who determines what is a good cause? I might think that it is, but you might disagree. Or the other way around."

Jacki shook her head. "You like mind games, don't you?"

"I like to ponder philosophical questions, and while you stay with me, we can have many stimulating conversations on various subjects."

Jacki regarded him with narrowed eyes. "I might not be the best choice for that. I didn't even go to college."

Kalugal reached for her empty glass and refilled it. "I didn't either, not officially. I sat in classes that interested me, paid professors to give me private lessons, and I read a lot. But since I had a lot of time to do that and I'm fairly intelligent, I gathered knowledge that is the equivalent of several degrees."

"I'm impressed." She lifted her wine glass. "To self-taught knowledge."

"I'll drink to that." He clinked glasses with her. "So, what's your decision?"

"When is the exchange scheduled for?"

"Seven in the morning tomorrow."

"So if I give you my answer at six in the morning that should be fine."

"I'd rather you gave me your answer by tonight, so I could call Kian ahead of time, but I don't want to pressure you."

She snorted. "Right. No pressure at all. If Kian lets you talk to your mother, you will not have an incentive to release me later. I might be stuck here with you forever. And just so you know, I still don't trust you."

"I understand. But I'm sure Kian would think along the same line and insist on safeguards. He will probably want to talk to you once a day to verify that you are still okay with staying. And don't forget that each day will cost me twenty-five grand."

"That's what worries me the most. For that amount, you could have a bunch of Stanford professors sitting in your living room and discussing philosophical questions with you."

"Ah, but I don't want to hear their opinions. I want to hear yours."

"Why?"

"Because your perspective is more important. To me, you represent the human race. The professors, with all due respect, are living in their ivory towers, and their opinions on things are shaped by their privileged existence. They think that they understand the struggles of the common people, but they don't."

"And you do?"

"I don't either. That's why I need you."

The satisfied expression on Jacki's face told Kalugal that he'd hit the jackpot. Finally, she could see herself contributing something that he lacked but needed.

Jacki

I must be nuts, Jacki thought as she followed Kalugal into the tunnel leading from the bunker to the house.

She already knew that she was going to say yes because he'd made it impossible to say no. The guy was a master manipulator, and yet she believed that he needed her.

It just made sense to her.

If she were in Kalugal's proverbial shoes, living isolated from human society, in the company of other women who were strange creatures like her, Jacki would want to have at least one normal human male around to mix things up.

Heck, she couldn't imagine herself living in a houseful of women like in some damn boarding school for girls. Despite the many negative experiences that she'd had with men, Jacki wasn't a man hater because she'd had many more experiences that had been positive.

Most men were okay. They were just as sensitive and as vulnerable as women when it came to love. She still remembered how utterly devastated a couple of her foster brothers had been after breakups. In fact, they had taken it harder than the girls and had mourned the death of their relationships for much longer.

Contrary to popular belief, women were more emotionally resilient than men. Maybe it was because they were more cautious, more guarded, and expected to get hurt, while the guys did not.

"Normally, my men and I dine together, but for now, it's going to be just you and me, Rufsur and Phinas."

"Did I meet Phinas?"

He chuckled. "You did. The first time you and Jin tried to corner me outside that cigar lounge, he was there with Rufsur and me."

She cast him an apologetic smile. "I didn't think that you would make the connection. We worked damn hard to change the way we looked. What gave us away?"

"The horrid makeup was the first clue. The other was your height. You are both tall."

As they entered the dining room, Rufsur was already there, and she also recognized the second guy. Both got up from their seats as if she was some dignitary.

"Hello, Phinas." She offered him her hand. "I'm Jacki."

He dipped his head. "I know."

Rufsur looked at her, then at Kalugal, and then back at her. "Is everything okay?"

She nodded. "Kalugal explained why he acted that way."

"I would love to hear that," Rufsur murmured under his breath.

"He did it to verify that the tether was gone. If Jin was still spying on Kalugal or on me, she would have told Kian about what happened, and he would have been too enraged to keep quiet about it."

"So am I forgiven?" Kalugal pulled out a chair for her.

"Not yet. I expect a lot more groveling."

Phinas seemed satisfied with the explanation, his head bobbing up and down in agreement, but Rufsur wasn't. His lips pressed into a thin line, he unfurled the napkin with a loud pop and draped it over his knees.

Kalugal took his seat at the head of the table. "Jacki might be staying with us for a little longer."

Rufsur's head snapped toward his boss. "Are you giving up on talking with your mother?"

"It's Jacki's choice whether she agrees to stay with us for a few more days. She is no longer a hostage, and therefore Kian has no reason to withhold contact with my mother from me. Jacki can leave whenever she pleases."

That was news to her. "I can?"

Kalugal nodded. "I hope that you will decide to stay, but if you wish, you can walk out of here right now, and no one is going to stop you."

"I don't get you." Jacki lifted the napkin off her plate and placed it on her thighs. "When did you decide that?"

"A moment ago."

"You are full of surprises, Kal."

He arched a brow. "Kal?"

"Yeah, Kalugal is a mouthful."

Phinas hid his smile by lifting his glass to his mouth. Rufsur cast her a glare but said nothing.

Someone wasn't happy about her and Kalugal's reconciliation.

Poor Rufsur. After practically crying on his shoulder for over an hour, Jacki might have given him the impression that she'd chosen him as her confidant and savior. She couldn't blame him for feeling angry at her sudden change of heart.

From his perspective she must have appeared fickle, but from hers she'd just needed someone to talk to, and he'd been that someone. Besides, Rufsur wasn't there when Kalugal had apologized, and he hadn't heard his boss offer to donate twenty-five grand to the clan's charity for every day she stayed in the mansion.

He also didn't know that she was a fugitive, and that Kalugal's offer solved the problem of her having to find a place to hide.

"Kal. I like it." Kalugal smiled. "I'm not sure my mother would, though. She gave me my name."

"Does it have a meaning?" Jacki asked.

"In Sumerian it means big king."

She chuckled. "Your mother must have been clairvoyant. It fits you to a T."

Kalugal

"Let me show you to your room." Kalugal offered Jacki a hand up.

"Can I go back to the library?"

"I thought that you found the selection of books disappointing."

"I was looking for something to entertain myself with, but your admission about being self-taught inspired me. What if I can do what you've done? I was a good student in high school. I just didn't have the means to continue to college."

"Aren't there scholarships available for needy students with good grades?"

"Yeah, but they don't cover everything. I figured I would work for a couple of years and save up money, but that was a mistake. I never made enough to put money aside."

"That's a shame." Kalugal lifted his hand to put on the small of her back but then dropped it.

He'd promised not to touch her.

Instead, he motioned for her to start walking. "Let me show you to your room first, and then you can go to the library whenever you please. You can also go to the kitchen if you are hungry and get a snack. I want you to feel at home here."

As they climbed the stairs to the second floor, Jacki stopped and looked down the wide corridor stretching in both directions. "Do your men usually sleep in the bunker or in the house?"

He wasn't ready to reveal how many warriors he had, so he opted for a half-truth. "Some have rooms in the house, and others prefer the bunker."

"I bet it goes according to rank. The officers get to stay in the house, and simple soldiers have to stay in the bunker."

"It's a mix. Rufsur stays in the house, and Phinas prefers the bunker." Kalugal opened the door to the room he'd decided to put Jacki in.

Originally, it had been designed as his upstairs office for when he didn't feel like going to the large one downstairs, but he hardly ever used it for that or anything else. It was just a small room with a beautiful bookcase, a desk, and a leather couch.

There were no spare guest rooms in the house. So instead of moving a couple of his men out of their bedroom, he asked for the couch to be replaced with a proper bed, and the computer moved to his downstairs office. There was no closet, though. Right now, Jacki had nothing to put away, but if she agreed to stay, she would need a wardrobe, which he would gladly provide for her. Or better yet, she could use his closet.

"It's such a beautiful room." Jacki walked toward the French doors and opened them. "It even has a balcony with a chaise. I love it."

It was the smallest room in the house, but she regarded it as if it were palatial accommodations.

"This used to be my second-floor office," he admitted. "All the rooms in the house are spoken for, so I had a bed put in and the couch taken out. I hope you don't mind."

She turned around. "You shouldn't have gone to all that trouble. The room in the bunker is great. I wouldn't have minded staying there, especially since I might be leaving tomorrow." She narrowed her eyes at him. "Wait a minute. Have you been planning this all along? Because you offered to take me to a guest room this morning."

"I didn't plan anything. I just wanted you to be near me for the remainder of your stay, and I don't like sleeping in the bunker."

Casting him a doubtful look, Jacki walked over to the only interior door and opened it. "This is your bathroom."

"Yes. The master bedroom is on the other side of it. The office doesn't have a dedicated bathroom, so you'll have to use mine."

"How convenient." Jacki grimaced. "I'd rather sleep in the bunker." She walked out of the room.

He followed her out into the corridor. "I vowed not to touch you without your permission, so it doesn't matter that we are sharing a bathroom. We are not going to use it at the same time. Besides, the room in the bunker is no safer than this one. I can enter it anytime I want, and so can my men."

She had nothing to worry about from them either, but implying that she would be safer staying close to him might convince her to take the room next to his.

"Your hearing is really good, right?"

"Excellent."

"So if anyone opens my door uninvited, you will hear it, right?"

"If I'm in my room, yes. If I'm in the bunker or in my downstairs office, I might not." He smiled. "But since I'll want you with me when I'm not sleeping, that's not a problem. You'll accompany me wherever I go."

She arched a brow. "What about your precious secrets? You can't work with me there."

He waved a dismissive hand. "Most of what I do is not a secret. And if you want to learn about stock trading, you might even find it interesting."

She snorted. "With what money?"

"I can teach you to trade on paper. That's the best way to start instead of risking money before you know what you are doing."

"I have to admit that I'm not interested in stocks. Does your bathroom lock from the inside?"

"It does. But you must realize that a simple door with an ordinary lock will not keep an immortal out if he wants to get in."

"A locked door will signal that the bathroom is in use and that you shouldn't come in."

He nodded. "Naturally."

"Fine. I'll take the room. The balcony is really nice."

Jacki

As Jacki tossed and turned, she wondered whether Kalugal's silk pajamas had something to do with her inability to fall asleep.

They felt wonderful against her skin. But even though they were brand new and he had never worn them before, just the thought of how he would look in them was enough to fill her head with naughty thoughts.

Damn, after what he had done, she shouldn't be thinking about him like that at all, but he'd apologized so sincerely and then made her that incredible offer just so he could spend more time with her.

Even if all that was an elaborate ploy to eventually seduce her, no one had ever gone to so much trouble for her.

She couldn't help but feel flattered, special.

And wasn't that what she'd always wanted? For a guy to fall for her head over heels and be willing to do anything for her?

Except, that was a fantasy, and the reality was much different. The kiss that Kalugal had forced on her hadn't been passionate, not on his part.

Upon further reflection, Jacki realized that she'd misinterpreted what he'd said about hating kissing her. Kalugal had hated forcing her into it and pretending that he'd been about to do much worse.

There was no way he would have made her such a fantastic offer if he wasn't attracted to her.

Great, so they were attracted to each other, but that didn't solve anything. He was still immortal, and she was still human, and there could be no happily ever after for them.

Could she survive a month with Kalugal without succumbing to his charm and having sex with him?

Would it be so bad if she did?

Yeah, it would. Because when it was time for her to leave, she would not only be heartbroken, but also disappointed in herself.

Outside, the sky was getting lighter, and a glance at the clock by her bed confirmed that it was a little after five in the morning. She'd promised Kalugal to give him an answer by six, and she was still undecided.

Well, that wasn't true.

Jacki had known all along that she was going to accept Kalugal's offer, she was just trying to make her fears go away.

But that wasn't going to happen in the next hour. Besides, she had never allowed fear to run her life before, and she was not about to let it do that now.

This was her chance to do some good. All she had to do was to keep her heart locked and her desire subdued. How hard could it be?

And if it got to be too much, she could just walk away. The longer she survived, though, the more money would go to the rescued victims of trafficking.

She wasn't a weakling, and she could manage a week or two.

After all, she had a lot of experience pushing guys away, and if she thought of Kalugal as just another guy who wanted her in his bed, it should be a piece of cake to keep him at arm's length.

Kicking the blanket off, Jacki got out of bed and padded to the bathroom door. It was quiet on the other side, which hopefully meant that Kalugal wasn't there. Still, she opened the door only a crack and peeked inside.

The coast was clear.

Quickly, she tiptoed to the other side of the bathroom and engaged the lock on the door leading to Kalugal's bedroom.

As she brushed her teeth, it felt strange to stand at the double sink vanity and look at the other side and see Kalugal's neatly arranged stuff.

She liked that he wasn't a slob, and that his hairbrush was clean of hairs, and his toothpaste was folded and put away in its container. There was no maid service in the mansion, so the bathroom wasn't spotless because someone came in and cleaned it. Kalugal kept it like that.

Except, she was sure that he didn't clean the floors or his toilet or do his own laundry. One of his men was probably in charge of that.

Maybe she could do that while she stayed in his house?

That would send a clear message that this was a business arrangement and not a seduction in progress.

She was going to earn her keep and take on a share of the work like everyone else in the household.

Smiling, she reached for Kalugal's brush and ran it through her hair. She was going to be one of the guys, or rather a sister. After the many foster families she'd had, it was a role Jacki knew how to play well.

Kalugal

Kalugal opened his eyes and listened to the sounds coming from his bathroom.

Jacki was awake.

It felt oddly satisfying to imagine her brushing her teeth next to his vanity, using his hairbrush because he didn't have a spare one he could give her, stripping out of his pajamas and stepping into the shower...

Damn. He shouldn't think about her in the nude.

He banished the last image from his head by shifting his thoughts to his upcoming conversation with his mother. What was he going to talk with her about?

Condensing the past ninety-odd years into a ten-minute conversation was impossible, and he wasn't even going to attempt it. Should he choose a few highlights?

Or maybe it would be best to let her do the talking and just listen.

After all, Kian would be privy to their conversation, so it wasn't as if he could share any secrets with his mother. In fact, he could use it to throw more smoke in Kian's eyes.

Was it all smoke, though?

Maybe forming some sort of alliance with the clan wasn't such a bad idea. They could offer him no real protection from his father, but they still had many more men than he had. There was strength in numbers.

Kalugal didn't want his cousin poking his nose into his business, but having him on standby in case he needed Kian's cooperation was not a bad idea.

When Jacki was done in the bathroom, he waited several minutes longer to make sure the coast was clear before entering. Naturally, he didn't bother locking the door leading to her room.

He didn't mind her accidentally walking back in and seeing him nude. On the contrary. She might see something she liked.

When he was done, Kalugal got dressed, walked out the front door of his suite, and knocked on Jacki's door. "May I come in?"

She opened it. "Good morning. Is there a chance of getting some coffee around here?"

"Follow me." He waved a hand. "There is always coffee in the kitchen."

"How does it work?" She fell into step with him. "I mean the household duties. You have no maid service. Is there a rotation of chores?"

"Some of them are on rotation, and others are permanently assigned. Atzil is our cook, and he also keeps the kitchen stocked and clean. The men are responsible for keeping their rooms and bathrooms neat, and Phinas occasionally performs a surprise inspection to make sure that they do. The common areas of the house and the bunker, as well as my quarters, are on rotation."

He and Jacki weren't the first to get to the dining room, and a couple of the men were already there. They nodded politely at Jacki.

"Good morning," she said, her tone of voice implying that she wasn't happy about them having company.

"If you prefer, we can have coffee in my room."

He had a coffee maker in his suite's bar, but it hadn't occurred to him to invite Jacki to the master sitting room. She might have gotten the wrong idea and become all prickly again.

"Do you have something to eat in there as well?"

"Will cookies do for now? I can ask Shamash to bring us breakfast when it's ready."

"That would be great." She cast an apologetic glance at the two men. "There are a few things I need to discuss with you in private."

"Of course." He dipped his head.

When they took the stairs, Jacki asked, "Who does the laundry?"

"Shamash does mine, and the rest of the men do their own."

"Is Shamash your valet?"

Kalugal smiled. "He is my personal assistant."

"It's just a fancier name for the same thing. It doesn't matter what you call it."

"It matters to Shamash." Kalugal opened the door to his suite. "After you."

"You are so polite."

Was she mocking him?

"Would you prefer me not to be?" He motioned for her to sit on the couch and walked over to the bar.

The sitting room was separated from his bedroom by a door, but he had left it open and noticed Jacki glancing at his bed.

"No, I like it that you are polite, and I also like it that you made your own bed. Or has your assistant done it?"

"I believe in leading by example, and since I demand that my men make theirs, I can't have someone else do it for me."

"Nice." She sat up straight and jutted her chin out. "If I am to stay here for a while, I would like to contribute by taking over some of the chores. I can do laundry, I can change bedding, I can clean floors, I can cook, serve meals, you name it. The more tasks you can give me, the better."

For a long moment, Kalugal just looked at the woman sitting on his couch and debated what the right answer was.

The good news was that she'd officially accepted his offer, but he didn't want her to be a maid in his house. She was to be his companion, and that was how he wanted his men to think of her.

If she was a Dormant whose transition he could induce, she would become his wife and life-long companion. He didn't want his men to remember the lady of the house doing household chores.

On the other hand, this was precisely why clever Jacki was offering to perform domestic tasks. It was a clear message to him that he shouldn't expect anything more from her.

The best thing was to refuse but put the blame on someone else. "You are my guest. Kian would not be happy if I turn you into a maid."

"Why would he care about what I do?" Jacki crossed her arms over her chest. "It's my business if I want to pay for my keep by doing the laundry or cooking or serving meals. I'm not the charity case that you are contributing to, and it's not part of our deal. And please don't say that it is because I will just walk out of here."

Stubborn woman.

Jacki needed to change how she saw herself, and he was going to help her do that.

Like in the musical *My Fair Lady*, he would be for Jacki what Professor Higgins was for Eliza. A mentor, a guide, and in time, a love interest.

Jacki

Jacki waited for Kalugal to respond, but for a long moment, he just looked at her face, studying her.

His close scrutiny was unnerving. What did he see when he looked at her like that?

An attractive woman?

A stubborn and unreasonable person?

Was it a mistake to offer him her maid services?

Jacki had a feeling that it was. How was he ever going to see her as an equal if she insisted on serving him?

But then, maybe it was for the best if he didn't.

Kalugal was a snob, so if he regarded her as a servant, he would not consider her as a potential lover.

She didn't trust herself with him.

All that charm and good manners were softening her up, and when the time came and he wanted more from her, Jacki doubted her ability to say no.

The silence was broken by the coffeemaker announcing with a loud beep that it was done brewing.

Kalugal took out the two cups and brought them over to the coffee table. "Perhaps we could reach a compromise." He went back to the bar and pulled a bag of cookies out of the under-counter fridge, together with a container of cream.

"Sugar?"

"Yes, please." She rewarded him with a smile.

It felt nice to be served by the big boss himself, and it made her feel important, which was silly.

Kalugal was just being polite.

He brought over a small container of cubed sugar and pulled one cube out with a tiny pair of silver tongs. "How many?"

"Two, please."

He dropped the two cubes into her coffee and handed her the creamer. "How good of a cook are you?"

"I'm very good, and I know how to cook large quantities. How many men will I need to cook for?"

"Just one. Me. And you don't have to. It's entirely up to you."

"Why don't you want me to cook for your men?"

"Atzil would not appreciate you taking over his job."

"Why? It's only temporary. It would be a vacation for him."

Kalugal shook his head. "He wouldn't like it, and neither would the rest of my men. We have a routine that we are comfortable with. It's not prudent to disturb it. But if you cook only for me, that's a different story. The men wouldn't mind that." Kalugal opened the fancy bag of cookies and emptied it onto the small silver tray he'd brought to the table.

"That's because they would think that there is something going on between us."

He didn't deny it. "It's better that way. Right now, you have only Rufsur to contend with. Unless the men believe that I'm interested in you, every male in this house will try to woo you."

She hadn't thought about that.

"What about you?"

"What about me?"

"Are you going to try to woo me?"

His perfect lips curling into a smirk, he glanced at her from under lowered lashes. "You are a beautiful woman, Jacqueline. And you are also smart, brave, and direct, which I find very refreshing. You intrigue me."

Talk about feeling flattered.

But he hadn't answered her question. Nevertheless, she needed to give him the same preemptive speech she'd given Rufsur.

"We are not from the same species, Kalugal. There is no future for us, and I don't do hookups."

He arched a brow. "Never?"

"No exceptions. I'm going to stay with you for a couple of weeks and give you the human perspective you said that you were interested in. Then I'm going to leave, and we will probably never see each other again."

Lifting the small porcelain cup to his beautiful lips, he took a small sip of coffee and then put it back down.

"We've digressed from the subject we've been discussing, which was you cooking my meals during your stay. Are we agreed on that?"

That was a clever way to avoid addressing the elephant in the room, but she wasn't going to press the issue. Kalugal might not think that she was serious about her no-hookups policy, but he'd soon learn how adamant about it she was.

He'd said that he wouldn't touch her unless she initiated it, and that wasn't going to happen.

"You seem to be big on compromise. How about I cook for you, Rufsur and Phinas? In every military organization, the officers dine separately. I think Atzil and the rest will not have a problem with that either."

"They might. Let's try it for a day or two and see how it works."

That was better than nothing. "Okay."

Kalugal grinned and offered her his hand. "Then we have an agreement?"

She really didn't want to take it, but refusing would be rude.

"We do." Hesitantly, she placed her palm in his and waited for the bolt of lightning to strike.

It didn't, and no electric current zapped between their palms either. Instead, a wave of warmth unfurled in her belly and quickly rose to her cheeks.

"Wonderful." Kalugal let go first and pushed to his feet. "I will let Kian know about the change of plans."

"He will probably want to speak with me."

"He might. If he does, I'll come back to get you. While you wait, Shamash will bring up breakfast."

"Thank you."

Kalugal

As Kalugal closed the master suite's door behind him, he was still reeling from what had just happened. For a long moment, he stood rooted in place and tried to process his strange reaction to something as mundane as touching a woman's hand.

It had been the strangest thing.

Before, when he'd kissed Jacki, he had been so focused on his act and so emotionally closed off that the kiss had stirred nothing in him. He'd been like an automaton, his body a separate entity from his mind, a mere tool to execute his plan.

But when she'd placed her palm in his, accepting his offer and in a way also accepting him, something inside him had shifted, or rather melted. He didn't know how to describe the strange sensation. It was as if a warmth had entered his body, finding its way to his heart and wrapping it in pink cotton candy.

It was an absurd analogy, and yet that was the best he could come up with. The sensation was soft, sweet, and feminine.

Shaking his head, Kalugal forced his feet to start moving. He had a phone call to make, and it was already six-twenty, which didn't leave him much time. At seven sharp, Kian was going to connect him to his mother.

Or not.

Kalugal had half an hour to convince his cousin to accept the new deal.

It was a no brainer for Kian, and he should grab it with both hands, but Kian wasn't even-keeled and rational like Kalugal. The guy had a temper, was prideful, and overprotective of his people. He might imagine that there was some grand scheme behind Kalugal's offer and refuse it.

Naturally, he had a plan, but it had nothing to do with the clan, and therefore was of no concern to Kian.

Kalugal wanted to seduce Jacki, and if she transitioned, marry her. This was his chance to acquire an immortal mate and have immortal children with her. That option hadn't existed for him until Kian had unintentionally dropped Jacki into his lap.

It was more than that, though.

He liked Jacki. There was something about her that appealed to him on a visceral level. He had never before felt such a strong pull toward any other female.

Perhaps it had to do with her being a Dormant. Could it be that she emitted a different kind of pheromones that his body recognized as biologically compatible?

Jacki had put it succinctly. If she was human, there was no future for them because they belonged to different species, but she might be more than that.

In time, he would tell her, but not yet. If she chose to be with him, it would be because she desired him as a man and had fallen in love with him, and not because he could give her immortality.

On the face of it, he was being hypocritical. When he thought about seducing her, it was because she was a potential Dormant and could give him immortal children. Her beauty and the zest that he found so appealing were secondary considerations, and so were deeper feelings.

After a lifetime of keeping women at an emotional distance, it was difficult for him to switch gears and allow himself to feel things for her. Protecting himself from entanglement with females he couldn't have a future with had become second nature to Kalugal.

It was a defense mechanism.

If Jacki wasn't a Dormant, he would have to let her go, and it was better that he didn't develop any deep feelings for her.

And if it didn't work out between them, either because she wasn't a Dormant or because of personal incompatibility, Jacki wasn't his only option.

The truth was that once he established a truce with Kian, he could get access to the clan's females, who were already immortal and probably just as eager for immortal partners as he and his men were.

That being said, he hoped that Jacki was the one, but that was dependent on many factors, with her transition being just one of them. Kalugal wasn't an easy to please guy, and in order for them to work, Jacki had to pass several tests.

He liked her looks and was attracted to her, which was the entry-level requirement, and he also liked her personality. She was outspoken and assertive, and yet, he could sense a softness in her that yearned for a safe place to blossom.

Jacki's life circumstances had forced her to keep that side of herself suppressed, hidden, protected behind her outward prickliness. But when she felt safe, which given his earlier actions would take a lot of work on his part, he would coax that softness to the surface.

Kalugal suspected that this was the reason why Jacki didn't do hookups. She was afraid of losing the emotional detachment that she worked so hard on maintaining. It was a shield that she had erected to protect herself from the harsh realities of her life, and if she let it slip to allow someone inside, she could get hurt.

But that just added favorable points to the package.

Jacki would not share his bed unless she fell in love with him, and the challenge of winning her heart was just as exciting as seducing her.

Kian

The phone call from Kalugal arrived earlier than Kian had expected, but since Turner was already in his office, it wasn't a problem.

"I'm going to put him on speaker."

Turner nodded.

"Good morning, Kalugal."

"Good morning. We don't have a lot of time before the call, so I'll make it as brief as I can. I've negotiated an agreement with Jacki. For every day that she voluntarily stays in my house, I'm going to donate twenty-five thousand dollars to your charity organization. The funds can either go toward renting a new sanctuary for victims of trafficking that is closer to home or toward any part of the program that needs funding. I leave the decision of where to direct the funds to your discretion."

Kian and Turner exchanged puzzled glances.

Kalugal wanting to keep Jacki wasn't a big surprise. After he'd learned that she was a possible Dormant, he probably wanted to induce her himself. But the surprise was what he was offering in exchange.

Turner smiled and lifted his hand, palm up, indicating that Kian should haggle on the price.

Kian nodded. "Naturally, I'll need to hear from Jacki that she agrees to the deal. But let's assume for a moment that she does. How long are you planning on keeping her?"

"For as long as she wants to stay. I told her that she is no longer a hostage and can leave at any time."

"Why the sudden change in tactic?"

"You know the reason."

"You need time to seduce her. Does she know that?"

"No, and I want to keep it that way. You didn't tell her that she is a possible Dormant, and neither did I after learning about it from Julian. If she falls in love with me, I want to make sure that her feelings are genuine. It would be because she wants me, and not because I can give her immortality. And there is also the issue of her immunity. Since I can't make her forget anything, I need time to build trust that will go both ways. I can't let her into my life before I know that she is one hundred percent loyal to me."

"I can't find fault with that. But you shouldn't induce her without her consent."

"I won't. Jin told me how to prevent it from happening. When everything else falls in place, I'll tell Jacki the truth and ask her if she wants to be induced. Although why wouldn't she?"

"Transition could be deadly, and instead of gaining immortality, a Dormant could forfeit his or her short human life. Jacki is young and healthy, so she should be fine, but the older the Dormant, the riskier it gets. People should be aware of that and make their own decision."

"I agree."

"Good. So we have that settled. But I think twenty-five thousand a day is too low for what you are getting. Jacki doesn't know that, but I do."

"How much do you want?"

"Double."

Kalugal chuckled. "I didn't expect you to be so greedy. Let's make it thirty."

"I know that you will pay any price for a chance of having an immortal mate. I could've asked for more."

"That is true. But it is also true that we have a long road in front of us, and you wouldn't want to alienate me by making unreasonable demands before we made any headway in our negotiations."

Damn, the guy was good.

"How long are you going to keep paying up? I know that you don't plan on doing it forever."

"Until Jacki transitions or we determine that she is not a Dormant and she leaves. I'm quite certain that I will need no more than a month for that, but if I do, I'll double the contribution for the second month. Twenty-five a day for the first one, and fifty for the second. I think that's a good compromise."

"I can live with those terms."

"I also want you to lift the blockade. Since Jacki is staying with me out of her own free will, you and I no longer have a conflict, and there is no reason for you to keep a force here. I have a business to run, and I don't want you in it."

"I bet. But as long as you have Jacki, I will need to keep a minimal force in place to make sure that you don't get up and run away with her. I want to know where she is at all times. Secondly, I want to talk to her every day to verify that she is still okay."

Kalugal

Kalugal glanced at the clock. They were running out of time, and Kian still needed to verify that Jacki was indeed staying out of her own free will.

Placing his hand over the receiver, he motioned for Phinas to get closer. "Get Jacki here. She is in the master suite."

"Yes, sir." As usual, Phinas's stoic expression revealed nothing.

"Don't mention what you've heard to anyone. Especially not to Rufsur, and not to Jacki either. She doesn't know that she's anything other than human."

"Yes, sir."

It was so much easier to work with Phinas, but Kalugal preferred Rufsur's company. Phinas was more of a yes man, while Rufsur was a good sounding board. He didn't let Kalugal's intelligence intimidate him, and he wasn't afraid to voice his opinion.

Except, that was a double-edged sword.

Rufsur didn't accept Kalugal's prior claim on Jacki and thought that it was okay for them to compete over her. He needed to have a talk with the guy and lay down the rules. Rufsur would no doubt bristle for a while, but he would have to get over it sooner or later.

"Are you there?" Kian asked.

"My apologies. I had to send one of my men to bring Jacki over. We are running out of time for the scheduled phone call with my mother, and we still have a few items to iron out."

"We can finish up after the call, but I need to talk to Jacki before I allow it."

"Of course. But before we continue, I want your assurance that your men will not interfere with my day-to-day operations. Also, when I take Jacki out shopping or to restaurants and shows, I don't want your men trailing behind us."

"You'll have to order stuff online and dine in. Jacki is a wanted woman and you can't take her out in public. At least not without a proper disguise."

Kalugal straightened in his chair. "Wanted for what?"

"She can explain later. Is she there yet? We have mere minutes to spare."

"One moment, please."

Kalugal rose to his feet and opened the door right as Phinas was about to knock.

Looking at Jacki, he wondered what she could possibly have done to be wanted by the police. Was she a thief? A murderer? An embezzler?

If she was an untrustworthy person, he would have to cancel the deal despite all of her other positive attributes. Maybe that was why Kian had agreed so readily to his proposal?

Dormants were rare and precious, and by letting Kalugal keep Jacki, Kian was depriving his own clansmen of a possible life partner.

The logical conclusion was that he didn't want a criminal to become part of his clan. Except, there was no time to find out what Jacki's crime was and, if necessary, cancel the deal.

Still, he could do that later, after he talked with her and found out. Worst case, he would have to pay for one day of her stay and then send her back to Kian with a 'thanks, but no thanks' note.

"Come in. Kian is on the line and he wants to talk to you." Kalugal motioned for her to take the seat he had vacated. "The speakerphone is on."

She sat down and leaned over the device that he'd left face up on his desk. "Hi, Kian. Did Kalugal explain the deal to you?"

"He did. But I want to hear it from you in your own words, so I know that we are all on the same page."

"It's simple. For every day that I stay here, Kalugal will donate twenty-five thousand dollars to the clan's charity for the rescued victims of trafficking."

"How long do you intend to stay?"

She chuckled. "How much will it cost to build a shelter in California? Kalugal says that Alaska is a miserable place for that and that the victims deserve better. I agree."

For a moment, Kian didn't say anything, and Kalugal imagined him calculating the costs in his head.

Building in California was expensive everywhere, even inland, and not only because of the land cost. The state and its various cities charged insane amounts for the numerous permits and fees they demanded, nearly doubling the cost of construction and pricing decent housing out of most people's reach. No wonder it had the worst homeless crisis in the States.

It was one of the many things that would change when he took over the world. Kalugal would do away with corrupt politicians who were lining the pockets of their donors, like by approving so-called building projects for the poor with price tags of over half a million per unit.

What a joke that was.

The problem was that the Californian homeless situation was just one small drop in the enormous worldwide bucket of things that needed fixing, and he didn't trust humans with implementing his policies. Corruption and nepotism were rampant everywhere, and the misuse of taxpayers' money was criminal.

The solution Kalugal envisioned was managing everything with the help of artificial intelligence, but the technology was decades away from being ready.

Good thing that he was a patient man, and that time was on his side.

"A year," Kian eventually said, confirming that he'd been calculating the costs in his head. "Are you planning on staying that long with Kalugal?"

Jacki

A *freaking year?*

Jacki knew she wouldn't survive that long. Heck, she wasn't sure she was going to survive a month.

"No, I'm not. Will a month's worth of donation be enough for a down payment?"

"You don't have to do that, Jacki. Not unless you like Kalugal and want to spend more time with him. I won't say no to his contributions, but I don't need them."

Kalugal put his hand on her shoulder. "Stay as long as you are comfortable. Don't feel obligated to fund Kian's charity."

She turned to look up at him. "You are the one funding it, not me. But let's see how it works out. I might stay a week, or a month, or two."

"Good," Kian said. "I'm glad that we have reached an understanding with five minutes to spare. I will expect a phone call from Jacki every day, and after the call to Areana, I'll provide you with bank information for the wire transfers."

"Goodbye, Kian. And send my regards to Jin."

"I will." He ended the call.

"Thank you." Kalugal gave her shoulder a little squeeze. "If you don't mind, I would like to speak with my mother in private, or as privately as I can with Kian listening in."

"Of course." Jacki jumped to her feet. "I'll be in the kitchen."

"Okay. When I'm done, I'll come to get you."

Kalugal hadn't even asked her why she was going there, but that was because he was literally out of time.

Not wanting to intrude on Kalugal's first conversation with his mother even for a moment, she grabbed Phinas by the elbow and headed for the door. "Can you introduce me to Atzil?"

"Certainly."

When they were out in the corridor, Jacki cast him an apologetic smile. "Sorry about dragging you out of there, but Kalugal needs to be alone for that."

Phinas nodded. "I would have left without your intervention." He looked at her with curious eyes. "I understand that you'll be staying with us for a while. "

"Yes. Kalugal explained that he needs a human's perspective on certain things. I'm not sure what they are, but I'm happy to help in exchange for his very generous donation to a worthy cause."

"What are you getting out of it?"

She shrugged. "Nothing monetary. It just makes me feel good to know that I'm contributing to the cause."

Phinas seemed doubtful, but he didn't press the issue. "Why do you want to meet Atzil?"

"I convinced Kalugal to let me cook for him, you and Rufsur while I'm here. I want to talk it over with Atzil and figure out how we can both use the kitchen without stepping on each other's toes."

"Are you a good cook?"

Jacki smiled. "You will soon find out."

"I can't wait to sample your cooking. But don't tell that to Atzil."

"I won't." She let out a breath. "I can imagine how excited Kalugal is about talking with his mom."

Phinas nodded. "I'm glad for him. I wish I could talk to my mother, but she is long gone."

"She wasn't an immortal?"

"No."

"So your father was an immortal?"

"It doesn't work like that."

"So how does it work?"

"I don't know what I'm allowed to tell you. You will have to ask Kalugal."

Right, as if he was going to tell her anything. As it was, she already knew too much, and because of her immunity, they couldn't erase the knowledge from her head.

Kalugal's speech about her being free to leave was nonsense. She might be able to leave his house, but she would be collected by Kian's men and taken back to that underground facility, or wherever the clan was.

Jacki no longer thought that either of them would kill her, but she was certain that she would never be free to live out her life as a human among other humans.

When Kalugal had said that Kian was never going to let her go, he might have done it to convince her that she would be better off staying with him, but he hadn't been lying.

Actually, it worked in his favor. With Kian taking care of the problematic immune, Kalugal could appear like the good guy who was not holding her against her will.

It wasn't the end of the world, and Jacki could definitely see the upside of being taken care of. Her days of worrying about paying rent and having enough left over for food were over. But she'd already had that in the program and had chosen to leave it behind for freedom.

Apparently, she'd just exchanged one form of captivity for another. Both had their advantages and disadvantages.

The program had given her financial security, but the director had selective breeding plans in mind that she had no wish to be part of. Living among immortals, on the other hand, meant a life of spinsterhood unless she eased up on her convictions. She couldn't have a future with any of the men, and the only type of relationship she could have would be as a temporary lover.

Forget about being a wife or a mother.

But wait, maybe she could at least have children?

Would they be immortal?

Phinas had said that his mother had been human. Jin wasn't immortal either, and yet she and Arwel seemed very serious about each other.

Was there a way to make it work?

Kalugal

As Kalugal waited for Kian to connect him to his mother, he decided to keep the conversation with her as positive as possible.

The troublesome questions that burned in his heart would have to wait for another time. Like how she could live with Navuh and not seek a way to get out of the harem, especially now that she could solicit the help of her sister to get her out. Or why would a goddess bind her life to a mere immortal?

The truth was that there was no point asking her those questions at all because he knew the answers, and it would only upset her.

There were no male gods left for Areana to choose from, and Navuh was next in line as the most powerful immortal ever born. If that was the only criterion for choosing a husband, then Areana had chosen the best one available.

Secluded in the harem the way she was, Areana might not have been aware that her mate was a cruel despot who ruled his people with an iron fist, and who had no regard for human lives. With her, he might have been indeed as loving and as respectful as she had claimed he was.

Was that what she'd said, though?

Things were a little blurry after all this time, and what Kalugal had heard her say as a five-year-old boy might have morphed into something different over the years.

What he remembered clearly, though, was her telling him how much she loved him and his brother and that, in his own way, their father loved them too. Removing them from the harem and separating them from their mother had been done to protect them.

Still, Areana had feared for him and had told him to keep his unique abilities secret from his father. Which meant that she hadn't been entirely oblivious to the kind of man Navuh was.

And yet, she'd said that she loved him, and she had made Kalugal swear that he would never use his power against his father.

Chuckling mirthlessly, Kalugal swiveled his chair around and looked out the window. It seemed that she'd left him a loophole, though. He didn't think his vow had included not killing his father by conventional means. But the problem was that he couldn't be sure of that. He remembered vowing not to use his power of compulsion against Navuh, but he might've vowed not to kill him as well, and over the years the memory had changed.

When his phone rang, Kalugal snatched it off the desk. "I'm ready."

"We are patching you through," Kian said.

"Kalugal?" His mother's melodic voice was loud and clear, and exactly like he had remembered it.

His throat suddenly constricted, he managed only to whisper, "I'm here."

She started sobbing quietly. "I thought that I would never get to talk with you again. This is a miracle." She took a shuddering breath and regained her composure. "How have you been, my son? Has life been good to you? Better than it was in the Brotherhood?"

"Running away was the best decision I've ever made. Thank you for planting the idea in my head when I was a small boy. I am free, I am my own man, and I don't have to answer to anyone. I struggled only for a short time at the beginning, but I found a way to make money, and my men and I live very comfortably."

"Yes, Annani told me about you making a fortune on the stock exchange. You were always clever."

"Thank you. How have you been? How is Tula?"

"You remember her? We are both fine, keeping each other company. Life is uneventful in the harem. Or rather it was. After Annani had tried to rescue me, and I was given this communication device, things became much more interesting. She keeps me informed on everything that is happening in the world."

This was news to him.

Kian had said nothing about the clan trying to rescue Areana. He'd only said that they'd managed to smuggle a communication device to her.

"What happened to the rescue, did it fail?"

She laughed, the beautiful sound confirming beyond a shadow of a doubt that he was indeed talking with his mother.

As a child, he'd thought that his mother had a beautiful voice because she was a beautiful woman. As an adult, he should have wondered about the otherworldly quality of her laugh, but the idea that Areana was a goddess had been too preposterous to even tickle at his awareness.

"I didn't need rescuing. Annani thought that your father was mean to me and that I had suffered for thousands of years at his hands. But she was wrong. I love your father, and he loves me. He is good to me."

That was debatable, but Kalugal had promised himself not to touch on the subject during his first conversation with his mother. Instead, he moved to the rescue operation. He was consumed by curiosity and a little envious of Kian. The guy had come up with an actionable plan to rescue Areana while Kalugal had never figured a way to do that.

"I'm sure that it wasn't Annani herself who organized the rescue. I assume it was Kian?"

"Your brother was the one who came up with the idea for infiltrating the harem, and Annani was the one who ordered Kian to implement it."

Talk about big news. His brother had been involved in the rescue?

Covering up for his surprise, Kalugal chuckled. "Annani couldn't have ordered Kian to do anything. She is just a figurehead. He runs the show."

Areana laughed again. "You haven't met my sister yet. She is very much in charge, and what she says, goes. Kian might argue, but in the end he has to do as she commands."

Sly Kian. He had bluffed about being the clan's leader, the same way he had bluffed about hurting Areana if Kalugal hurt Jin.

"Apparently, I have gotten the wrong impression. I thought Kian was the head of the clan."

"He is. Most of the time, Annani doesn't interfere. But she is the Clan Mother, and if she wants something done, it gets done."

His mother sounded both proud and fond of her sister, whetting Kalugal's appetite to meet her in person.

"I wonder if you can do me a favor and tell Annani that I would like an audience with her."

If Annani was indeed in charge, then he didn't need Kian's permission and could go straight to the boss.

"I will ask her. Did you have a chance to meet Lokan?"

"No one has told me that it was a possibility."

"Then you should certainly do that first." Her voice broke. "My boys together at last. It will gladden my heart to know that you've become friends and allies. And maybe one day, the bonds of friendship could blossom into brotherly love."

Wendy

When the door mechanism activated with a hiss, Wendy expected Bowen or Leon to come in. It wasn't their regular time, but there could be no one else. The guards came in only to deliver her meals, and since those consisted of wrapped sandwiches and coke cans, they had no reason to come back and collect dishes. Everything except for the tray went into the trash bin.

The person who entered wasn't one of the guards, though. It was a woman, and she had one of those professional fake smiles plastered on her face.

Had Kian sent a social worker to talk to her?

Wendy doubted that.

Keeping her prisoner was illegal, so it wasn't like they could involve anyone from the outside.

"Hello, Wendy." The woman walked over to her and extended her hand. "My name is Vanessa, and I'm a therapist."

"You mean a shrink? I'm not crazy."

"I didn't say that you were." Vanessa sat on the other side of the couch. "Kian sent me to talk to you."

Wendy shrugged. "I have nothing to say." She cast the therapist a sidelong glance. "Are you here to erase my memories? Because that will be the best thing for everyone. After you do that, you can drop me off somewhere, and if my mind hasn't turned into mush, I will call the director again and ask him to send someone to pick me up. Case closed."

"Do you want to go back to the program?"

Damn. Wendy hated shrinks and their stupid questions. Would she have called her uncle and told him where to find her if she didn't want to go back?

"Of course, I want to go back. In the program, I have a great-paying job and a secure future. Over here, I have nothing."

"What about Vlad?"

Wendy's heart squeezed painfully, but she affected a shrug. "He hates me now, so that's water under the bridge."

"What if he doesn't?"

"I'm not going to give away my job security and my future for a boy, no matter how sweet he is. That would be stupid."

"Why do you think that?"

Wendy narrowed her eyes at the therapist. "Would you leave your cushy therapist job for a guy? Especially if you knew that no other place would hire you because you can only treat paranormals?"

Vanessa nodded in understanding. "I get it. You think that other than your paranormal talent, you have nothing to offer."

"I don't think that. I know that."

"You are still a very young woman. You can become whoever you want to be."

"Not really. My father will only pay for community college, and I will not qualify for financial aid to complete my education because he's not poor. Besides, why would I bother to study anything when the program pays me a huge salary anyway? Without any education, I'm getting paid as much as a doctor who's just starting out."

"Why did you run, then?"

She hadn't.

Wendy had joined the group to spy on them and gain favor with her uncle. If she wanted to advance in her job, she needed to go above and beyond, and that was exactly what she had done. After all, she was supposed to be the director's eyes and ears in the program.

But that wasn't what she was going to tell the therapist.

"It was a stupid decision, which I regretted almost immediately. I just got carried away."

Vanessa tilted her head. "I doubt it. You could have asked to get dropped off."

Damn. The therapist might be an empath or a telepath, and to fool her, Wendy needed to go deeper into her lies.

Not a problem. All she had to do was to turn them into truths in her head.

"I was scared. I didn't know who you people were. You kept us locked up in here, didn't allow us access to phones, and put guards on us. What was I supposed to think? That you would let me go if I asked nicely?"

Vanessa smiled. "We were right to do that, though. Kian suspected from the very beginning that one of you might be a mole, and that's why we kept you away from phones and didn't let you out."

"I'm not a mole. I just want to get out of here and go back to the program."

The therapist shifted, so she was facing Wendy directly. "Mey told me that you love the outdoors. Is that true, or did you just use it as an excuse to get away from the cabin?"

"It's true. I love the mountains, just not getting up there. Those narrow roads were scary."

"I know what you mean. They scare me too. But if you love the outdoors, it must be difficult for you to be underground."

"I hate it."

"And yet you want to go back to the program, which is located in an underground facility the size of a small city."

Wendy shrugged. "That's a small price to pay for security. As I said, my number one priority is having a well-paying job and a secure future. Everything else is secondary."

Vanessa arched a brow. "Even love?"

"Love is overrated. It leads people to make bad decisions that can ruin the rest of their lives."

"Do you know someone like that?"

"My mother. Not that I know her. She left when I was a baby."

"What was her bad decision?"

Wendy rolled her eyes. "Marrying my father, of course, and her second mistake was having a baby with him."

"If you can't remember her, how do you know that marrying your father was the bad decision? Maybe she had other issues that you were not aware of?"

"Perhaps. I don't know. She became addicted to drugs, and then she left. I think that she escaped into the drugs first and only then gathered enough courage to run."

"Do you resent her for it?"

Wendy rolled her eyes. "What do you think? Of course I do."

"Every person reacts differently. You seem to understand her reasons, which is very mature of you."

"I know what her reasons were, but she should have taken me with her instead of leaving me to be raised by a monster."

"Now we are getting somewhere. Was your father abusive?"

Wendy nodded. "He's a good-looking guy, and everyone thinks that he is so charming, but when no one is looking, he turns into a monster. He must have made her life so intolerable that she turned to drugs to numb the pain and then just left. But she should have taken me. If she couldn't have taken care of me herself, she could have dropped me off at an orphanage. That would have been better than growing up with him."

Her mother should have called her older brother, and he would have helped her or at least taken Wendy and raised her himself. Her uncle had said so after she'd joined him in the program.

But he hadn't known about the abuse. He hadn't even known what happened to his sister. She hadn't kept in touch, and after leaving Wendy, she'd disappeared.

Her mother had probably died from an overdose soon after leaving. That was most likely why she had never come back for her baby girl.

"Perhaps that is true," Vanessa said. "But you can't know that for sure. Maybe your father's inner monster didn't come out until after she'd left. Perhaps she had other reasons for running."

"Like what? Hooking up with another jerk that she fell in love with? That could be. Her decision-making process was fucked up."

"You have every right to be angry at your mother and at your father. They have both failed you. But that doesn't mean that every person you care about is going to do the same."

"This is never going to happen to me again. I won't let myself care for anyone enough to give a damn when they let me down."

Kian

"Come in, Vanessa." Kian motioned for the therapist to take a seat. "I assume that your meeting with our little mole was illuminating?"

Vanessa was a busy lady. Coming over to his office instead of heading back to the sanctuary and giving him an update in person instead of over the phone meant that she had something important she wanted to discuss with him.

"It was, but that's not why I decided to spend the night in the village. It's because of Vlad. Jackson told me that he is not in a good place, and I thought that I'd stop by his house and have a chat with him." She smiled. "That kid is like a son to me."

"I'm surprised that he is taking it so hard. He barely knows the girl."

Vanessa lifted a brow. "How long did it take you to fall for Syssi?"

"That's different. We were fated."

"Maybe Vlad and Wendy are fated as well."

Kian rose to his feet and walked over to the fridge. "If they are, Vlad has my sympathy. I detest liars." He pulled a beer out. "Can I offer you something to drink?" He stepped aside so she could see the contents of the fridge.

"I'll take a Perrier."

After handing her the bottle, Kian sat on the other guest chair. "So, what have you learned?"

"It was just a friendly talk, not a therapy session." She twisted the cap off. "Otherwise, I wouldn't be able to share with you what I've learned."

"Obviously."

It was just semantics, but it was important to Vanessa to make the distinction.

"I know that you are busy, so I'll make it brief. When Wendy was just a baby, her mother left. She was raised by an abusive father, and she doesn't trust anyone. She sees the program as a safe haven that will protect her from all of life's troubles. It provides her with a place to live, pays her a very generous salary, and she probably sees herself climbing the organizational ladder and staying on for the duration. She is willing to sacrifice everything for this perceived safety."

"She is young and naive. There is no such thing as guaranteed safety, not even for government employees. That program might shut down for any number of reasons. There could be budget cuts, someone might discover the shady things the director is doing, the director might pass away, and so on."

"My thoughts exactly, but I didn't point it out to her. She was too riled up to listen to reason, but I will bring it up next time, with your permission, of course."

"Why do you need my permission?"

"I was getting to that. I have an idea for how to approach this situation, but naturally, it needs your approval."

"Go on."

"I checked with Bowen, and he says that Wendy is susceptible to thralling. He had no problem erasing the keep's location from her head, and he verified that she had no recollection of where it was. We can test it further by erasing small memories."

"Where are you going with this?"

"When Wendy realizes that her future would be much more secure with the clan than it could ever be with the program, she'll no longer want to go back. She likes Vlad, and she doesn't like hurting him, but she believes that she'll be throwing her future away if she lets herself fall for him."

"If he was her fated mate, nothing else would have mattered."

Vanessa smiled. "Every person is different, Kian, and Wendy carries around baggage that would topple an elephant. She is clinging desperately to the only security she's ever had."

"What do you suggest we do with her?"

"Give her and Vlad another chance. Wendy loves nature, and she loves the mountains. I think we should send her and Vlad to our cabin, along with Ingrid and Richard and a couple of Guardians. It will provide a completely different environment from the one she grew up in and from the paranormal program. It might help her see the world in a different light."

"Are you going to visit her there? I'm not a therapist, but I can't see a lifetime of baggage getting cured by fresh mountain air."

"Of course not. I can have Skype sessions with her. But fresh mountain air combined with Vlad's love might be the magic potion that Wendy needs."

"You'll need to talk it over with Vlad. I doubt that he's willing to give Wendy another chance."

"That's why I'm heading to his place next. But I wanted to get your tentative approval first."

Cradling the unopened beer in his hands, Kian leaned forward. "Normally, I wouldn't have minded giving Wendy another chance. But two issues give me pause. She managed to fool Edna, and that's very troubling. I don't think I could ever trust her. And the second issue is exposing Vlad to more heartache. If he gives her another chance and she disappoints him again, he'll be crushed."

Vanessa sighed. "But at least he won't live with what-ifs. He'll have closure."

"And what about Edna?"

"I have a theory about that, but I need more time with Wendy to be sure. It might be a coping mechanism that she's developed."

"Like a split personality?" Kian popped the cap off the beer and lifted the bottle to his lips.

Vanessa shook her head. "It would have to be more than that to fool Edna."

"Do you have a hypothesis?"

"I talked with Edna, and from what she's described, I suspect that Wendy flooded her own psyche with painful memories to distract her. The things that Wendy let Edna see convinced her that she knew the girl's reasons for leaving the program, and since the next layer was all about suffering, Edna didn't go digging deeper. She was sure that what she had seen was enough."

"That sounds like a very clever technique for someone as young as Wendy."

"Don't forget that she'd spent months in the company of other paranormals, and she also got training on how to protect herself from mind invasions. She knew exactly what to do."

"Fascinating." A light bulb went off in Kian's head. "If little Wendy can protect her mind from getting invaded, then maybe there is a way to block Kalugal's compulsion?"

Vanessa smiled indulgently. "It's not the same thing. Wendy is susceptible to thralling and shrouding like most humans. What I suspect she did was to throw a mental smokescreen over her emotions. That's not going to help you against Kalugal."

"There must be a way."

"I'm sure there is. You can train your mind to resist, but it will take time and a lot of practice, and we don't have anyone who can teach it."

"What about Lokan?"

"He can compel humans, not immortals. In order to train your mind to resist compulsion, you need someone with that ability to keep attacking you with it. It's like developing a mental muscle. You need resistance to grow it."

"Perhaps I can ask Annani, but that's a long-term solution. Right now, I need to come up with a way to communicate with Kalugal while shielding myself from his compulsion."

"Easy. Compulsion is transferred through sound waves, so you can do the same thing that the Guardians in the blockade did. Put in earplugs and communicate with Kalugal via text."

Kian should have thought of that before, but he knew why he hadn't.

It was his damn pride.

To tell Kalugal that from now on they would only communicate through text was like admitting his inferiority, which Kian loathed to do.

Except, it seemed that there was no better option.

Vlad

"Hello, Vlad. I'm glad that I caught you home." Jackson's mom walked in and put her purse on the counter.

"Hi, Vanessa. Can I offer you a cup of coffee?" his mom asked.

"Thank you. I could use a little boost."

His mother didn't look surprised by Vanessa's visit. Had she asked the therapist to come over and talk to him?

Everyone was blowing this incident out of proportion. So a girl he used to like had betrayed his trust.

Big deal.

It happened all the time. Maybe not on such a grand scale, but whatever. It wasn't as if they had been in a relationship. Vlad had known Wendy for a total of four days. He'd get over it.

When the coffee was served, Vanessa and his mother chitchatted for several minutes, but he knew they were just trying to ease up into the real reason for Vanessa's visit.

"I went to see Wendy earlier." Jackson's mom put her coffee cup down and turned to him. "We had a long chat, and I think I can help her. Or rather we can help her together."

"With what?"

"Wendy thinks that the only safe place for her is in the program. She doesn't trust people. She's afraid to form emotional connections because she expects everyone to let her down, and the program provides her with the security she's never had before."

There was nothing in what Vanessa had said that made him want to forgive Wendy, let alone help her. "Why are you telling me that? If she was so happy there, let her go back to the program."

"I don't think she was happy. Otherwise, she wouldn't have jumped on the opportunity to escape. Later, she got scared and decided that it was a mistake."

Ever since he'd returned to the village, Vlad had been thinking a lot about Wendy's motives for betraying her friends, and what Vanessa had suggested was one of the scenarios that he had come up with. But it hadn't been the only one or the best. The one he'd eventually settled on was much more sinister than that.

"Or Wendy might have tagged along because she was a mole, and the first chance she got, she called her boss and told him where he could find her friends. She'd been planning this for a long time, pretending to like me so she could manipulate me. Why would you want to help someone like that?"

Vanessa nodded. "That had occurred to me as well. But even if that's true, her motives are still the same. Her loyalty to the program comes from a place of fear. That's the only home she knows, and that's where she thinks she belongs. It's her safety net. That's an illusion, of course, but that's what she believes. And because of things that happened in her past, she is willing to sacrifice everything for that false sense of security."

Vlad tried to imagine himself in Wendy's shoes. The clan was his home, his family, and his safety net. Would he give all of that up for a girl? Even one whom he loved?

He wasn't sure.

A guy like him would have a hard time surviving on his own in the human world, but that was because he looked like a damn vampire. Wendy was a pretty girl who could blend in anywhere.

Except, she might have felt like an outcast on the inside, and that was what mattered.

"How are we going to help her?" he heard himself asking.

Vanessa rewarded him with a bright smile. "I'm so glad that you found it in your heart to forgive her, and that you are willing to give her another chance."

He shook his head. "I'm willing to help Wendy. I didn't say that I forgave her."

"I understand. We will take it one step at a time. First thing we need to do is get Wendy out of the prison cell in the keep's underground. She's wilting in there, all alone, with nothing to do but watch television all day long. I convinced Kian to let us use the clan's cabin. It's an isolated location, so Wendy will have nowhere to run, but she will be surrounded by nature, which I believe will be therapeutic for her. You, Richard, and hopefully Ingrid will go with her, along with a couple of Guardians, of course."

Vlad wasn't sold on the idea. "I've already missed several classes, and also shifts in the bakery. I can't just pick up and go."

"I can write you a doctor's note for your teachers, and I can talk to your boss about rescheduling your shifts." She leaned toward him and winked. "He owes me a favor or two."

"When and how long?"

"Let's start with the weekend and see how it works. If, after that, you still don't want anything to do with Wendy, we will send her back to the program."

That hadn't been part of the deal. "I don't want to be responsible for her future. It's up to her to decide what she wants to do, and you and Kian can decide if you want to trust her."

Vanessa leaned even closer. "Let's cut to the chase, Vlad. Do you have feelings for Wendy?"

"I had. But then she used me and made a fool out of me."

"I think that they are still there, but you've been hurt, so you shoved them into a corner and built a wall around them to block them."

Unfortunately, Vanessa was right.

"They can stay there until they shrivel and die."

"Or maybe they can come out and be given a new life. What if you and Wendy are fated for each other? Do you want to pass on this opportunity and have someone else attempt her induction?"

She couldn't have shocked him more if she had told him that he'd been elected President, and a limo was waiting outside to take him to the White House.

"Is that what it's all about?" his mother asked. "You think that Wendy is the one for Vlad?"

Vanessa nodded. "I'm not talking as a psychologist, and this is not my professional opinion. I'm talking as your friend, Stella, and as Vlad's honorary aunt. Given the way things have been going since Amanda found Syssi, the Fates have been working overtime to find mates for us. I believe that it's Vlad's turn to find his happily ever after."

Jacki

Atzil wasn't happy to share the kitchen. "I've been cooking for everyone since the very beginning, and I haven't heard any complaints." He cast a sidelong glance at Phinas. "Right?"

Phinas lifted his hands in a peace sign. "I'm not complaining."

"It's not about you." Jacki put her hand on Atzil's bulging bicep. The guy was built like a pro-wrestler and had the bearing of a drill sergeant with a buzz cut to match. "It's about me. I will go nuts with nothing to do. I offered to do the laundry or wash the dishes, but Kalugal wouldn't have it. Cooking for him, Phinas, and Rufsur was the only thing he agreed to." She leaned closer. "But I can also be your kitchen helper. He doesn't need to know. I can peel and cut and clean pots. I will make your life easier."

Atzil pursed his fleshy lips. "I could use some help around here."

"So, do we have a deal?"

He arched a brow. "Do I have a choice?"

"Nope." She offered him her hand. "Deal?"

He shook it, his large hand grasping hers gently.

The guy wasn't tall, but he was stocky, and he must spend hours in the gym on a daily basis. Even his neck was muscular, and his jaw was so broad and square that it looked like it could slice bread.

"Let me show you where everything is, and what you are allowed to touch and what you are not."

When the short tour was over, Kalugal walked into the kitchen. "I need a word with you, Jacki."

She nodded and turned to Atzil. "Thank you for showing me around."

"Jacki and I will eat in the library," Kalugal said. "Can you send someone with a tray when lunch is ready?"

"You've got it, boss."

"Thank you." Kalugal motioned for her to accompany him.

As they walked down the corridor, Jacki wondered whether Kalugal was planning to revoke her cooking privileges.

He hadn't looked happy when he'd walked into the kitchen and saw her talking with Atzil, but then it might have nothing to do with her. Maybe his talk with his mother had been disappointing?

"Please, take a seat." He waved his hand at the couch.

Sitting on the edge, Jacki felt like she'd been summoned to the principal's office for sentencing.

But for what crime?

"How was your conversation with your mother?"

"Too short." He walked over to the bar and poured himself a drink. "Can I offer you something?"

"Do you have soft drinks in there?"

"Perrier or coke?"

"Coke, please."

He pulled out a can and handed it to her. "When I told Kian that I wanted to take you out shopping and dining, he said that you are a wanted woman and that I should have you shop online and order in. Would you like to tell me what that is all about?"

Jacki let out a breath.

So that was what had Kalugal's panties in a wad. He thought that he'd just invited a criminal into his house, and on top of that he was paying twenty-five thousand dollars a day for the privilege.

No wonder he was pissed.

"It's not what you think. I ran away from a job, not the police. But since my employer was the government, and I was part of a paranormally talented team that they'd assembled after a painstakingly long and expensive search, they want me back."

"Why did you run away?"

Jacki popped the ring pull and took a sip. "The director of the secret paranormal program had a brilliant idea. If he could pair up compatible talents, they could produce super-powerful children. His recruiter was a compeller like you, and she helped him with that. I'm immune to mind manipulation, so I wasn't affected, but Jin dated a guy she would have never chosen if not for the compulsion. Not only that, they drafted very young people, teenagers. Anyway, I figured out pretty quickly that they were never going to let any of us out. So, when Jin's sister found her and offered to help her escape, I asked to join them."

"Was the program located in a secret and isolated facility?"

"It's not really secret, but it's not well known. It's a huge underground compound the size of a small city that was built as a fallout shelter. Someone came up with the idea of utilizing it for various secret programs during peacetime, and ours was just one out of many. Nevertheless, we were sworn to complete secrecy, and none of the families knew where the recruits had been taken. My teammates were compelled to keep the secret by that recruiter I told you about. Naturally, I wasn't, but I pretended that I was. I figured out early on that I should keep my immunity to myself."

"How did Jin's sister find her?"

"That's a long story."

"I'm in no hurry, are you?" He took a sip from his drink.

"Damn, where to start? I assume that you already know that immunity is not my only talent, right? I'm sure that you had a recording device hidden somewhere in the room I shared with Arwel, and that you heard me talking about it."

He nodded. "I didn't hear you say it, but I was told that you mentioned having visions of the future."

The guy was clever with his words. He neither confirmed nor denied the hidden recording device.

"Mostly, my visions are pretty useless because they are never about my own future. They are usually about the futures of people I know, but hardly anyone listens to me when I warn them about something that's about to happen to them. They think I'm nuts or that I'm making it up. But when I told Jin that her sister was coming for her during one of our Saturday leaves, she listened. Probably because she knew that paranormal abilities were real. It's hard for those that don't have them to accept that some people can see the future, read thoughts, see auras, or tether their consciousness to someone they touch. Although that one's unique. No one has ever heard about a talent like Jin's."

Kalugal smiled indulgently. "Does it make you nervous to talk about it?"

"Why do you think so?"

"Because I've never heard you talk so fast."

Jacki nodded. "I'm not used to talking about my paranormal abilities so freely. But what really makes me nervous is talking about the abilities of others. I feel like I'm betraying their trust, but that's stupid because you already know all about that."

Kalugal

Jacki was being honest with him, and Kalugal felt that he should respond in kind. To build trust, it had to go both ways.

"Frankly, I don't know as much about paranormal abilities as you might think. Most immortals can thrall and shroud to some degree. It's a survival mechanism that is necessary for living hidden among humans. My abilities are stronger than most, and I inherited them from my father, who is even more powerful than me. Other than that, I know that some immortals have strong empathic abilities, and others have telepathic or both, but that's about it. I've also never heard about tethering or about hearing echoes of conversations embedded in walls."

Jacki shook her head. "It worries me that you are telling me all that."

"Why?"

"Because you can't make me forget anything. It's like the murderer showing his face to the victim. It doesn't matter if she sees it because he is going to kill her anyway."

Instinctively, Kalugal leaned forward. "I'll never harm you, Jacki. You have my word."

She shrugged. "I don't think that you are going to kill me, but you are not going to let me go either. And if you do, Kian won't. I'll never be free again."

"Free to do what?"

"Live among humans."

He was tempted to tell her that she didn't belong with them, but it was too early for that.

"What's wrong about living among immortals? We are not so bad."

"So you are not denying it?"

"I'm neither denying nor confirming. Let's take it one day at a time, shall we? Maybe you'll decide that you are more comfortable living with immortals than with humans. You won't have to hide your paranormal talents anymore, and you'll be free to express yourself in any way you want. Normal, or paranormal. That's liberating."

She smiled. "You're right. I've never considered that angle."

"Things are rarely black and white, or even shades of gray." He waved his hand. "They are as nuanced and as varied as all the colors of the spectrum."

"I like your analogy."

Kalugal wasn't an empath, but after many years of negotiating business deals, he was good at reading human emotions. Jacki's speech had slowed down to its normal speed, which meant that she was no longer nervous, or at least not as anxious as she had been at the start of their conversation.

"You've told me about how you knew that Jin's sister was going to show up and help you escape, but you still didn't tell me how she knew where to find Jin."

"I don't have all the details about that. What I know is that they somehow found the recruiter, caught her, and got her to tell them where they could find Jin."

"Interesting. I assume that by 'them' you mean the clan?"

Jacki smiled. "They told me that they were a group of paranormally talented people who were saving others like them from the government's clutches. That seemed a reasonable explanation to me. And then you spilled the beans when you told me that Arwel was an immortal. He told me a little about your history, but I still don't know much about you." She chuckled. "Talk about a trip down the rabbit hole."

"You are taking it remarkably well."

"What else am I supposed to do? Freak out? That's not going to help me."

"Very true."

The door to the library opened, and Rufsur came in, holding a large tray. Shamash followed behind him with a smaller one.

"Where do you want me to put it?"

"Over there." Kalugal got up, walked over to the games table, and moved the chessboard to its dedicated stand.

Rufsur put the tray down and pulled out a chair. "Miss Jacqueline?"

"Thank you." Jacki rewarded him with a bright smile.

Shamash put the other tray down. "Enjoy your lunch." He turned around and walked out.

Regrettably, Rufsur stayed.

Pulling out a chair for himself, he sat down. "I told Phinas to come, but he chose to dine with the men today." Rufsur unfurled a napkin and draped it over his thighs.

Kalugal wasn't happy.

He and Jacki had been making good progress, and Rufsur was intruding. "Why don't you join Phinas?"

"Nah. Phinas told me that Jacki is going to cook for the four of us and that we are going to dine separately from the men. I like that." He cast Jacki a charming smile. "When should we expect your first creation?"

"If it's all right with Atzil, I can make today's dinner."

"What are you going to prepare?"

"I'm not sure yet. I need to check what I have to work with."

"I'm sure that whatever you make is going to be a treat."

As Kalugal listened to Rufsur laying on the charm, he decided that he would have no choice but to have a serious talk with his second-in-command. He would have preferred for the guy to bow out gracefully, but Rufsur was playing dumb and pretending that he wasn't aware of Kalugal's claim on Jacki.

Still, he would have preferred to avoid issuing a command in regard to a personal matter. Perhaps Rufsur would back off if Kalugal told him that Jacki was a possible Dormant and that he planned on marrying her if she was?

Or, he might not.

Rufsur might argue that he had noticed her first and had as much right to pursue her as Kalugal.

In a democratic organization, that would have been true, but not in Kalugal's. He was the leader, and his men were there to serve him. He hadn't forced any of them to stay, and those who had chosen to do so were generously compensated for their services. But that didn't mean that he owed them anything other than their wages.

It was true that they were like brothers to him, but even among brothers, there was a hierarchy, and they were not equals.

Bottom line, Jacki was his, and Rufsur would better get it through his thick head sooner rather than later.

Rufsur

When they were done with lunch, Jacki put her plate on the tray and reached for Rufsur's.

"I've got it." He lifted his and Kalugal's. "But you can help me carry the smaller tray to the kitchen."

Kalugal cast him an annoyed glare, but he pretended not to notice. Now that Jacki was sleeping in the boss's old office, getting to talk to her privately would be next to impossible, and Rufsur needed to know where he stood with her.

If she'd chosen Kalugal then he would step aside, but if she hadn't, let the best man win. The boss was tough competition, but he had his flaws, and Jacki was smart enough to realize it.

For starters, the guy had an ego the size of the Milky Way, and he wasn't nearly as much fun to be with as Rufsur, if he said so himself. Kalugal tried to project an easy-going attitude, but that was a thinly disguised act. He was intense, way too cerebral, and valued his damn artifacts more than he valued relationships. He preferred spending time in his dusty archeological digs to having fun with his friends in clubs and chasing women, which was every normal immortal male's favorite activity.

For an immortal, Kalugal was still very young, but he had the soul of an old human.

Jacki lifted the smaller tray with the empty cups and bottles. "Lead the way."

"When you are done, please come back here," Kalugal said. "We are not finished with our conversation."

"Do you mean Jacki or me?" Rufsur knew the answer to that, but he asked anyway, knowing that it would irritate Kalugal.

"Jacki. You have work to do."

"Yes, sir."

When they were out in the hallway, Jacki leaned closer to him. "Is everything all right between you and Kalugal?"

"Sure." Rufsur grinned. "He doesn't mind a little competition." His words were meant for Kalugal's ears more than Jacki's.

Jacki affected an incredulous expression. "Is that what this is all about? You guys are competing for my attention?"

Thinking about how to answer her, Rufsur walked into the kitchen and headed for the sink. For some reason, Jacki had sounded angry. A beautiful young woman like her should be used to guys fighting over her. It was flattering, not insulting, and it was natural.

Leaning against the counter, he waited for her to put the cups in the sink.

She grabbed a dishtowel and started to wipe the tray clean. "How old are you, Rufsur?"

"In immortal terms or human terms?"

"Actual years that you've spent on this earth."

"One hundred and thirty-two. But just so you know, that's considered young for an immortal."

"And how old is Kalugal?"

"Younger by several decades."

Atzil, who up until now had been listening to their conversation, ducked into the walk-in pantry and quietly closed the door behind him.

Jacki either hadn't noticed his departure or just chose not to acknowledge it. "Still, that's old enough to act like adults and not like teenage boys." She leaned against the center island, facing him.

He arched a brow. "Fighting over a woman is not childish. As long as a man is not taken and thinks that he has a chance, he'll keep competing for the most desirable females. It's in our nature." He smirked. "The best man wins the best woman and so forth. You could think of it as an evolutionary process. Survival of the fittest."

She put the tray aside and looked him up and down. "You are reducing relationships to animal instincts. Thinking people are more complicated than that, and many factors influence their choice of a desirable partner."

He waved a dismissive hand. "You've just confirmed what I said. Who do you think the best female is? For every male, it's a different set of attributes. The best woman for me is not necessarily the best for another guy, but high quality is high quality. There will always be stiff competition for that."

Jacki shook her head. "You don't know me. I can be a horrible person, selfish and stupid. Like every other male, you see the exterior, and you don't care about anything else."

"You are not selfish because you ran after Kalugal and me to save a guy that wasn't even your boyfriend. And you are not stupid either."

She chuckled. "I'm surprised that you think that. Running after you and your boss to save Arwel was incredibly stupid. I don't know what I was thinking. I had no chance."

"In retrospect, you know that you didn't, but at the time, you thought that we were regular human guys and that you could take us on. You had bear spray, and it might have worked on someone with slower reflexes. I found your courage admirable, and so did Kalugal."

She grimaced. "Lucky me."

"I think that you are. You have two great choices, but naturally I think that you'll be happier with me. I'm more your type."

"Oh, yeah? And you know that how?"

"Simple. You are more like me than like Kalugal."

She narrowed her eyes at him. "In what way?"

"Easygoing, unassuming, not stuck-up, quick on your feet, loyal, resourceful. Like me, you are the live-and-let-live type of gal. You and I, we jive."

He wanted to add good-looking but stopped himself in time. Jacki thought that men wanted her only because of her beauty, and that was probably true, but he liked the whole package, and he wanted her to know that it was more than her looks that he was attracted to.

"Thank you. Those were all very nice things to say, and I'm glad that you've noticed them about me, but I'm not interested in a romantic relationship with you or Kalugal. I would very much like to be friends with you both, though."

"Do you think it's possible? I know that I'm attracted to you, and so is Kalugal. And you are attracted to one or both of us as well."

She crossed her arms over her chest. "I am not."

"Did you forget about this?" He tapped his nose.

Her cheeks got red. "Damn you and your sense of smell. You are like dogs." She huffed out a breath. "My excitement wasn't in response to either of you. The library reminded me of a sexy scene from a movie."

"Which one?"

"I don't remember the title, and it doesn't matter. You are both immortal, and I'm human. It could never work with you or with Kalugal, so you'd better get it out of your heads."

Jacki

Rufsur smiled. "Okay, I get it. But if Kalugal and I were not immortal, who would you have chosen?"

Jacki didn't have to think hard. She liked Rufsur, but Kalugal was the one she craved.

"But you are immortal, and I don't like what-ifs. They are a waste of time and mental energy." She wiped her hands on a dishtowel. "I need to go back to Kalugal. With how much he is paying for my company, I shouldn't make him wait."

Pushing away from the counter, Jacki didn't look at Rufsur as she walked out of the kitchen. Hopefully, he'd gotten the hint and would stop pestering her.

It was a pity that they couldn't be friends, though. He was a decent guy and good company when he wasn't trying to charm her into agreeing to a date, or whatever he hoped to achieve.

Even if she were inclined to accept, Kalugal wouldn't have allowed it.

Rufsur was walking a tightrope with his boss. She'd noticed the glares Kalugal had been casting at him and wondered how far their friendship would stretch before it snapped.

Perhaps she should have been more forceful with her refusal. Except, she couldn't have been clearer without crossing the line into rude and turning Rufsur into an enemy instead of an ally.

But then that was the trouble with men. As long as they thought they had a chance, they acted all nice and helpful, but the moment they got rejected, they made a complete one-eighty.

With a sigh, Jacki opened the door to the library and walked in.

Kalugal hadn't moved from his spot next to the games table, and as he lifted his head and looked at her, the damn butterflies in her stomach took flight.

"You wanted to see me?"

"Always." He smiled, and the butterflies went into a flapping frenzy.

Pretending that it was business as usual, Jacki pulled out a chair on the other side of the table, sat down, and waited.

"Tell me more about the program. How many people were in it, and what kind of talents they had."

"Why do you want to know?"

"It bothers me that the government has paranormals. It's a new threat to immortals on both sides."

"How so?"

Kalugal crossed his legs. "As long as claims of supernatural powers were ridiculed and dismissed, we had nothing to worry about. Even if someone noticed something out of the ordinary and reported it, no one would have taken it seriously. The fact that the government is collecting paranormals means that's no longer the case. We need to be even more careful than we've been up to now."

She nodded. "You're right. I had no problem believing you when you told me that Arwel was immortal. It was almost on the same level as if you'd told me that he was Russian. I would have been a little doubtful because he had no Russian accent, but I wouldn't have dismissed it completely either. I don't think that I would have been as open-minded about it if I didn't have a paranormal ability myself and hadn't met others who were like me."

"That's only one part of the problem. The other part is the kinds of talents the people in the program have. Powerful telepaths, for example, could potentially tune into the minds of immortals. Someone with the ability to remote view could potentially uncover the clan's village or my father's island."

Jacki frowned. "There was one guy who could read auras, but he didn't notice anything unusual about the immortals. Or maybe he did and just didn't say anything."

Kalugal leaned back and crossed his arms over his chest. "That's why it is important for me to know exactly who is in that program and what their powers are. I also need to know how the clan sprang you and Jin free. Kian and I might have to put our heads together and figure out a way to get the rest of the trainees out and then shut that program down."

Jacki straightened in her chair. "If you could do that, it would be awesome. But Kian said it would have been too dangerous to take everyone with us because it would have triggered a massive manhunt, and he didn't want the government breathing down his neck."

"That's a consideration. But first, I need to know all the facts."

"Where do you want me to start?"

"At the beginning. How were you, Jin, and the others recruited?"

Kalugal

When Jacki had finished telling her story, Kalugal was even more alarmed than before.

He got up and poured himself another drink, then pulled out a can of coke and handed it to her without asking if she wanted it.

"Thank you. So what do you think?"

"I anticipated advancements in artificial intelligence that would complicate things for immortals on both sides, but I thought that we had more time. I've also known that the American government as well as others around the globe were collecting information, but up until now, it was a futile pursuit because it was impossible to sift through the massive amounts of data. It seems that they've overcome that obstacle with technology. Instead of having hordes of people analyzing the information, they have bots doing it much faster and more efficiently. I find it very troubling that they have programmed the bots to respond to trigger words mentioning paranormal abilities."

"Don't you have a secure satellite network like Kian and his people have?"

"I do. And I assume that my father is smart enough to have one as well. But that's not going to help us when the information gathered will include the feed from countless surveillance cameras. With bots analyzing the feeds, it will become very difficult for us to hide who we are."

Artificial intelligence wouldn't be affected by his various shrouds. Traveling as Professor Gunter or any of his other personalities would become impossible without the use of elaborate disguises that included prosthetics.

Kalugal had known that it was coming, but he'd hoped to be the one in charge by then. If he were the puppet master, he could divert the information gathering and processing any way he wanted, which was precisely how he planned to take over.

Except, it seemed that he had to redouble his efforts before it was too late.

"What can you do about that, though? Infect the government's computers with a deadly virus?" Chuckling, Jacki popped the top of the coke can.

"That's actually a brilliant idea."

"I know." Jacki smirked. "But there is a difference between coming up with an idea and implementing it.

Who can even do that?" She eyed him from under her lashes. "Can you?"

He laughed. "Not personally. I know how to do some basic programming, but nothing at this level. I can find people who can, though."

"Immortals?"

"Humans. I don't know any immortal hackers."

"Kian has one. William is a freaking genius. I bet he can do it."

"William? I spoke with someone by that name. He said that he was in charge of communications. Is that the same guy?"

Jacki nodded. "He is really good with computers, and he has another guy he works with named Roni. I think that Roni is even better at hacking. He was the one who found you at the club."

"Fascinating. So the rumors about the clan having advanced technology are true. I always thought that it was part of my father's propaganda."

"Or maybe they just have more talented people."

"That could be. But in either case, it seems that cooperating with Kian would be beneficial to me."

Jacki grinned. "I'm so happy to hear you say that. I feel like in a small way I'm helping to bring you two closer."

"Not small at all." He leaned across the table with the intention of taking her hand, remembering at the last moment that he'd promised not to touch her. "If not for you, I wouldn't be donating to Kian's charity, which I'm sure made him regard me more favorably."

"I think that you would get along. He is a very different person from you, but I see some things you have in common."

"Are you basing your opinion on his actions, or have you met him in person?"

"I've met him. He came with the team that helped us escape from the program."

She hadn't mentioned Kian in her story, but then she hadn't mentioned the other team members either. In fact, he had a feeling that she'd tried to reveal as little as she could about the particulars of the escape.

"I'm surprised that he joined the team going out on such a minor mission."

Jacki smiled. "He planned on it being a ski vacation and an information-gathering trip, and he even brought his wife along. He didn't expect to find us right away."

"His wife?"

"You didn't know that Kian was married?"

"I don't know much about the clan. How did he meet her?"

Jacki shrugged. "I have no idea. It didn't come up in conversation. Some of the other Guardians brought their wives and girlfriends as well. They really thought it would be a nice vacation."

The more Kalugal learned, the more he wanted to find out. "I assume that the wives were immortal?"

"It would make sense. At the time, I didn't know that they were not human. Later, Arwel told me about the fangs and the glowing eyes, but he said that immortal females didn't have fangs or venom. Though to tell you the truth, I didn't notice anything strange about the men or the women. They behaved like regular people, other than the paranormal abilities, that is. But since those were nothing new to me, they didn't raise any red flags."

Kalugal's mind was on the wives and how they'd been found. Had they all been Dormants who transitioned? Or had the clan found unaffiliated immortals?

Jacki couldn't answer those questions for him. To get answers, he would have to play nice with Kian. The question was, what would his cousin demand in exchange for the information?

Perhaps more contributions to his charity?

Just as having more time with Jacki, that would be money well spent.

Jacki

It hadn't escaped Jacki's notice that Kalugal had reached for her hand and then pulled back at the last moment. He really was going to refrain from touching her unless she initiated it.

Well, he could keep on waiting because she wasn't going to do that.

She had no intention of encouraging him.

Right.

Damn. It was hard.

Until she'd met Kalugal, it hadn't been difficult to stick to her vow to never hook up with a guy unless he loved her and was willing to commit to her. Except, none of the guys that she'd briefly dated could compare.

Kalugal was a sexy devil with sinful blue eyes, the most kissable lips, and a haughty attitude that, for some reason, made him even more irresistible.

Talk about the alpha to top all alphas.

Kalugal gave Kian a run for his money. Not that she'd been attracted to Kian. First of all, the guy was married and off-limits. And secondly, he was too much of a straight arrow, way too serious, and gruff. Jacki liked Kalugal's charming bad-boy vibe.

Besides, she'd never been into guys with type A personality. Usually, they were obnoxious jerks who thought that the world revolved around them, were bossy, and not interested in anything that anyone other than them had to say.

Who needed that, right?

Except Kalugal listened to her attentively, he appeared to value her opinions, and he treated his men with respect. Other than the forced fake kiss from the day before, he hadn't acted like a jerk at all.

On the contrary. He'd been the perfect gentleman.

Jacki knew he wasn't, though. He was naughty, devious, and sensual, and if she was completely honest, she liked that side of him more than the perfectly-mannered one.

Despite her best efforts to silence the small voice in the back of her head, it kept whispering that she would love for Kalugal to initiate another kiss, and if he made sure to get her consent first, she wouldn't even mind if he was a little forceful.

And how stupid was that?

That fantasy was not going to become a reality unless Kalugal declared his undying love for her and offered to marry her. But since those two conditions were as likely to be met as pigs growing wings and taking to the sky, she had to banish the annoying thoughts before he got a whiff of what was going on with her.

That damn sense of smell of his was a major inconvenience, and if Rufsur had been able to detect her arousal, Kalugal must have too.

It was so embarrassing, and she couldn't even come up with a good excuse for it. They'd been discussing the threat new technology posed to immortals' ability to remain hidden, not comparing notes on *Fifty Shades*.

Still, Kalugal hadn't said anything, so maybe his sense of smell wasn't as good as Rufsur's?

That was doubtful given his superiority in everything else. He'd probably noticed but refrained from commenting because he was more of a gentleman than his second-in-command.

"What are you thinking about?" Kalugal asked.

Damn.

"Technology," she blurted the first thing that popped into her head. "It's amazing, and I love everything about it, but it's also scary. Like what you've said about the surveillance cameras collecting information and bots analyzing it. It could be both positive and negative. Like it can help reduce crime because the bots could alert the police in real time, but it would also mean loss of privacy on a colossal level. Imagine a prospective employer having access to how many times you've cussed in the last year or whether you were rude to anyone. That would affect everyone's behavior. People would become even faker than they are now."

Luckily for her, Kalugal found the topic more fascinating than the scents she was likely emitting.

"You are a very smart lady, Jacki. What you are describing is already happening. Have you heard about China's social credit system?"

"No. What's that?"

"People accumulate positive and negative scores based on their behavior. The data are collected by various means, including what people spend their money on, how long they spend on leisure activities instead of being productive, and also their behavior. Everything gets recorded by countless surveillance cameras that are spread all over the major cities. In addition, currency and credit cards are being phased out, and the only way to pay for things is through a phone application. That way, the government knows what people are spending their money on and can also block them from purchasing certain things, like train tickets or airfare."

"What else do they do with that information?"

"According to the score, privileges are granted or taken away. It starts with small things like the internet speed in a person's home getting throttled, to big things like getting banned from using public transportation. It affects job prospects, the kind of schools a person's kids may be accepted to, etc. It's the ultimate Big-Brother-watching."

"Scary. It gives the government complete control over its citizens." She let out a breath. "But that can only happen in China because the population has no say in the policies and they just have to take it or else. It will never happen here, so that's not something you should worry about."

Kalugal smiled indulgently. "Never is a strong word, and it's already happening here on a smaller scale. Everything you do online leaves a record and can be accessed, even things that you delete or think that you were browsing anonymously. People's homes are full of electronic gadgets that gather information on them. For now, it's used primarily for commercial purposes, like advertising that is custom-tailored to your interests, but it can be very easily adapted for other uses."

As Jacki contemplated what she'd just learned, Shamash knocked and then entered the library. "Atzil is asking if you want to eat your dinner here or in the dining room."

"It's dinner time already? How long have we been in here?"

Kalugal rose to his feet and offered her a hand up. "As the saying goes, time flies when you are having fun. I'm glad that you enjoyed my company."

"I did. I hope that you enjoyed mine as well, but I wanted to prepare dinner and didn't notice that it was getting late."

He smiled. "I'm glad. I had the most pleasant afternoon, and I wouldn't have given up a moment of it even for the best gourmet dinner. I'm looking forward to many more conversations with you." He led her out of the room.

"Me too." And she meant it. Kalugal was a pleasure to talk to. "Are we eating in the dining room?"

"Yes. I think it is time I introduced you to my men."

Kian

As Kian's phone rang, he glanced at the caller number and let it go to voicemail. It was nine o'clock in the morning, so it was probably Jacki calling from Kalugal's number, but he didn't want to take chances.

Kalugal had already spoken with Areana earlier in the morning, and Turner had been there for that, but he had to leave for his office in the city. The way they had solved the communication problem was Kian letting Kalugal's calls go to voicemail and returning them only after getting Turner on the other line.

Thankfully, no one had died because the missions Turner had been working on had been delayed by a couple of days while he'd been helping manage the crises. Kian had enough on his guilty conscience without adding that to the pile.

"I'm here," Turner answered. "You just need me in the background, right?"

"Yes. I'm returning Kalugal's call. It's probably Jacki reporting in as scheduled."

"I'll put my side on mute."

"Thanks."

Kian placed the call.

"Hello, cousin. Are all my phone calls going straight to voicemail?"

"Until we find a better solution, yes."

"What if I give you my word that I will not attempt to compel you?"

Kian hesitated for a moment. "I'm not ready to trust you yet."

Kalugal sighed dramatically. "That's regrettable. Did you receive my wire transfer?"

"Yes, and the accounting department should have sent you a receipt. Donations to our charity organization are tax-deductible. I assume you are paying taxes?"

Kalugal chuckled. "That's one of life's certainties. Luckily, you and I don't have to worry about the other one."

"True. Is Jacki there?"

"Yes, I'm handing the phone over to her."

"Hi, Kian." She sounded upbeat.

"Good morning, Jacki. How is your stay with Kalugal so far?"

"Illuminating. We had a long and fascinating conversation yesterday about emerging technology and how it can affect personal freedoms. When I told Kalugal about the program Jin and I were in, and how the government is finding paranormal talents, he became very concerned. I hope that's okay. I mean that I told him about it, not him being concerned."

"It's fine. I was going to tell him about it myself."

"He says that he's going to call you in a few minutes to talk about it."

Kian was surprised that Kalugal hadn't put the call on speakerphone, and that he was keeping his distance to give them some privacy. He could hear Kalugal, but his voice was muted as if he were on the other side of the room.

"Tell him that I'll call him."

"He asks that you wait ten minutes before calling. He has something that he has to do first."

"No problem. Anything else you want to tell me?"

"No, that's it. I convinced Kalugal to let me cook lunch and dinner for him and his two lieutenants. I don't want to feel like a freeloader, especially since he is paying a fortune for my company."

Kian stifled a chuckle.

Kalugal didn't need a cook, he needed a mate, and he was paying for a chance at that.

"Whatever works for you, Jacki. We will talk again tomorrow."

"Goodbye, Kian."

He waited the ten minutes Kalugal had asked for and called back. "I assume you wanted to talk to me in private?"

"Indeed. I want to talk to you about the government's paranormal talents program, and I didn't know what you were comfortable discussing in front of Jacki."

"What's on your mind?"

"We can't let the government continue with the program. We have to sabotage it somehow."

That was unexpected. Kalugal still didn't know about the connection between paranormal talents and Dormants, so that couldn't be what he was so upset about.

"Why are you so concerned about it?"

"I'm surprised that you are not. If the government is collecting people with extra perception abilities, it means that the higher-ups are no longer denying the existence of paranormal phenomena. Reports of strange happenings will be taken seriously. A remote viewer can see your village or my father's island and report it. A telepath can tune in to any immortal and learn of our existence. In the past, no one took those people seriously, and they were assumed to be either charlatans or mentally unstable. Now, those reports will get investigated."

"I haven't met a remote viewer that talented yet, and the chance that a strong telepath will cross paths with an immortal are slim to none. There aren't that many of us."

"Still, I believe that allowing it to continue is hazardous. You should have taken all the trainees with you instead of only four. That would have gotten the director in trouble, and the program might have been shut down already."

"Or it could have triggered a massive manhunt."

"What has been done to find the four you got? Was there a massive hunt for them?"

"Not really. In fact, I was surprised by how little has been done to look for the program's escapees, but I think I have the answer to that. One of them was a mole."

"How did you find out?"

"She stole a phone from a boy who befriended her and called the director. We were very careful with the three we helped escape with Jin, so she didn't have much to report. But at least now I know why there was so little done to try to find them. The director just waited for his spy to call in."

"Did you check them for trackers?"

"Of course. They were clean."

"That doesn't make sense. A lot of effort went into collecting these people. If I were the director of that program, I would have made sure that I could track them."

"Don't forget that they were kept in a secret facility and that their once a week outings were supervised. Not only that, with the exception of Jacki, they were all under compulsion not to interact with anyone outside the program. And according to her, she managed to hide her immunity. Jin was the only one she confided in."

Kalugal

Kalugal smiled. Jacki was smart and resourceful. Hiding her immunity had been the right thing to do.

"I'm still suspicious. After all, we are dealing with the government, and they have access to the latest technology. They might have implanted the trainees with trackers that are undetectable by conventional means. What did you use to check them?"

"Bridget, the doctor you spoke with when Jin got sick, ran them through her medical equipment. I don't remember what exactly she used. It was either an ultrasound or a CT scan."

"Still, we can't rule out the possibility of undetectable trackers. If you value your village's secret location, which I know you do, don't let any of them in there."

"Too late. Jin is already here."

"Did she transition?"

"Not yet."

"Tell her and Arwel that I wish them good luck."

"That's nice of you." Kian's tone was mocking.

"I'm a nice guy. If anyone is the villain in this story, it's you. I was just living my life, minding my own business, and then you decided to send a spy to tether me. What happened after that is on you."

"I can't argue with that. But that doesn't make you a Boy Scout."

Kalugal chuckled. "From what I've read, Boy Scouts are not all that nice either. The organization filed for bankruptcy because of all the sex abuse lawsuits it was slapped with. Perhaps you should include former scouts in your rehabilitation charity."

"I wish I could help every victim, but regrettably, I can't. I can't even put a dent in the damn trafficking in my own city. We eradicate one cell, and another pops up someplace else. It's incredibly frustrating."

Kian was repeating the mistake of many other do-gooders. He was addressing the symptoms instead of the underlying disease.

In contrast, Kalugal's plan was to cut off the rotten weeds at the roots by depriving them of nourishment, aka funds.

Once paper money was eradicated and all monetary transactions were made electronically, he could easily shut down the accounts of traffickers, terrorists, scammers, and all the other leeches that were feeding on the blood of innocents. He would starve them like the malignant parasites they were until they shriveled down, fell off, and died.

If he had access to the system that the government employed to flag trigger words, he could implement his plan much earlier. But that was most likely not doable. He would have to develop and fund a similar system on his own, and unless there was a significant breakthrough in technology that made it simpler and less costly to build, it would take him several more decades to achieve his utopian future.

Except, Kian would probably see Kalugal's vision as dystopian rather than utopian because it would come at a stiff price in the form of reduced privacy and autonomy.

Whether the trade-off was worth it was a matter of opinion, and Kalugal would love to have a philosophical discussion about it with his cousin.

Naturally, he would present it as a hypothetical.

"We should meet, Kian. Or at least have a video conference. I'm at a disadvantage. I don't even know what you look like. I was told that you have my portrait, and I'm very curious to find out how you got it."

"We had a forensic artist draw it from someone's memory of you."

"My mother's, I presume?"

"It was done long before we found out that Areana was even alive."

"Who gave my description, then?"

"It was a member of the Brotherhood who crossed over to our side. He remembered you quite vividly."

"You said that you started looking for me as a favor to my mother. Was that a lie, Kian?"

"I wasn't looking for you when the portrait was drawn, and it was not commissioned by me. One of my men hired the forensic artist."

"What possible reason could he have had for that? Did he have all of Navuh's sons' portraits done?"

"No. We had the others. They were done by another member of the Brotherhood who crossed over to our side and who happens to be a talented artist. But he didn't remember you well, and he lacked the skill to draw a portrait from someone else's memory."

His cousin seemed to be getting tangled in the web of his own lies.

"That still doesn't compute, Kian. If you were missing one portrait, it would make sense for you to hire the forensic artist to draw mine. But you say that you didn't and that one of your men commissioned it."

Kian sighed. "At the time, I wasn't interested in you because you ran away and were no longer part of the Brotherhood. I was only interested in the current leaders. My Guardian's interest in you was personal. Evidently, you had induced his mate's transition without realizing it. She turned immortal and had no idea why or how."

For a long moment, Kalugal processed that piece of information in stunned silence.

"That's one hell of a coincidence, and how the hell did she know it was me?"

"She met one of your brothers by chance and recognized him from his portrait. He looks like you, even though you are not really related. Back then, I didn't know that, of course. I thought that you were all half-brothers. Now I know that Navuh selects human males that look like him to work in the harem so he can claim the sons of the other immortal concubines as his. Long story short, his portrait triggered a distant memory, one thing led to another, and her mate commissioned the artist. She recognized you from the sketch."

"I have to admit that I'm excited. It's like finding out that I have a child I didn't know about. Can I meet her?"

"I don't think her mate would be okay with that."

"When did it happen, and what's her name? Maybe I remember her."

"I doubt that you remember Eva. It was more than fifty years ago."

Kalugal leaned back in his chair and grinned. "I remember her. Gorgeous lady. Brunettes are usually not my type, but she was stunning. She was also difficult to thrall. I should have suspected something."

"She's an incredible lady."

To think that he had missed out on a chance of securing an immortal wife, or mate, which was apparently the proper term. Except, Eva hadn't been right for him.

She was beautiful and smart, but something about her had been off-putting. Despite her outward femininity, she'd given out a masculine vibe. Then again, he hadn't really known her. They'd hooked up for one night, and he had never seen her again.

Poor Eva. She must have been so confused when she'd realized that she wasn't aging. He wondered what explanations she'd come up with for that.

Talking with her would be interesting.

"Perhaps a phone call with Eva could be arranged? With your immune on the line of course."

Kian

On the one hand, Kian was glad that Eva had left an impression on Kalugal. On the other hand, her seduction might have been done with the help of thralling or getting her drunk, and that was unforgivable.

"I don't think so. You took her virginity."

"With her full consent. And that's another reason I remember her so well. I'm not fond of deflowering virgins. She initiated the sex and didn't tell me that she was a virgin. I wouldn't have touched her if I had known. But with how bold she acted, I was sure that she was experienced."

"She was drunk."

"Wow, she really remembers a lot about that night, but not accurately. She said that she was a little tipsy, but she seemed in full control of her faculties. After discovering that she was a virgin, I admit that I thralled her to forget more than I usually do, but I did it for her sake. Those were different times, and good girls were supposed to wait for their wedding night. I figured that if she didn't remember losing her virginity, she wouldn't have to fess up to it."

"You were a young man back then. You might have misjudged her intentions."

"I didn't. Eva was more than a full participant, and after the fact, I did the best I could for her."

"You might have underestimated how drunk she was."

"I did not. Eva doesn't remember much from that night because of my thrall, not because of the alcohol. If you let me talk to her, I can jog her memory."

"Or compel her to forget even more of that night."

"Kian, would you please climb down from that branch? We have to start trusting each other, and I think that we've made good progress during our talks. We need to take it to the next step and meet in person. Our mothers are expecting it." He chuckled. "At some point, Annani is going to put her foot down, and you will have to obey her wishes."

Kian grimaced.

He'd heard Areana tell Kalugal about who was the real head of the clan, busting the bluff that it was him. "She usually asks nicely first."

"I'm sure. But we both want to please our mothers regardless of who's in charge. And I would also like to meet my brother."

Kian had been expecting that request as well.

"He is back in Washington. For now, Lokan is straddling the fence, and it's crucial that his involvement with us remain top secret. If your father finds out, he might kill him for treason."

"I told you. I don't have any contact with Navuh. Lokan's secret is safe with me."

"That might be true for you, but what about your men?"

"They have as much to lose as I do if they are discovered by Navuh, and if there was a traitor in their midst, my father would have known where to find me and would have sent for me a long time ago."

"Are you willing to bet your brother's life on that conviction? What if your father was content with you being away and just wanted to keep an eye on you?"

"Not likely. But I'll restrict the knowledge of Lokan's secret to my two lieutenants, whom I trust with my life. When we meet, I will need them to accompany me."

Kian chuckled. "I see that your mind is set on a face-to-face meeting. What are you plotting, Kalugal?"

"You keep insulting me unjustly. If you wish, we can keep talking on the phone, but I don't see why you are so afraid of me. You can bring your immune to the meetings. I've heard that he is a brilliant strategist, and you've told me that he is a champion chess player. I would like to meet him as well."

"He is busy at the moment."

"I would like to say that we have time, but we don't. We need to brainstorm the government issue. Those paranormals that you left behind need to be freed, and the program needs to be shut down. I'll gladly lend my unique abilities to the effort."

That was an unexpected surprise, and a pleasant one.

Except, Kian still didn't trust Kalugal's motives.

"I'll discuss it with Turner. I need to figure out a way for us to sit down together with proper safeguards in place."

"Can I at least talk with my brother? You can arrange for a three-way call like you did with my mother. Or you can give him my number and leave it up to him to decide whether he wants to take the risk to call me or not. He might want to meet me before our summit, which would really please my mother."

A summit. Kian liked that term, but he didn't like Kalugal going behind his back and asking Areana to request an audience with Annani on his behalf.

"Speaking of your mother. If you wanted to talk to mine, you should've cleared that with me first."

"I wasn't sure you would convey my wish to the goddess."

"So you went over my head. That's not the best way to build trust, cousin."

"True that. From now on, all requests will be addressed to you first."

"Good. I will ask Lokan if he wishes to talk to you, and if so, how he wants to go about it."

"Thank you. I appreciate that."

Annani

Annani lifted the cup of tea to her lips, smelled the aroma, grimaced, and put it back on the table.

Frowning, Alena sniffed at her own cup. "What's the matter, did I get the recipe wrong?"

"No, it is the same as all the other times you tried to soothe me with it. I have grown tired of the taste and of the artificial calmness it brings about. It is not really soothing as much as it is numbing."

"That's not my experience. I find it mildly calming, like listening to classical music."

"Maybe it affects you differently. You are naturally calm, while I am not. I wonder which of the herbs produces the effect. We should give Merlin the list of ingredients and have him analyze them."

Unperturbed, Alena sipped slowly from her cup. "I find it odd that after drinking this tea for thousands of years, you are suddenly concerned with what's in it."

Crossing her legs, Annani put her hands on her knees. "It might have lost its effect on me, or maybe I am just too agitated for it to work. I am tired of sitting on the sidelines and witnessing my son and my nephew circling each other like a couple of stags. I should go there and force them to sit at the negotiations table. It is in everyone's best interest for us to forge an alliance with Kalugal and his men."

"The problem is that Kalugal has a dangerous power, and Kian is afraid of getting near him. Not that I blame him. I wouldn't trust my own mate with the power to take over my will. I don't know how Kalugal's men deal with that."

"They trust him not to use it on them, that is how. He must have proven himself to them."

Alena shook her head. "As I said, I wouldn't want someone with the power to compel anywhere near me, even if he professed his undying love to me, and we were bonded mates."

"It raises an interesting moral question. As an immortal, you have that same power over humans. Does it mean that they should shun you?"

"If they knew about it, they would." Alena smiled. "Thralling is not the same as compelling, but it's similar enough. That's one of the many reasons for keeping who we are and what we can do a secret. If word got out that creatures like us existed, we would be hunted down and killed. Humans like their position at the top of the food chain, and they will do anything to keep it."

"Yes, you are right. I just wonder how the Dormants react once they realize that their mates can control their minds."

"You could ask Syssi."

"I will do that the next time I visit, which I plan on doing very soon. I need to be there as a safety precaution for Kian. Kalugal cannot compel me, while I might be able to compel him. My presence will level the playing field."

"Kian would never agree to that. What if Kalugal can overpower you?"

Annani huffed. "Inconceivable. I am not like my sister. I am a powerful goddess, and he is just an immortal."

Alena arched a brow. "You don't know that. It would be a very unpleasant surprise to find out that he can compel you."

"He asked Areana to convey his wish for an audience with me." Annani reached for the tea. "If I refuse, it would insult him, and it would also give the impression that I am afraid of him. Both are unacceptable."

"Then we have a problem. Maybe we can go on a trip to Europe or South America and use it as an excuse for why you can't grant Kalugal his audience."

"I am not going to run off like a coward." Annani put her cup down and pulled her phone out of the hidden pocket in her gown. "I am calling Kian."

"Oh boy." Alena chuckled. "I think I should leave you to it. I don't want to hear you two yelling at each other." She rose to her feet.

"Sit down." Annani pointed at the armchair. "I know that you prefer to avoid conflict, but that is a luxury a leader cannot afford."

"That's why I'm not a leader. I'm happy to be your companion and to help run the sanctuary."

"That is a leadership position. And there will come a time when you will have to make difficult decisions and stand your ground when facing opposition."

With a sigh, Alena returned to her seat. "Fine. Just try to be civil. Kian has been through a lot over the last week, and his nerves are frayed."

"I will do my best."

Except, as soon as Kian answered the phone, Annani's good intentions flew out the window. He sounded exasperated even before she said anything, and once she was done, his answer was precisely what Alena had predicted it would be.

"Not happening, Mother. Are you not aware of the risks?"

"There is no risk to me. Kalugal cannot compel me."

"And you know that how?"

"Because his father could not do that, and Navuh is more powerful than Kalugal. He has an entire island under his control."

"Did Navuh ever try to compel you?"

"He might have. But since he had no effect on me, I do not know if he tried."

"That's all you have? That doesn't prove anything."

Annani sighed. "If Navuh had the power to compel me, he would have used it when he came with Mortdh to my father's palace. Mortdh wanted to convince Ahn to uphold his promise and to order me to marry him instead of my beloved Khiann. Back then, Navuh was Mortdh's obedient and devoted son. He would have done everything to help his father."

"You don't know that. If he was smart, and we know that he is, he kept his compulsion ability a secret from Mortdh. Using it on you would have tipped his hand. That's one option. The other is that he wasn't as powerful back then. His powers might have grown over the five thousand years since you last saw him."

"That is possible. But Kalugal is still young. In fact, he is about the same age now as his father was then. Which means that I am more powerful than him. Do not forget that my powers have also grown over the years."

"Have you ever tried to compel more than one person at a time?"

"No."

"Kalugal compelled all the Guardians who were connected to Arwel's earpiece in one shot. Can you do that?"

"That is the best idea you have had so far. I am going to test my compulsion power on my people and check how many I can control at once."

"I'm glad we came to an understanding. Let me know how it goes."

Annani felt her anger rising, but she kept her voice neutral. "You assume that I will fail. I assure you that I will not, and I will have Alena witness and verify the results."

"I trust you, Mother. I'm only concerned with your safety. You are the engine that keeps the clan going. Imagine what would happen to us if Kalugal managed to compel you to surrender yourself to Navuh."

"He would not do that even if he could."

"We can't risk it."

Jacki

In the kitchen, Jacki chopped parsley for a garnish while humming along to Atzil's rendition of *'The Girl from Ipanema.'*

"...Yes, I would give my heart gladly. But each day as she walks to the sea..."

After the initial awkwardness of sharing the kitchen had passed, it was fun to work alongside him. The place was big, and they each had their workstation, so it wasn't as if they were stepping on each other's toes.

Still, Jacki made sure to compliment him on everything she possibly could, so he wouldn't kick her out. It was easy to do. Atzil was an extremely fast chopper, he kept his work area meticulous, and best of all, he sang while he cooked, and he was good.

"You sound exactly like Frank Sinatra."

"Thank you. I'm surprised that a young girl like you even knows who he was."

"I'm twenty-two, so I'm no longer a girl. I used to work in a diner that played an oldies track, and I liked humming along to Frank."

He smiled. "I'm one hundred and seven years old, so you are a girl to me."

Jacki shook her head. "I took a trip down the rabbit hole. You all look like you are in your late twenties or early thirties. That's so confusing."

"Immortality comes with many benefits."

"Are there any negatives?"

He nodded. "We are isolated. Contact with humans is best kept to a minimum."

"Because they might get suspicious if they notice oddities about you."

"Correct. Like if I cut my finger while chopping onions, it would heal in less than a minute. And there are other tells. I need to make sure that my eyes don't start glowing and my fangs elongating as soon as I see a sexy lady."

He cast her a sidelong glance. "You know that's what happens when an immortal male is aroused, right?"

She nodded. "Arwel told me a little bit about it. But I've never seen it, nor do I want to." She shivered. "No offense, but I'm not into vampires, and fangs would scare the hell out of me. What do you do when that happens?"

"I need to hold it off until I get her alone. Then I can erase the memory from her head. But if it happens while there are a lot of people around, I'm screwed. I don't have the boss's ability to affect many humans at once."

"That sucks."

"Yeah, but that's not the worst part. Since there are no immortal females, I can't even dream of one day having a family. It gets lonely."

"That's because you escaped from your community. Is there a way to get some of the immortal females out?"

He shook his head. "It's complicated. I'll leave the explanation to Kalugal. I don't know how much he wants you to know."

"I'll ask him over lunch." Jacki put the finishing touches on her salmon dish, adding the parsley garnish and several slices of lemon. "How does it look?"

"Very nice."

She had no experience in preparing fancy dishes, so she'd winged it, and Atzil had given her a few pointers even though he cooked pretty much in the same way she used to in the foster homes. Uncomplicated recipes in large quantities.

"I'm going to serve it in the library."

He nodded.

"Do you think the guys mind the new arrangement?"

"Only because you are not eating with them, and they are jealous of Kalugal, Phinas, and Rufsur. We don't dine all at once anyway because there isn't enough space in the dining room. We have a schedule."

"Good." She lifted the tray. "I don't want to cause unnecessary strife."

"Let me help you carry it."

"Thanks." It was big and heavy, and she was grateful for his offer.

When they entered the library, Kalugal and his lieutenants weren't there yet, which was good since she had time to set up the game table to look like a place to eat and not play chess.

But when ten minutes had passed, and neither of the guys showed up, Jacki started to get annoyed. After all the work she'd put into preparing a nice lunch, it was getting cold.

She was about to walk out and march into Kalugal's office when the door opened, and her three lunch companions entered with packages piled high in their arms.

"What's all that?"

"I ordered clothing and other necessities for you," Kalugal said.

She gaped at the mountain of bags and boxes the men put down by the door. "When? And how did you know my sizes?"

Smirking, Kalugal pulled out a chair for Jacki, waited for her to be seated, and then pulled one out for himself. "I got the sizes by checking the clothes and shoes you arrived in. And I ordered things from a local boutique and had one of my guys pick everything up."

She glanced at the large pile by the door. "It looks like you've bought out their entire stock."

"Everything they had in your size."

Wow.

"Thank you. But that's way too much. When am I going to wear all that?"

Rubbing his chin, Kalugal pretended to ponder the question. "You can wear a different outfit for every meal. That's breakfast, lunch, afternoon tea, and dinner. Four a day. And then you can change into a fifth outfit, something leisurely for the evening."

"Don't be silly. I'm not going to do that."

"It's up to you. After you go over the purchases, let me know if you are still missing anything, or if I need to exchange items for a different size."

"I will, thank you. Now let's eat before everything gets cold."

When lunch was over, Kalugal told Rufsur and Phinas to carry her things to her room, which Jacki suspected was a clever way to get rid of them as soon as he could. He wanted her all to himself.

"Where am I going to put everything? There is no closet in my room."

"I'll clear a section of mine for you. The entrance is through the master bath, so you'll have privacy getting dressed."

"I see that you thought of everything."

He smiled. "I'm a thorough guy."

Jacki folded the napkin and put it on the table. "I need to cook you something really fancy for dinner. I don't know how else to thank you."

"My thanks will be seeing you in those beautiful clothes." He looked her over. "Nothing can detract from your beauty, but what you are wearing is like framing a masterpiece in cheap plastic. It won't do."

She chuckled. "That's a great way to insult me while giving me a lovely compliment. How long did it take you to come up with that?"

Smirking, he waved a hand. "It's not a line that I pulled out from my sleeve, it's an observation. Would you put a thousand-dollar perfume in a fifty-cent container? You wouldn't. It would be an insult to the perfume."

"Okay. I get it. Thank you again. I can't wait to check the stuff out."

"Give me a few more moments of your time, and then you can go."

She felt a blush creeping up her cheeks. "That's not what I meant. I'm not in a rush to leave."

Kalugal

Jacki's peachy blush was gorgeous. But what Kalugal loved the most about it was that it signaled Jacki's softening toward him. She was lowering her shields, and the thorny outer layer was practically gone. She was allowing herself to feel arousal, which she'd been fighting hard to stifle before.

Frankly, he hadn't expected her protective walls to start crumbling so quickly. Especially not after the stunt he'd pulled the day before, not to mention the whole abduction and sticking her in the trunk of his car episode.

It seemed that Jacki was the forgive and forget type of girl, who didn't hold grudges.

Just another reason to love her.

Not that he did, but if she transitioned, he would allow himself to feel more for her. Until then, Kalugal was going to keep an emotional distance.

Falling for a human was a rookie mistake, and so far, he'd been careful to avoid that pitfall.

Jacki was getting under his skin, though. And at the rate things were going, keeping his heart out of the seduction would be more difficult than with any other woman he'd seduced before.

Perhaps he should speed the seduction part up. It was a necessary step in proving or disproving Jacki's dormancy. The sooner it was done, the better. If she turned out to be just an ordinary human, he would have less of a hard time letting her go if he hadn't spent a long time with her. And if she transitioned, it would be a game changer.

Once that happened, he could fully commit to her and their relationship.

"I should have asked for a kiss," he murmured.

Jacki's head snapped toward him. "What did you say?"

Hearing the alarm in her voice, Kalugal decided to make light of it. "As a thank you. Just a small kiss on the cheek." He turned his profile to her and tapped the hollow with his finger. "Right here." He turned the other way. "And maybe one here as well. A triple kiss would be the best. One here, one there, and then one more here."

She narrowed her eyes at him. "I'm trying to think if your request violates your promise to me. Technically, you are still leaving it up to me to touch you first, but you are demanding it, so it's not really up to me."

"It is entirely up to you." He sighed dramatically and affected a sad expression. "That's okay. You can make me a nice dinner instead."

Shaking her head, Jacki chuckled. "You are playing on my conscience and it's working. I'll kiss you on the cheek if you sit on your hands."

"Done." He turned his head.

"And you must promise to keep sitting on them and not grab me."

"I wouldn't dare."

"Okay." Jacki rose to her feet and leaned toward him. "Here it comes." She pecked him on the cheek.

"Now the other one." He presented his right cheek, and she pecked it too.

"One more?"

"No, that's enough." She hurried to sit back down. "Thank you for keeping your promise."

"I always do."

Except, he was a master loophole finder. Now that Jacki had touched him, he was technically free to touch her. But he wasn't going to use that loophole. Having her kiss him was a first tiny step toward intimacy, and then there would be another one, and then one after that.

The idea was to encourage closeness while building trust.

It was like coaxing a skittish kitten to come for a pet. It might hiss and even scratch, but with a soft tone and a gentle touch it would soon start purring.

"I wanted to ask you something." She reached for the napkin and twisted it between her fingers. "Phinas said that his mother passed away a long time ago, so she wasn't an immortal. But when I asked him about his father, he said that it doesn't work like that. I'm confused. How are immortals made?"

"A little bit of magic."

"Come on. I'm serious."

"The immortal genes are passed only through the mother. Phinas's mother was a carrier of those genes, but they hadn't manifested."

He was getting dangerously close to revealing too much too soon, but he didn't want to lie to her either.

"So she was basically a human, right? And his father was a human as well."

"That's mostly correct. Phinas's mother appeared human, but she was partly immortal."

"Was she aware of that?"

"I don't know. I never met Phinas's mother."

That wasn't a lie; she was long gone by the time Kalugal was born. Except, as a female Dormant living in the Dormants' enclosure, she had known that she was different.

What she might not have known was that she could've been activated.

As far as he knew, the island's female Dormants were led to believe that only males could transition. He'd been twelve when his father had taken him out of the Dormants' quarters to start his training in the warriors' camp, but he still remembered the place fondly. Even though the women's lives hadn't been easy, he didn't remember the place as somber or sad.

"Are there many carriers of the immortal gene among humans?" Jacki asked.

"Not many."

"How do you find them?"

"I don't know. I've never searched for Dormants. The dormant females on the island are the daughters of other Dormants, and so on. My father had them from the very beginning."

Jacki grimaced. "He kept them as breeders."

She was smart, figuring it out from the few details he'd revealed. If he wanted to keep Jacki's possible dormancy a secret from her, Kalugal needed to be careful.

"My father is not a nice man."

"Still, I don't understand how those women could produce immortal offspring. Are the boys born immortal, and the girls are not?"

"None of the children are born immortal. They need to be activated."

"How?"

Leaning forward, he smiled. "That's a secret I can't reveal."

"Can't or won't?"

"Both. It's better that you don't know too many details."

Jacki let out a breath. "I'm not deluding myself that I'm ever getting free, so it doesn't matter how much I know about you. If I leave here, Kian will pick me up. My choices are either to stay with you or with the clan. I will never be allowed back to humanity."

"As I said before. Never say never. You don't know what tomorrow will bring."

"I'd rather be prepared than disappointed."

Jacki

With that damn sexy smirk lifting his perfect lips, Kalugal leaned toward her. "Whatever happens, I can promise you one thing. You won't be disappointed."

What the hell was that supposed to mean?

Of course, she was going to be disappointed.

As much as Jacki tried to stifle her attraction to him and not have silly what-if thoughts, she wasn't made from granite, and Kalugal was slowly but surely burrowing his way into her stupid heart.

Once he got tired of trying to seduce her, he would send her off to Kian, and that would be the end of her vacation in fantasy land.

She might be a Cinderella, and there might be even a glass slipper in the packages Prince Charming had ordered for her, but there was no fairy godmother to sprinkle magic dust over her and turn her into an immortal, or Kalugal into a human.

She'd better not get carried away and start thinking of herself as a princess. Cooking, washing dishes and floors, and dusting would remind her that she was a Cinderella without the happy ending.

"Can I go up and make room in your closet for the new wardrobe you got me? Or do you want to come with me and show me where I should put the stuff."

"I'll come if you need me, but if you can manage by yourself, it would be better. I need to get back to work."

Hallelujah.

Jacki had to offer, but she was glad that he had other things to do. It was difficult enough to be alone with Kalugal in the sprawling library. The closet was too intimate.

"When would you like to eat dinner?"

"I usually dine at eight, if that's okay with you."

"Perfect. It will give me enough time to try everything on and prepare dinner as well. Any special requests?"

"Surprise me. You're an excellent cook, and I enjoyed myself tremendously."

It was sweet of him to exaggerate. Her cooking was good but simple, and a guy like Kalugal had probably dined in the best of restaurants.

"Thank you. If you need me, I'll be upstairs."

"I will see you at dinner." He pushed to his feet and offered her a hand up.

When she took it, he brought it to his lips and kissed the back of it. "Thank you. I had a lovely time."

As the library doors closed behind Kalugal, Jacki let out a breath. Absentmindedly caressing the back of her hand, she wished for the feel of his lips on her skin to linger.

You're such a fool, Jacki.

Angrily, she collected the dishes, dropped them on the tray, and was about to lift it when Shamash walked in.

"I'll take it."

This time, she wasn't going to argue. "Thank you."

"You're welcome." He took the tray and walked out.

As she hurried upstairs, Jacki was excited about trying on her new clothes. It was frivolous, and she shouldn't, but she couldn't help it. As someone who got most of her outfits in thrift shops, getting new designer outfits was a once-in-a-lifetime treat.

Besides, she was curious to see what Kalugal had chosen for her. If half the boxes and bags contained sexy lingerie, and the other half clingy dresses and short skirts, she would know where his mind was. His choices would reveal his intentions toward her.

When she opened the door to her small room, the pile of boxes looked even bigger. The guys had left some on the bed, some on the desk, but most of it on the floor, barely leaving any room for her to navigate her way to the bed.

Jacki started with those first, and with every new package she opened, her heart beat a little faster. So many beautiful things, all elegant without being over the top, sexy without crossing the line into slutty, and the fabrics were mostly made from natural fibers, which she preferred.

Kalugal had exquisite taste, or what was more likely a top-notch personal shopper.

An hour later, she had everything out and grouped. Jeans and other everyday clothes were in one pile, more elegant pants, skirts, and blouses in another, and so on.

There were also eight pairs of shoes, flats and heels, a couple of dresses for evenings out, four silk pajama sets, five sweaters, two robes. And the lingerie sets were the kind she would have bought for herself if she had the money. Soft, not too revealing, but still sexy.

Definitely the work of a female personal shopper. There was no way Kalugal would have known to choose that kind of lingerie for her.

Now it was time for the fun part. Trying everything on. But since her room didn't have a mirror, she had to do that in Kalugal's closet.

Not a big deal.

Anyway, she had to put her things away.

His closet was larger than the entire apartment she'd shared with two other roommates, and it was more than half empty. The problem was that Kalugal's things were scattered throughout, so the first order of business was to organize them in sections according to function.

It shouldn't have taken her long, but Jacki couldn't help sniffing each outfit for the faint residual smell of his cologne or holding his dress shirts to her cheek and imagining that she was embracing Kalugal.

Pathetic.

She was acting like a teenager with a crush.

Finally, when his things were all sorted and organized, she started on what she'd come up there to do, which was trying her new things on and then putting them away.

Not everything fit perfectly, but most did, and she wasn't going to bother with exchanging anything.

Jacki had never felt as elegant and as put together before, except for her hair. The long waves were pretty, but the classy and luxurious outfits called for a more sophisticated hairdo.

She'd never had a professional cut and style her hair, but that wasn't in the cards because she couldn't leave the house. Besides, even if she could, she didn't have money to pay for it. But perhaps she could pin her hair up, or maybe blow dry it straight?

Except, a thorough search of Kalugal's bathroom failed to produce a blow dryer, and the shopper had forgotten to include round hairbrushes in her acquisitions. She also hadn't bought any makeup.

Normally, Jacki didn't bother with it, but the new outfits whetted her appetite for putting more care into her appearance.

Running her hand over the skirt of the beautiful knee-length black dress she'd put on, Jacki turned sideways to check out how she looked in profile. She had heels on, and they made her legs look long and shapely, and her butt lifted and tight.

The black pumps were at least three inches tall, but she had no problem walking in them even though she wasn't used to wearing heels.

Jacki was all dressed up but with nowhere to go.

With a sigh, she stepped out of the pumps and put them on the shelf with her other shoes.

It would have been fun to Skype with Jin and show her each outfit as she tried it, but Jacki had no cell phone, and she wasn't going to ask for one because it was too risky to call Jin from Kalugal's house. If he had Jin's number, he could call her and compel her to come to him.

Perhaps she could ask for a laptop and send Jin an email with pictures of the outfits. Neither Kalugal nor Kian should have a problem with that.

Kalugal

"Wow, Jacqueline." Rufsur whistled as Jacki entered the office. "You should start an Instagram page."

She rolled her eyes. "Right, as if I could show my face on social media. But thank you for the compliment."

"Was everything satisfactory?" Kalugal cut in.

"Everything is great. Thank you, and also convey my thanks to your personal shopper. She did an amazing job."

"I don't have a personal shopper. Why would I need one?"

Given Jacki's raised brow, she didn't believe him. "If you say so. But some of the things that you got me no guy would have chosen."

He chuckled. "You are right. I asked the boutique owner's advice on some of the things. She was a great help, and I don't mind thanking her for you."

"Is she a good friend?" Jacki sounded jealous.

"I don't have human friends. I have acquaintances who know me as one of the personas I assume, and not the real me."

"That sucks."

"It is what it is." He leaned back and gave her a thorough appraisal. "You look very chic."

She looked down at the loose blouse and skinny pants she'd chosen. "No more fifty-cent containers for your twenty-five-thousand-dollars-a-day perfume."

Behind him, Rufsur snickered. "That's a good one, boss."

Was it, though?

Kalugal wasn't sure whether Jacki was flattered or insulted by his analogy, and he didn't want her to think that he objectified her. But trying to fix it now would only make it worse. Instead, he decided to change the subject.

"Are you missing any items?"

"A few small things like hairbrushes and some makeup. I was wondering if I could borrow a laptop." She shifted from foot to foot. "I can put the things in the cart, but I can't pay for them."

"Of course you can." He opened his desk drawer and pulled out his wallet. "Use this." He handed her a corporate MasterCard.

She looked at the name. "Calvin Rothman?"

"One of my many aliases." He reached into the drawer again and pulled out a tablet. "You can use this to make your purchases."

"Is it code protected?"

"It's new, and I didn't activate it yet. It's yours."

"Thank you. Can I send emails from it?"

"You'll need the Wi-Fi password."

"Can I have it?"

"Who do you want to send emails to?"

"Jin. But I don't have her email address. I was hoping to ask Kian to get it for me in our next phone conversation." She smiled. "What's the point of having beautiful new outfits if I can't model them for my friend?"

"You can model them for me."

Jacki chuckled. "I walked right into that one, didn't I? I meant a girlfriend."

"Is that something that women normally do?"

"Of course. Women don't get dressed up for guys, they do it to impress other women, who can actually appreciate how much effort has gone into it."

"Do you?"

She shrugged. "I'm not that much into fashion. I like to be comfortable and not worry about ruining expensive clothes while I work. It's all about functionality for me."

Kalugal pushed away from the desk and got up. "That's the old you." He put his hand on the small of Jacki's back and walked her out of the office. "This is the new you." He waved a hand over the stylish outfit. "The way we dress influences the way we think about ourselves, and the way we see ourselves influences the way we carry ourselves, which in turn determines the way other people perceive us."

"You assign a lot of importance to appearances. Where are we going?"

"I thought that you'd like to have afternoon tea with me. We could continue our conversation from before."

"I would love to. But don't you have work to do?"

"I do, but I'm taking a break. That's one of the benefits of being my own boss." He opened the library doors. "Games table or couch?"

Jacki glanced at the couch and shook her head. "Games table."

"Do you still have bad memories from that piece of furniture?"

"It's not that. I just don't want to accidentally spill something on the gorgeous upholstery."

"Good save." He pulled out his phone. "I'm texting Atzil to serve us tea in here. Any preferences? Would you prefer coffee instead?"

"Coffee, if you don't mind. Trying on clothes is surprisingly exhausting. I need a little boost of energy."

He typed the message and put the phone away. "Was there enough space for your things?"

"Plenty, but I reorganized your wardrobe. I can show you later where everything is." She looked at him from under her lashes. "I hope you don't mind."

"Mind? I love it. I feel pampered. This place lacks a woman's touch. Feel free to reorganize anything that doesn't meet with your approval. You are the lady of the house now."

For once, Jacki didn't have a retort ready and just gawked at him. "Okay..."

Experimentally, he patted her hand to check her response and was glad when she didn't withdraw it.

Not wanting to push his luck, Kalugal leaned back in the chair. "Back to our discussion about dressing the part."

"I wasn't aware that I was on stage."

"We are all on stage all of the time. Even when we are alone. Let me give you an example. I have a hobby which I'm quite obsessed with. Digging for artifacts. The persona I use for that purpose is good old Professor Gunter." He changed his voice to sound older and affected a slight German accent. He then pushed his belly out and adjusted his pants.

Jacki laughed. "You're good. That's really playing a part."

"Thank you." He dipped his head. "Since I travel through airports as Professor Gunter, shrouding myself is not enough, and I have to put on an actual disguise. But it's more than just the rumpled brown suit and hat. I talk and walk like an old man, and because people react to me as if I were an older gentleman, I often find myself thinking as one. I smile indulgently at the kids running around and making havoc, and I call young women *liebchen*. When I come home, I shower and change, which helps me wash away that persona and become myself again."

"You lead a complicated life."

"I do. But at least it's not boring."

"I guess. I would love to travel to foreign countries, but digging in the dirt is not my idea of fun."

"*Et tu, Brute?* Rufsur shares your opinion on that." He leaned closer to her and smiled. "Maybe you'll change your mind after I show you my collection. You see, the digging part is not much fun, but I hire locals to do that. The exciting part is finding something fascinating, a piece of the puzzle to unlock forgotten secrets."

Kian

"I spoke with Ingrid." Vanessa walked into Kian's office. "She can't go." Pulling out a chair, she sat down and put her purse on his desk.

Kian arched a brow. "Can't or won't?"

"It's both. She said that Richard is fun, but that she doesn't feel the connection. He is not the one for her. She would have gone to help out with Wendy and Vlad, but she has that new hotel project you assigned her to. If you want it to be ready by the end of the month, she needs to work nights and weekends to catch up on the work she missed during the lockdown."

"So what do we do now?"

"We need to find someone else who wants to give Richard a chance. I'm going to pay him a visit, make an assessment, and then try to match him with the right female. Ingrid called dibs on him because she was there when he arrived. We didn't give anyone else a chance to get to know him."

"Good luck."

"What's your impression of Richard?" She pulled a tablet out of her purse.

Kian grimaced. "I'm not good at those things. Maybe you should talk to Syssi. Her opinion about people is usually much more positive than mine. Or you can ask Amanda. She is not as kind as Syssi, but she is more forgiving than me. But the best one to ask is Edna. She probed him."

Vanessa rolled her eyes. "I will call each one and ask them their opinions, but I want yours as well. Syssi will focus on the positives, Amanda will be neutral, and you will focus on the negatives. That will give me a good picture. And then I'll complete it with Edna's deeper assessment."

Kian chuckled. "According to Edna, there is nothing deep about Richard. He is a what-you-see-is-what-you-get kind of guy."

"That's not a bad thing." Using a stylus, Vanessa scribbled on her tablet. "What else?"

"He is not afraid of hard work, which is the one thing that I like about him. He's decent looking, I would say that his intelligence is above average, and that's about it. Edna said that he'd never loved anyone, romantically that is, which seemed to shock him because he was convinced that he'd been in love. He'd even gotten engaged, but

Eleanor compelled him to break it off with his fiancée and join the program. He's still pissed about it."

"Rightfully so." Vanessa kept scribbling for another minute. "Anything else?"

"He and Jin dated, but that was because of Eleanor's compulsion. Jin said that he was okay, but that she would have never dated him without Eleanor's intervention. That's all I got. Did you ask Ingrid what she thought of him?"

"I did. It's in my notes." Vanessa put the tablet back in her purse. "I'm heading to the keep, and from there, I'm going to the halfway house."

"How is that project going?"

"Very well. Julian was the right choice to head it." She smiled. "Yamanu's karaoke nights are a hit. The girls love him."

"I'm glad it's working out, and we have a new donor who is funneling twenty-five thousand dollars a day into the charity. I'll leave it up to you to decide how to use the money."

She sighed. "There are so many things I want to do that it's hard to prioritize. I'll work on it next week. First, I want to solve the issue of the new possible Dormants and their integration into the clan. We can't leave them hanging in limbo."

"I agree. What's your progress with Vlad?"

"He agreed to go to the cabin, but when I called this morning and asked him if he wanted to come with me to the keep to visit Wendy, he declined the offer. His excuse was that he has classes he can't miss, but I think that he is just not ready to face her yet."

"Poor kid. He doesn't deserve the heartache."

"That's true. But on the other hand, Wendy might be his fated one, and that's worth jumping through some hoops for."

Jin

Jin pushed the sunglasses up her nose. "It's so annoying that I have to put on a disguise to leave the village."

Not that the sunglasses were such a chore, and other than that, she'd just gathered her hair in a ponytail. But it was still pissing her off that she had to hide like a criminal when she'd done nothing wrong.

Mey glanced at the rearview mirror and frowned. "It might be nothing, but that Ford truck has been following us for a while now."

Instinctively, Jin slid lower in her seat. "What are you going to do?"

"Evasive maneuvers. Instead of heading straight to the keep, I'm going to the mall first, and we are going to spend a long time looking for a parking spot. If he follows us there, we are in trouble."

For the next several minutes, Mey drove in silence without increasing the speed or trying to get away, but she kept glancing at the rearview mirror.

When at the next intersection she turned left and the truck continued straight, Jin let out a breath. "He wasn't following us."

Mey didn't look relieved. "I'm going to drive around for a little bit to see if he comes back. He might have done it on purpose."

"You are like a real spy. I'm glad that you are driving and not me. I would've freaked out and started speeding away."

"I didn't want him to know that we'd noticed him. By the way, when are you getting your own car?"

"I'm not in a hurry." Jin shifted up in her seat. "The autonomous driving part still scares me. Besides, I'm treating this time as a honeymoon. Arwel and I are working on my transition, and once I enter it, I'll be out of commission for several days at least. I see no point in starting anything before that."

"Did you make any progress on our business plan?"

"Sorry." Jin smiled sheepishly. "I'm busy doing other stuff. There is no rush, right? You are an immortal, and soon I will be too. We have all the time in the world to pursue our dream."

Reaching over, Mey patted her arm. "You are right. Enjoy your time with Arwel. I'm a little bored, but I can take

Yamanu up on his offer to help out in the halfway house." She smirked. "I could teach the girls to do the runway walk."

Jin perked up. "That's a great idea. We could make a collection of clothes and bring them over for dress-up fun. It'll work great in conjunction with Eva's makeovers."

"I thought that you were busy doing other stuff."

"I am. This is for after my transition. The only thing I'm trying to achieve before that is fixing Wendy and Richard's situation."

"What about Jacki?"

Jin sighed. "I don't know what to think about that girl. Maybe one of Kalugal's men will have better luck with her. She didn't respond to any of the Guardians."

"I hope so."

After passing through the mall, Mey seemed satisfied that they were no longer being followed and checked her GPS. "We are almost there."

Less than ten minutes later, she turned into the parking entrance of one of the high rises. Pulling out a visitor's pass from the center console, she showed it to the guard, and they were let right in.

"Is this the keep?"

"No. It's one of the buildings on the other side of the street. We are going to use a tunnel to get there."

"Sounds complicated. I've been through the tunnel on the way out of the keep, but I wouldn't know how to find the entrance."

"I have the instructions written down."

Jin smirked. "Is the note going to combust once you choose to accept the mission?"

"Sort of. It's in my notes on my phone, and if I lose it and someone tries to tamper with it, the thing will erase all data and self-destruct."

"Isn't that dangerous?"

"Nothing will happen to it on the outside. Just the inside components melt or short circuit. I didn't ask how exactly it would happen."

As they arrived at the lowest parking level, Mey pulled out a card and lifted it up so the electronic eye could see it. A moment later, the gate rolled sideways, and they drove in.

There were only three other cars there, and the walls were lined with crates.

"I remember this place." Jin opened the door. "This is where the limo waited for us when we left the keep."

"Yamanu told me that there are two of them, so you might have used the other one." Mey locked the car. "They look the same, though."

Stopping in front of a door marked as storage, Mey pulled out her phone, and after checking her notes, she punched in the code. They walked in, closed the door behind them, and only then opened the second one that led into the tunnel.

"I don't know what I'm going to say to Wendy." Jin fell into step with her sister. "I spent all morning trying to come up with the right approach. I don't want to go in there and berate her. I'm sure she's gotten enough of that."

"Vanessa saw her yesterday."

Jin hadn't known that, which was upsetting. She should have been kept in the loop on all things concerning her friends.

"What did she say?"

"I haven't spoken to her. Yamanu just mentioned that the therapist was working with Wendy." Mey sighed. "I still can't believe what she did. The girl is either an amazing actress or has a split personality disorder. She and Vlad were hitting it off, and I had such high hopes for them."

"That's what I keep thinking. If she didn't want to leave the program, why did she beg us to take her along?"

"Maybe she changed her mind later. Or perhaps she chickened out, or maybe she realized what she was leaving behind and got cold feet. Where else would a nineteen-year-old girl get a job that pays as much?"

Jin huffed. "Yeah, but all that money is meaningless if she never gets to spend it because she is enslaved for life and made into a breeder for a new superior generation of paranormals."

Mey lifted her hand. "That's precisely what you need to tell her."

Kian

"Syssi, what a nice surprise." Kian pushed away from his desk and walked over to his wife. "I thought that you were going to use your day off to go shopping for maternity clothes." Pulling her into his arms, he was careful not to squeeze too hard.

Her belly was only starting to show, but he was always mindful of the precious life growing inside of it.

"Amanda said that I'm being ridiculous." Syssi rubbed her tummy. "I think this is getting rounder because I eat more and not because of the pregnancy. Twelve weeks is too early to be showing. Anyway, I decided to stop by your office and invite you for a cup of coffee at the café before I go."

"I'm glad." He glanced at the pile of work waiting on his desk. "Spending time with my wife in the middle of a workday is a rare treat. Everything else can wait."

The only thing he didn't like about it was that they wouldn't be alone.

It was mid-morning, so the café wasn't full, but several of the tables were taken, and he had to smile and say hello.

It was a beautiful day, and the sun was up, but it bothered his eyes, and Kian had forgotten to take his sunglasses with him. "Do you mind if we sit in the shade?"

"Not at all." Syssi walked over to a table that was under the canopy of a tree. "Is this good?"

"Perfect." He pulled out a chair for her. "What would you like?"

"Just a cappuccino. I'm still full from breakfast."

"That was hours ago. I'll get you a Danish."

She chuckled. "Overeating is not good for the baby."

For a moment, he looked confused, but then he shook his head. "One Danish does not count as overeating."

She sighed. "How can I say no to such delicious temptation."

Her suggestive tone had a predictable effect, and Kian had to stifle a retort that was not appropriate for a public place.

Instead, he headed to the counter. "Good morning, Wonder."

"Hello, Kian." She greeted him with a bright smile. "I don't usually see you here during the day."

"Syssi has a day off."

"That's awesome. What would you like?"

After placing the order, Kian returned to the table and pulled out a chair. "Wonder is going to bring our order when it's ready."

Syssi smiled. "Her cappuccino making skills have improved so much that she's giving me serious competition."

"Not a chance. Yours are the best."

"Thank you." Syssi took her jacket off and hung it on the back of her chair. "It's getting warmer. Your mother is going to enjoy the weather when she comes for a visit."

He cringed. "I hope she doesn't. But if Kalugal and I don't get together soon and negotiate a co-existence agreement, she might. She's got it into her head that she can shield me from his compulsion."

"She probably can."

"Probably is not good enough. I'm not going to risk it."

"You can't tell her what to do, so if you don't want her to come, you need to hurry up and set up a meeting with Kalugal."

"I'm working on it. I could take Turner with me, but if Kalugal compels my bodyguards and me, Turner is not going to be able to help. I think that the only viable option is a teleconference. I won't need Anandur and Brundar with me in the room, and if Kalugal tries something, Turner can cut the connection."

Syssi frowned. "I'm not an expert on these things, but I don't think it's going to work. You and Kalugal need to get to know each other and develop trust. And you can't do that without a face-to-face meeting. Teleconferencing is not going to give you the same multi-sensory input that you would get when you are physically in the same place as him. And in your case, you have all those extra senses that will help you evaluate Kalugal. It makes me think about this generation of texters who have lost their ability to actually connect to people."

Kian chuckled. "I saw a clip of a group of friends sitting around a table in the mall's food court and texting each other instead of talking."

Syssi tapped her forehead. "That gives me an idea. What if you wore earplugs while meeting with Kalugal? You could both have tablets and text each other instead of talking, but at least you would be sitting at the same table. All these subconscious clues and the scents he is going to emit will be available to you."

"That's brilliant." He took her hand and brought it to his lips. "I don't know why Turner and I haven't thought of that."

"Sometimes, it is easier for an outsider to see a solution than it is for those with their noses in the problem."

"Maybe I can take it a step further. I need to talk to William."

"What do you have in mind?"

"An earpiece that absorbs outside sounds but doesn't transmit them as is, but alters the wavelengths, stripping the compulsion component away."

Syssi looked doubtful. "First of all, we don't know what compulsion is and on which wavelength it's transmitted. You can't strip down something that you can't isolate. And secondly, a device like that will take a long time to develop, and you can't wait because Annani is breathing down your neck."

Unfortunately, Syssi was right.

"Then I'll have to use your suggestion and communicate with Kalugal via texting, which is going to be really weird when sitting across from him."

She waved a hand. "I might be wrong. Talk it over with William; maybe he can come up with something."

"Here are your cappuccinos." Wonder put down the tray with their order. "I couldn't help but overhear your conversation, and I have an idea."

"What is it?" Syssi opened a sugar packet and poured it into her cup.

"Give Turner a taser. If Kalugal tries something, Turner can zap him."

Kian chuckled. "I could also get Kalugal one of those dog collars that are remotely controlled, but I don't think it's going to be conducive to encouraging trust and cooperation between us."

Jin

As Jin and Mey entered Wendy's room, they found her lying on her stomach on the bed and watching the tube.

She turned her head to look at them, but her eyes seemed vacant. "What are you doing here?"

Jin sat on the couch. "We came to visit you."

Mey sat down next to her and crossed her arms over her chest.

"Why? So you can yell at me?" Wendy turned her head back to the screen.

Jin wasn't a psychologist, but even she knew how Wendy had interpreted Mey's pose. With a slight shake of her head, she touched her sister's knee.

Mey got the hint, let out a breath, and put her arms down.

"Can you pause that for a few minutes?" Jin asked. "I want to talk to you."

Reluctantly, Wendy pointed the remote at the screen and paused her program, but she stayed in the same pose and turned her head only slightly to cast Jin a sidelong glance.

"I'm not going to yell at you or berate you. I just want to understand why."

"I already told the therapist everything. You can ask her."

"I want to hear it from you. Why did you ask to join the escape when you didn't want to leave the program?"

"I thought that I did, and then I changed my mind. Giving up the best job I would ever get was the stupidest thing I've ever done."

"I disagree. You made the right decision and then got cold feet. That's all."

Wendy lifted on her forearms and slung her legs over the side of the bed. "How can you say that? There is nothing for me on the outside. What other job is going to pay me that much money and give me a safe place to live as part of the compensation package?"

"And what are you going to do with all that money? How are you going to spend it if they never let you out? Not only that, you will become a breeder for the enhanced paranormals the director and his bosses want to produce. That's slavery, not a job."

Wendy grimaced. "Put like that it doesn't sound so great, but at least no one will abuse me. I might not be free, but I'll be safe."

"Who do you think is going to abuse you outside of the program?"

"Anyone who wants to. I have no family, no backup. I'm all alone."

"How about your father?"

Wendy shook her head. "I don't want to talk about him or ever see him again. As far as I'm concerned, he is dead."

Well, that explained a lot.

The abuser was obviously her father, and he was the reason Wendy had sought shelter in the program.

"Look, Wendy, the government program is not the only safe place in the world for you. This organization that Mey and I are now part of can give you shelter as well. They can't pay you as much as you've been making in the program, but they can provide you with a safe haven. No one is going to hurt you, and no one is going to use you as a breeder either."

Next to her, Mey cleared her throat and shook her head.

It was true that if Wendy wasn't a Dormant she couldn't join the clan, but Jin was positive that Kian would arrange something for her. He could give her fake documents and a job at one of the clan's many enterprises.

"Can I get that in writing?"

"You don't trust me?"

"I don't trust anyone. Why would the organization help me after what I did? They are better off dumping me somewhere."

"Everyone deserves a second chance. And Kian is willing to give you one. Just don't blow it."

Closing her eyes, Wendy let out a breath. "He shouldn't give it to me. Unless I know for sure that I won't end up on the street, I'd rather return to the program. I don't trust promises."

As aggravating as Wendy's stubbornness was, she was at least honest. As long as she didn't get assurances, she was going to cling to the program's supposed merits and ignore any other opportunities she might get.

Jin pushed to her feet. "I'll see what I can do. I'll talk to Kian and get him to commit to a concrete plan of action for you."

"In writing."

Mey chuckled. "You are putting too much faith in written documents. A signature is only worth as much as the signatory's willingness to deliver the goods."

"Or the fees you can afford to pay an attorney," Jin added. "In the end, it all boils down to trust. Do you trust Director Simmons, Wendy? The man who had Eleanor compel you, and the same guy who planned to breed you like a mare? Or do you trust the people who befriended you and were looking out for you?"

"I don't trust anyone," Wendy whispered.

"That's a good start." Jin leaned and kissed the girl's cheek. "I gave you a lot to think about. I hope you'll make the right decision."

Lokan

As Lokan's clan-issue phone rang, he took it out onto the balcony before answering.

"Is that Kian?" Carol followed him out.

"Who else?" Lokan accepted the call. "Hello, Kian."

"Good afternoon, or good evening your time. I have news from your brother. He wants to meet you."

Lokan tensed. "Did you tell him about me?"

"Your mother did. She wants her boys to meet and hopes that you'll become friends and allies. In her words, and I'm quoting, 'Maybe one day the bonds of friendship could blossom into brotherly love.'"

Lokan plopped down on the lounge chair. "Did Kalugal say how he wanted to do that?"

"He left it up to me. I think we should meet him together. That way, I can extend Guardian protection to you."

"Much good that will do if Kalugal decides to compel us."

"You should be immune to his compulsion. If your father's didn't work on you, Kalugal's shouldn't either. In fact, I'm counting on that. If he overpowers my men and me, you can help."

"I'm not at all certain that he can't compel me. I couldn't protect your people from his compulsion, which means that he is stronger than me."

Carol leaned over him and kissed his forehead. "Don't worry. I'll get a taser gun, and if he tries anything, I'll zap him."

Kian chuckled. "That's funny. Wonder had a similar suggestion. Your brother seems to court female aggression."

"That's because he's a threat to our men," Carol said.

"Syssi came up with a better solution. It's not perfect, but it could work. We put in earplugs and communicate with Kalugal by typing on tablets."

Snorting, Carol sat on Lokan's lap. "That's ridiculous. He is going to feel so damn superior."

Lokan pulled her against his chest. "Do you have a better suggestion?"

"Not off the top of my head, but I'll think of something."

"We don't have a lot of time," Kian said. "Our mothers are anxious for us to sit down and talk."

"If no one comes up with a better solution, the earplugs could work." Carol tucked a stray curl behind her cute little ear. "When and where?"

Lokan stifled a chuckle. His mate might look like an angelic pixie, but she was a fierce fighter and one of the bravest people he'd ever had the honor of knowing.

"San Francisco. It's better that we come to Kalugal and not the other way around. I'll rent a house for the occasion, so we can all stay over and talk freely away from human ears and eyes."

"How many men are you bringing with you?" Lokan asked.

"I didn't make any arrangements with Kalugal yet, but I'm going to insist on a maximum of three bodyguards for each of us. He doesn't need to know that yours are actually mine. That will give us a slight advantage. Six of ours against three of his. One of mine is going to be Turner, though, and he is not a Guardian, so it's five to three."

"What about mates?" Carol asked. "I want to come."

"Sorry, Carol. I don't want to endanger you or Syssi. But this could be a good opportunity for you to visit the village and spend time with our friends while Lokan is with me at the summit."

"Do I have a choice?"

"Not really. There is no way I'm exposing Syssi to Kalugal, and I'm sure Lokan feels the same about you."

"I do." Lokan kissed the top of Carol's head, hoping to stave off a tantrum.

"Can I come with Lokan to San Francisco and stay at a hotel? You can bring Syssi along, and we can hang out together. Maybe you could rent a conference room in the hotel instead of a house, and at the end of the day, Kalugal will go home while you and Lokan will stay in the hotel. I think it would work better. Maybe Callie and Wonder can come too. That would be fun."

Kian let out an exasperated sigh. "I'll give it some thought."

"Thanks. That's all I'm asking. Now that we covered the where, what about the when?"

"Annani and Areana are pressuring us to hurry up, so this weekend would be best, but I need to check with Kalugal if it works for him."

Carol shifted in Lokan's arms. "If it's going to happen over the weekend, you absolutely must include the mates. Right?" She lifted a pair of guileless eyes to Lokan.

"I'm all for it, love. But it's Kian's show, and he makes the rules."

"I'll let you know. In the meantime, make the appropriate arrangements. Reschedule meetings if you need to."

"I don't have anything scheduled for this weekend. The question is, how long will it take? I have meetings on Monday and every day for the rest of the week."

"Let's see how it goes. We might be done in one day, or we could keep talking without reaching an agreement for weeks. But none of us has the time for that. If it seems like it's going to drag on, we could schedule another meeting for the next weekend and so forth."

"Sounds good. I'll make flight arrangements for Carol and me to arrive Friday night at San Francisco."

Smiling triumphantly, Carol pumped her fist in the air.

Kian chuckled. "I didn't decide on including the mates yet."

"You will." Carol pushed off Lokan's lap. "Say hi to Syssi for me."

Jin

Jin waited for the door to Wendy's room to close before turning to Bowen. "Thank you for sticking around. I think it's good for Wendy to see familiar faces."

"Not mine. All she's getting from me are scowls."

"I know that you are angry and disappointed." Mey put her hand on his arm. "But try to be a little nicer to her. She is just a young girl who thinks that she's alone in the world, and that no one cares about her."

He huffed out a breath. "I've already gotten the same speech from Vanessa, and I'll tell you the same thing that I told her. I'm not a good actor, and I'm not the forgiving type either. The best I can do is ask Onegus to replace me."

Mey patted his arm again. "Just make a tiny effort to scowl less. Can you do that?"

Rolling his eyes, he nodded. "You are all getting sucked in by her innocent-poor-me act. Fool me once, shame on you, fool me twice, shame on me."

The guy was a lost cause.

"We should go." Jin threaded her arm through Mey's.

"One second." Mey resisted Jin's pull. "How is Richard doing?"

"He is with Vanessa. She came to talk to him."

"Why? Is he having a breakdown too?"

Bowen shrugged. "She said something about making an assessment."

"So you didn't call her?"

He shook his head. "Richard is doing fine. He is the reason I stayed on. I don't think it's fair to let the guy feel like he is getting punished for Wendy's crime, so I figured I'd stay and keep him company when Ingrid is not here. I'm training with him in the gym."

"That's very nice of you. Do you know when Vanessa is going to be done? I would like to say hi to him."

"Let me check." He walked over to Richard's room and punched in the code. "His door is not usually locked. I just closed it so they could have privacy."

When it opened, Bowen poked his head inside. "Mey and Jin are here. Can they come in?"

"Sure!" Unlike Wendy, Richard sounded happy to see them.

"I hope we are not interrupting," Mey said.

Vanessa smiled and waved them in. "Richard and I are done."

"I heard that you got sick." Richard pushed to his feet and pulled Jin into his arms for a quick hug. "How are you feeling?"

"Much better, but I still get tired doing nothing."

"Come." He guided her to the couch. "Sit down and tell me how you've been."

They spent a few minutes chatting, with Jin making up half of the details of what had happened with Kalugal.

When she was done, Richard let out a breath. "I'm glad that it's over and that no one got hurt. How are things going with Arwel?"

"Great."

"Is he the one?"

Jin nodded.

"I'm happy for you."

"I need to get going." Vanessa rose to her feet.

"Yeah, we are leaving too." Mey followed Vanessa's example and then offered Jin a hand up. "We can walk together to the parking garage."

As they entered the elevator, Jin turned to the therapist. "So, what do you think about Richard? Did he pass the test?"

Vanessa chuckled. "The reason I came to talk to him wasn't to test him. I wanted to get a feel for him, so I could match him with the right female."

"What about Ingrid?"

"She bailed." Vanessa punched the button for parking level three, which wasn't the one connecting to the tunnel. "I'm going to grab a cup of coffee from the vending machine. Care to join me? You could tell me more about Richard."

"We would love to." Jin glanced at Mey. "Is that okay? Or are you in a rush to go back home?"

"No rush."

"Awesome."

To get to the lobby, they had to exit the clan's dedicated elevator at the parking garage level, go through another room marked as storage, and then enter one of the regular elevators the rest of the building's occupants were using and take it up. It was a long roundabout way to get to the café.

"It used to be reserved only for us," Vanessa said when they got there. "But Nathalie decided to open it to the other occupants. So it's no longer as private as it used to be, but it seems that people are not too crazy about a coffee shop with no servers, so most of the time, there is no one there."

They found one guy sitting at a corner table and typing away on his computer.

Jin leaned closer to Vanessa. "He's not one of ours, right?"

"He's not."

After getting their coffees, they chose a table that was the furthest away from the human.

The irony of grouping herself with the immortals wasn't lost on Jin. She was still human, but she was already thinking in terms of us versus them.

"I understand that you and Richard dated for a while," Vanessa said. "Any insights about him that you would care to share?"

"He is okay." Jin tore open a sugar packet and emptied it into her coffee. "He is not very romantic, and he is not a great conversationalist, but he was a pretty attentive boyfriend. He also has a decent sense of humor, and he doesn't take himself too seriously. That being said, he thinks that he is a hunk and that most women find him desirable."

"He's not bad looking," Mey said. "He has a certain charm."

"Not everyone is a heartthrob." Vanessa removed the lid from her black coffee and took a sip.

"What's the deal with Ingrid?" Jin asked. "Bowen said that she still comes over."

"I talked to her about joining Richard in the clan's cabin, and she declined. She said that he's fun to be with, but he's not the one." Vanessa took another sip and then put her cup down. "I have someone in mind for him, but I don't know if she is interested."

"Anyone I know?" Mey asked.

"I don't know if you've met her. Stella is Vlad's mother, and she is a costume designer. She doesn't hang out in the village café, and she spends most of her time working at home."

Jin grimaced. "I don't think a creative woman would appreciate Richard. Someone who is business-oriented might be better."

"Stella is a businesswoman too. To get design projects, she needs to advertise and submit bids and make budgets. It's not just about the artsy side of things. The best part is that she works from home, so she could go with them to the mountains and work from there. Also, as Vlad's mother, she could go as a kind of chaperone, and if she doesn't like Richard, she doesn't have to engage with him."

"I like it." Jin leaned back. "I wish Arwel and I could join them."

Vanessa shook her head. "The cabin only has two bedrooms and a loft. Wendy can take one bedroom, Stella the other, and Richard can take the loft. The

Guardians will have to take turns on the living room couch."

"That's not going to work," Jin said. "The sofa needs to stay clear for romantic evenings. What do you think about the Guardians sleeping in a motorhome?"

"That could be a solution."

"Or, Arwel and I can get one, and Arwel will do the guarding. A head Guardian can count as two regular ones, right?"

Vanessa laughed. "I don't think Kian will go for that."

"We could have two motor homes," Jin offered.

"First, I need to talk to Stella and see if she is game. If she's not, I'll have to find someone else."

Jin felt a little offended on Richard's behalf. He was a decent guy and fairly good-looking, and he might be the one for somebody.

"I would have thought that the clan females would jump at the opportunity to snag a dormant male."

"You are right. But I can't post an ad on the clan's virtual board and ask who wants to go. There would be a stampede. I need to approach one female at a time and do it discreetly."

Director Simmons

"Come in, Elijah." The director opened the door and ushered his old friend in. "How is the new recruit doing?"

"I gave him the full battery of medical tests and implanted him with the nano-trackers. Eleanor took care of his mental adjustment."

"Excellent."

The nano trackers were Doctor Elijah Roberts' biggest achievement. They had their limitations, with their short range being the major one, but what they lacked in that area, they more than compensated for with their incredible miniaturization.

Smaller than grains of sand, they were impossible to detect because they didn't show on any imaging equipment.

The recruits had no idea that the so-called flu immunization shot, which they got their first day on the base, was actually a shot of tiny trackers. Those formed a detectable grid that had been personalized to each of them.

As long as they didn't leave the base for more than three days, the nanos remained inactive. But after seventy-two hours without the inhibiting chemical that was added to the trainees' meals, the nanos activated, formed the grid, and started transmitting. Because of the short range, the trackers were useless to anyone other than the government with its wide network of receivers and amplifiers.

The whole ingenious system was still in development, but Roberts was an old friend, and he had no qualms about testing his inventions on Edgar's trainees.

"What are you going to do about the escapees?" Elijah pulled out a chair and sat down.

"Hold on."

As he always did while talking business with his confidants, the director activated the noise machine to cover up their conversation.

Roberts crossed his arms over his chest. "It has been almost two weeks, and you haven't done anything to retrieve them yet."

"There is no rush. The missing recruits are not as interesting to me as the organization that helped them escape, and I wouldn't have known about them if my darling niece hadn't called and told me about them. I have a guy in Los Angeles snooping around."

Roberts shook his head. "Do you know the proverb about a bird in the hand being worth two in the bush? You're trying to catch too many fish with one net."

Elijah was fond of his proverbs.

"Since when are you the voice of caution? You were the one who came up with the idea for a paranormal talents department. We knew there would be risks involved and that most of what we wanted to do would never get approved."

They had come up with their plan more than fifty years ago when they were both young students. Back then, paranormal phenomena and mysticism had been in vogue, and they both had been fascinated by the possibilities. It hadn't been frowned upon as it was now, and even the first mission to the moon had incorporated mystical and mythological elements. Scheduling it for July twentieth hadn't been a random choice. It coincided with the birthday of the goddess Isis, the Egyptian goddess of the moon.

"We did that together, but you were always too gung-ho about things. I like to take my time and make sure I'm not caught with my hand in the cookie jar."

Edgar laughed. "Especially in today's world. We've stuck our hands in the wrong jars for many years." He sighed. "Ah, those were the days."

Roberts nodded. "Chasing skirts around the office used to be a favorite pastime of mine. Now you can't even give a chick a compliment without her running to Human Resources to complain about harassment. Remember Joe? He was forced into early retirement because some broad accused him of pestering her."

"It's a sad state of affairs when a decorated soldier like Joe gets the boot because of a petty grievance from an insignificant underling."

Roberts pursed his fleshy lips. "I hope that you are keeping your hands to yourself with Eleanor. She could turn on you without batting an eyelash."

"I wouldn't touch her if she was the only female on the base. The woman is useful, but she's a bitch on wheels."

The one who whetted his appetite was sweet, juicy Wendy, but he wasn't going to touch her either. It was beyond the pale even for an old lecher like him. Edgar drew the line at female family members, especially since Wendy was the only one left.

"Good. We need her, and she is not easily replaceable."

"I'm well aware of that."

"Your guy in Los Angeles, I hope he is a private contractor."

"Of course. We don't want to attract too much attention to our so-called pilot program. The last thing I need is for internal affairs to start asking questions and breathing down my neck. I told him to snoop around and see what he can find. The problem is that our escapees are scattered in several locations, and my guy is a small operator. I told him to hire one more man, so he can keep tabs on each of them."

Jacki

"This is a hymn to Inanna, the goddess of love." Kalugal pointed at the crumbling tablet fragments under the glass display.

Showing off his collection, Kalugal reminded Jacki of a boy from her elementary school who'd tried to impress her with his stack of rare Pokémon cards.

It was so endearing.

Damn, she would have had to be made from pure rock not to fall for the guy. He was handsome, sexy, smart, polite, and he seemed to really like her.

He wouldn't be showing her his prized possessions if he didn't. And he wouldn't be donating a fortune to charity for every day that she spent with him either.

Not that he wanted Jacki with him at all times. Kalugal was a busy guy, and he had work to do, but he took breaks whenever he could and spent every moment of them with her.

Jacki wasn't all that interested in archeological finds, but since it was important to Kalugal, she made an effort to ask questions and 'ooh' and 'ahh' on occasion.

"I was able to guess most of the missing verses except for this one." He tapped the glass over an empty spot with his finger. "That's the biggest missing piece."

"Do you understand the writing, or did you have it translated?"

"I taught myself Sumerian, but reading it is not as easy as reading a modern language. It's a system of logographic and phonographic symbols, which means that some of them represent syllables that form words, and some represent entire words. Not only that, the same symbols are sometimes used as phonograms and other times as logograms depending on the context."

Jacki chuckled. "Saying that it was complicated would have been enough."

"It's complicated. Am I boring you?"

"Not at all. It's fascinating." Except, what she was enjoying the most was seeing Kalugal excited. "So Inanna is like Venus, the goddess of love, right?"

"She's the goddess of love, sensuality, fertility, procreation, and war. The Akkadians called her Ishtar, the Phoenicians called her Astarte, the Greeks called her Aphrodite, and the Romans called her Venus. All those ancient civilizations worshipped basically the same pantheon of gods, but they gave them different names."

"So, if the Sumerians were the first, they were the ones who invented them."

He smirked. "They didn't make them up. The Sumerians knew the gods."

Her eyes widened. "Those were your ancestors, right? The Sumerian gods?"

"Yes."

"Wow. How did that work? Were humans slaves to the gods?"

"Not slaves. Worshipers. Each of the Sumerian city-states was governed by a god, and his or her temple was not only a place of worship but also the administrative center of the city. The contributions were like taxes, and the gods used them for various purposes. Some of it went into maintaining the temples and paying the salaries of the temple's servants, clerks, and the like, but most of it went into building roads and water canals and everything else that required collaborative work. We are lucky that the Sumerians kept excellent written records and that their writing wasn't limited to hymns and other religious purposes. A lot can be learned from financial ledgers."

That was truly fascinating. Kalugal's explanation had turned the crumbling tablets and dusty pottery into real, living history, and Jacki was curious to find out more.

"What I don't understand is why the goddess of love is also the goddess of war. Those two are opposites. Make love, not war, right?"

Kalugal's satisfied expression hinted that he'd been waiting for her to ask that.

"I wondered the same thing. But then it occurred to me that Inanna sounds a lot like Annani. Furthermore, Sumerian writing could be read from left to right and right to left."

He looked at her like a teacher who was waiting for his student to arrive at a conclusion based on what he'd said.

"I don't understand. What does the sequence of syllables in the goddess's name have to do with her being the goddess of love and war? Does the name mean war or love in Sumerian depending on whether it's read from left to right or right to left?"

Chuckling, Kalugal tapped his forehead with two fingers. "You don't know who Kian's mother is, right?"

"I haven't met her."

"Kian's mother is the goddess Annani, the head of the clan, and probably the Sumerian goddess of love and war."

She still didn't understand the connection. "Arwel said that all the gods were killed by your grandfather."

Kalugal grimaced. "Except for two. Annani and her sister Areana, who is my mother."

It took a couple of seconds for what Kalugal had said to register, and when it did, Jacki's hand flew to her mouth. "Oh, my God! You are the son of a goddess? And so is Kian? Actual goddesses?"

Talk about being outclassed.

The tiny grains of hope that Jacki had subconsciously allowed to sprout had just been torched. Kalugal was the freaking son of a goddess, a half-god, while she was a human nobody.

She should leave, like right now. Just walk out and wait on the street for Kian's men to pick her up.

With the instinct to flee kicking in, her legs started moving without her giving them a conscious command to do so.

Kalugal stopped her with a hand on her arm. "Where are you going?"

"I have to go."

Kalugal

For some reason, mentioning that he was the son of a goddess had scared Jacki instead of impressing her. The spike in anxiety was so intense that he had a feeling that her instinctive fight or flight response had kicked in.

"I have to go." She pulled her arm out of his grasp.

"What happened, Jacki? Nothing about me has changed. I'm still the same guy you were perfectly comfortable with a moment ago."

She snorted. "Comfortable? Not really. You are…" She waved a hand over him. "Just too much."

"Am I overbearing? Condescending? Tell me how to make you comfortable, and I will."

She let out a breath. "You are none of those things. It's not what you do. It's who you are. I'm just a simple girl, and hanging out with a half-god freaks me out."

He took her hand and brought it to his lips for a gentle kiss. "I'm just an immortal like the other immortals you have been unknowingly hanging out with for the past two weeks."

"You and your father are the most powerful immortals in the world."

"True, but it is also true that I inherited my powers from my father, who is just an immortal, and not my mother, who is a goddess. Kian told me that she's a very weak goddess, weaker even than the average immortal. So my half-godly status really shouldn't freak you out."

Nodding, Jacki let out a breath. "Okay. So the freaky one is your father, not your mother."

"Precisely." He wrapped his arm around her shoulders. "Let's go to my office. I'll pour you a drink, and you can tell me all the ways in which I am too much."

She rewarded him with a lopsided smile. "That would take a while."

"We have time." He led her out of his display room.

"I do, but what about you? Don't you have work?"

"For the time being, I'm in maintenance mode." He opened the door to his office. "I just keep an eye on my portfolio and do some trading when necessary."

"Is that because of me?"

He walked Jacki to the couch and motioned for her to take a seat. "In part. But I also don't feel comfortable venturing out while Kian's men are watching my every move."

"They are here because of me."

Smiling, Kalugal opened the bar doors. "Don't kid yourself. If you weren't here, Kian would have just made their presence more covert. What would you like to drink?"

"Do you have a beer?"

"Not the kind you would enjoy, but I can make you a tasty cocktail."

"That would be great. Thank you."

He made a couple of old fashioneds.

Jacki took the glass he handed her and sniffed at it. "What's in it?"

"Bourbon, sugar, bitters, and a little water. Taste it. It's good."

She took an experimental sip. "Nice. Not too sweet and not too bitter."

"Like me?"

Holding the drink with two fingers, she regarded him for a long moment. "You're not bitter at all, you're a little sweet and a lot of tangy."

"Tangy? What does that mean?"

"Flavorful and intense. Nothing about you is average."

"It's a good thing, right?"

She shrugged. "For you, yes. For others, it's intimidating. You are in a class of your own."

For the first time in his life, Kalugal regretted his superiority. It obviously bothered Jacki, but as much as he searched his mind for some imperfections he could fess up to, he could find none.

He could lie and make some things up, but he had a feeling she would see right through him. Besides, Jacki was a straight shooter, and she wouldn't like to be lied to even if it was a white lie. Still, he was far from a saint, and he could exaggerate his less than saintly behaviors.

"It's not easy to be perfect." He crossed his legs and assumed a haughty expression. "People think that I'm stuck up, or that I have a god complex, and it makes me less likable. Also, I'm not what you would call a do-gooder. I'm quite selfish and always look for what's in it for me. I'm not always honest, and I'm not overly concerned with upholding the law when it suits me."

She chuckled. "I know. I've heard that you use insider information to make a killing on the stock market."

"You see?" He lifted his hand. "I'm not perfect."

"I didn't say that you were. You were the one who did. But thank you for trying to make yourself seem more human."

"Human? What's so good about humanity? Have you read the news lately?"

Grimacing, Jacki took another sip from her drink. "I'm ashamed to admit that I haven't. Jin told me something about two vicious gangs that are becoming so big that they are spreading their tentacles all over the country. Apparently, they are all over the news, but I had no idea they even existed before she told me about them. One is called the Doomers and the other the Humans."

Snorting, Kalugal nearly spat out his drink. "Doomers and Humans? Both are indeed incredibly vicious."

"What's so funny? Jin said that they do ritual killings."

"Well, maybe the Humans do. I have it on good authority that Doomers kill without bothering with rituals."

Jacki

Jacki failed to see the humor in that. Two murderous drug cartels who did really gruesome, horrible things were no laughing matter, and Kalugal's chuckles were starting to annoy her.

"Are you making fun of me?"

"I'm sorry. It's just too funny. Doomers is the nickname that the clan invented for members of my father's organization. It's the acronym of its real name, which is the Devout Order of Mortdh Brotherhood. Jin must have blurted something about Doomers and humans, but since you were not supposed to know about immortals, she covered it up with a story about two rival gangs."

Thinking back to the conversation, Jacki realized that it was precisely what had happened. "Oh, she is good. I need to remind her of that. She also said that the Doomers were getting into trafficking."

A shadow passed over Kalugal's eyes. "You wanted to know why the goddess of love was also the goddess of war."

That was a quick change of subject.

Was his father's organization really involved in trafficking?

Jacki had a feeling that she was onto something, but instead of asking Kalugal about it and embarrassing him, she could later ask Jin. Except, she'd forgotten to ask Kian for her email.

"I do, but before I forget again, can you ask Kian for Jin's email address? I forgot to do that when I checked in this morning."

"Of course. I can call him right away."

Kalugal sounded eager, which confirmed Jacki's suspicion that he didn't want to talk about the Devout Order of Mortdh. The name was a mouthful, and it was no wonder that the clan had shortened it to the very appropriate Doom. After all, their leader was the son of a murderer, and his organization worshiped the god who killed all the others.

"First, tell me about the goddess of war and love."

Her request must have pleased Kalugal because his pinched expression relaxed, and he took another sip from his drink.

"Annani, or Inanna, started out as the goddess of love. But when she spurned Mortdh, to whom she was betrothed, she caused a war. Annani was what you would call a crown princess. She'd been promised to Mortdh since birth, which assured his ascension to the throne when the time came, and Annani's father stepped down. But then she fell in love with someone else and broke off the engagement, with her father's blessing I might add. The consequences for Mortdh were more than just the loss of face. He lost his promised position as the next leader of the gods."

"Arwel told me that he killed another god and was sentenced in his absence to entombment. That's why he bombed the other gods."

"That's correct. The god he killed was Annani's husband."

In her imagination, Jacki saw the two gods battling to the death over the hand of the princess. It was gruesome, but in ancient times it probably hadn't been considered criminal.

"But if it was a duel, why did he get sentenced to entombment?"

"It wasn't a duel, it was an assassination. Killing another god was not allowed. So even if Mortdh killed Annani's husband in a duel, he would have gotten the same sentencing."

"I see. So the goddess's love caused a war, and that's why she was given the dual-title."

Kalugal shrugged. "That's only my hypothesis. I might be wrong."

"It makes sense, though. Poor Annani. She must have been so heartbroken." Jacki eyed Kalugal from under lowered lashes. "Are you blaming her for what happened?"

He shrugged again. "She wasn't the one who dropped the bomb. My grandfather was. He must have been insane because there was no upside to what he did. Even if he had survived, what would have been left for him to rule? A desolate land with most of its population gone?"

"Did he love her?"

"It was a political arrangement. He didn't even know her. He was enraged because of the public humiliation and his ambitions getting thwarted."

"I will never understand people like that. How can anyone justify a massacre? Or even one killing? I couldn't care less about honor or power, or even humiliation, not enough to kill for."

"What about revenge? Could you kill to avenge a loved one?"

That was a tough question. "I don't know. I've never had a loved one. But if anyone threatened the life of my child, I think I could be capable of killing. I hope it never happens, but if it does, I hope that I won't chicken out."

"You won't. You're a fighter, Jacki. You came after Rufsur and me to save Arwel, and he was just a teammate, not someone you loved. You fought like a tigress, giving it all you had."

"Because there was no one else. I was desperate. Jin was crying, and even though she was frozen in a crouch, she begged me with her eyes to do something."

Kalugal tilted his head. "Maybe she is your loved one. You did it for her."

Jacki rolled her eyes. Like every guy who thought that he was all that, Kalugal assumed that if she hadn't jumped into bed with him already, she was into girls.

"I'm not a lesbian. The fact that I don't like hookups doesn't mean that I'm not attracted to men. I'm just choosy."

He smirked. "I was referring to sisterly love."

Great. Not only had she misinterpreted Kalugal's comment, but she'd also opened the door for the kind of talk that could get her in trouble. The solution was a quick change of subject. Kalugal wasn't the only one who could use that tactic to his advantage.

"Jin and I became very close in the program, and then even closer after we escaped it. I miss her. Can you call Kian and ask for her email? I want to show her all the fabulous clothes you've given me, and the cute room you've put me in. Did I tell you already how much I like it? It's so cozy and beautiful."

Kalugal regarded her with an amused expression on his handsome face, his intelligent eyes reading her like an open book.

By now, he knew that whenever she started blabbering, it was because she was nervous.

Kalugal

Jacki was adorable when she got nervous. Instead of her usual guarded reserve, she got more animated, her cheeks got peachier, and her eyes sparkled.

If only he could provoke a reaction like that without stressing her out. But then a little sexual tension was okay, and he could push her a little but not go as far as embarrassing her.

He wanted her to feel safe with him, but at the same time excited and eager.

A guy could dream.

Jacki had issues, but he lacked the insight or the tools to figure out what those issues were, and how he could help her to overcome them. Getting her to talk was the best tactic, and it seemed that the more nervous Jacki got, the more she talked.

Gently provoking her would be fun. "I'm so glad that you are enjoying your room. I like having you so close at night. It almost feels like we are a couple."

Jacki's blush spread from her cheeks to her décolletage. "Maybe a Victorian couple. Didn't married people sleep in separate beds back then?"

He chuckled. "I wouldn't know. I'm not that old."

"I know that you didn't live in the Victorian era, but since you seem so well-educated, and you love archeology, I thought that you must have studied history as well."

"I did, but the bedroom arrangements of Victorian couples didn't interest me."

"What did?"

"What I find fascinating about history are the major trends. Political, economic, philosophical, religious, etc. I'm interested in the macro, not the micro."

"I'm the other way around. I like to know how people from different cultures interact amongst themselves. I used to watch a Japanese reality show about a group of young people sharing a house. It was fascinating. They were so polite and so cordial to each other. It was very different from the way young Americans interact with each other."

"Why did you stop?"

"I got recruited into the program, and we didn't have time to watch television."

"What about when you were with the clan?"

She shrugged. "I didn't know that my new buddies were immortal. They told me that they were an organization of paranormally talented people. So much was going on that I lost interest in the show. But maybe I'll go back to it now. It's very calming to watch, and I don't have much else to do." She looked up at him and smiled sadly. "I'm kind of lonely. I know that you spend as much time as you can with me, so I'm not complaining, but I really miss Jin and Mey and also Kri and Vivian."

It seemed that Jacki craved female company, which was the one thing he couldn't give her.

Pushing to his feet, Kalugal lifted his phone off the desk. "I should call Kian and get you Jin's phone number."

"He's not going to give you that. Ask him for her email."

"It doesn't hurt to try." He placed the call, but as usual, it went to voicemail. "He'll call back in a few minutes. In the meantime, would you like another drink?"

"Yes, please." She handed him her empty glass.

"Another old fashioned?"

"Yes. I liked it a lot."

As he refilled their glasses, Kalugal's phone pinged with an incoming text.

Handing Jacki her drink, he read the message out loud. "From now on, please text me whenever you wish to communicate with me." Kalugal chuckled. "I wondered how long it would take Kian to figure out this simple solution."

Jacki shrugged. "Texting is not the same as talking on the phone. It's impersonal. But I guess that in your case it's the only way it can work. No one wants to be compelled."

"I offered him my word that I wouldn't do that, but he doesn't trust me yet." Kalugal put his drink down on the side table and read the text as he typed it. "Jacki wants to talk to Jin. She asks for her phone number."

"He's not going to do that," Jacki repeated.

The response wasn't surprising, and Kalugal read it out loud as well. "Nice try. She can send the texts to me, and I'll forward them to Jin."

Kalugal cast Jacki a sidelong glance. "Is that going to work for you?"

"I don't want Kian to read my texts. Ask him for Jin's email address."

"Okay. Here it goes." He started typing. "Jacki doesn't want you to read her conversations with Jin. She asks for Jin's email address instead."

Later, when Jacki wasn't around, he was going to ask Kian to remind Jin to refrain from mentioning Jacki's potential dormancy.

Things were going well, and she was starting to have feelings for him. Once those blossomed into love, he would reveal the possibility, but not before.

Jacki lifted a hand. "Don't send it like that. Erase the first part."

"Why? It's precisely what you said."

"I don't want to insult Kian."

"He would not get insulted by that, but I'll do as you wish." Kalugal erased the first part and hit send.

Watching the dancing dots, he waited for the response. "He is typing up a storm."

A minute passed before the return text arrived, and Kalugal read it out loud once more.

"I'll get Jin's email for Jacki, but I need to make sure that it's secure first. On another note, I spoke with Lokan, and we talked about scheduling a meeting with you this Saturday. Each of us will be allowed to bring three men with him, and we will communicate via tablets. Lokan and I and our men will have earplugs in to protect us from your compulsion. Let me know if it works for you."

Jacki pumped her fist up in the air. "Finally! You guys are going to talk face to face, and you are going to meet your brother. You must be so excited."

"I'm amused that everyone is so scared of me."

"What did you expect?"

He shrugged. "I would have liked to talk with my brother without Kian there and without earplugs. But if that's the only option, I'll take it."

"Baby steps, Kalugal." Jacki leaned toward him and put her hand on his arm. "This is only the beginning. Once the three of you get to know each other better, maybe Kian and Lokan would be willing to take a risk and talk to you without earplugs."

"I doubt Kian would. But I hope Lokan will." Kalugal texted back. *Let me know when and where.*

Jacki

"I was looking for you." Kalugal walked over to Jacki's workstation in the kitchen. "Kian sent me Jin's email." He handed her a note with two email addresses scribbled on it. "The first one is Jin's, and the second one is yours. I created a new one for you. Don't use your old one."

"Obviously."

It hadn't even crossed Jacki's mind that her old email address was probably scrutinized and that she shouldn't use it, but she didn't want Kalugal to think that she was dumb.

He leaned closer to the pot. "What are you making?"

She smiled. "What does it smell like?"

There was enough garlic in it to repel a horde of vampires, but she doubted that part of the legend was true. Besides, Kalugal wasn't a vampire. He had the fangs and the mental tricks vampires were famous for, but he didn't drink blood.

Or did he?

Arwel had explained that the fangs were designed to deliver venom and not to suck blood. He hadn't explained what the venom did, but she assumed it was either a paralytic or a poison like a snake's or a spider's venom. The immortals probably used it to fight each other, or maybe they had in the past when they'd been less civilized. She couldn't imagine Kalugal, with his refined speech and his elegant clothing, biting into the neck of an opponent.

The idea was ridiculous.

"It smells like spaghetti sauce," Kalugal said.

"Correct. Tonight, we are eating spaghetti with meatballs."

It was a simple dish, and given Kalugal's impassive expression, it wasn't on his favorites list.

He was such a snob. But she was going to change his mind. "I know that it's not the fancy stuff you are used to, but I promise that you're going to love it."

"I'm sure. How long until it's ready?"

"Half an hour tops."

He glanced at his watch. "I have at least two more hours of work, and I would rather finish what I have to do and leave the evening free, so I can spend it with you. Can we eat dinner at seven?"

After he put it like that, she couldn't refuse.

"No problem. I'll just reheat it. That's one of the advantages of simple cooking. To taste good, it doesn't have to be served as soon as it's ready. In fact, the flavors blend better when it's left in the fridge overnight."

"I have no doubt. So far, everything you've made was delicious." He sniffed at the pot again and then smiled at her. "Everything tastes better in the right company." He leaned closer and whispered in her ear. "Nevertheless, tomorrow you are taking a break from cooking, and Atzil is going to serve just you and me in the library. I want to dine alone with you."

As excited butterflies took flight in her belly, she wondered whether it was Kalugal's closeness and the scent of his cologne that had caused it or the prospect of dining alone with him.

The truth was that Jacki regretted including Rufsur and Phinas because they made the dining experience awkward instead of relaxed. She preferred spending time with Kalugal alone. He was such a pleasure to talk to, and he knew so much about so many things.

"Okay," she whispered back.

He smiled. "What, no arguing?"

"Nope." She leaned really close to his ear so Atzil wouldn't hear her. "I'm tired of Rufsur's sour mood and snarky remarks, and Phinas just doesn't say much. I like being with you."

Kalugal's face-splitting grin was adorable. He looked like he'd just won first prize in a competition, which in a way he had. Except, he had won it before it had even begun.

No one could compete with him.

Taking her hand, he lifted it to his lips and kissed it gently. "Thank you. I like being alone with you too. I could spend years looking into your beautiful eyes." He smirked. "No one has ever listened to what I have to say so intently. Your eyes are so expressive."

The heavy intimacy of the moment was broken by Atzil clearing his throat. "I'll be in the pantry for the next five minutes."

Chuckling softly, Kalugal looked at her lips. "I wish we could have given him a better reason for his retreat."

Damn.

The urge to close the scant inches between them was overpowering. He was standing so close to her that Jacki could smell his exquisite cologne despite the strong aromas wafting from her pot.

She wanted to kiss him so badly, but that would be a colossal mistake. She shouldn't have fessed up to enjoying his company that much. Now he would get ideas and get even bolder.

"Since we are not going to eat right away, I'll go to my room and start modeling for Jin the new stuff you've gotten me."

As Kalugal let go of her hand and took a step back, there was regret in his eyes. "Don't forget that I want pictures too."

"I won't."

Note to self. No sexy poses.

After Kalugal left, Jacki took a couple of minutes to collect herself, and once her heartbeat returned to normal, she turned the stove off and headed upstairs.

Selecting the best of the bunch, she spread the outfits on top of the closet's central island. She took a few pictures while posing in front of a mirror, and then had the brilliant idea to shoot a short video while turning this way and that.

When she was done, Jacki wrote Jin a short email asking how she was feeling and how things were going with Arwel. She then added a short recap of what had been going on with her and Kalugal, attached several of the photos and videos, and hit send.

Staring at the screen, Jacki was aware that there was no guarantee Jin was going to see her email anytime soon. She might be busy with her guy and with her new friends, or maybe working on her fashion line. Now that her mission was over and she was free, Jin could start on her new life.

Except, Jacki wondered how Jin was dealing with the fact that Arwel was an immortal, and she was a human. It seemed like neither of them was bothered by that, while for Jacki it was a deal-breaker.

The thing was, Jin wasn't like Jacki, and hooking up with a guy just for the fun of it was no big deal for her. Except, it was quite obvious that Jin's feelings for Arwel ran deep and that she wanted a long-term relationship with him.

When the tablet lit up with an incoming email, Jacki smiled happily.

Hi, girlfriend,

I'm so happy to finally be able to talk to you even if it's only through emails.

Arwel and I are doing great. We moved into a brand new house together, and since Arwel is on vacation, we are basically doing nothing other than making love, taking romantic strolls, eating romantic dinners, and meeting with friends.

Now back to you. You look amazing! And I'm not talking just about the gorgeous clothes. You are radiant. And the outfits, oh my gosh, are some of them Herve Leger? Kalugal must be really into you to fork out a small fortune on that, not to mention the huge one on Kian's charity.

I want all the juicy details, girl. And don't you dare play aloof and keep me in the dark.

Waiting with bated breath, Jin.

Jacki smiled and started typing a return email when it occurred to her that Kalugal might be spying on her communication with Jin.

After all, he'd created for her a new email address, and she was using his tablet as well as his Wi-Fi network. If he wanted to, he could tap into it easily, which meant that Jin was not going to get any juicy details.

Still, there was no harm in asking her about her relationship with Arwel and how they were making it work.

> *I'm sorry to disappoint you, but there are no juicy details. I'm here in an advisory position. Kalugal wants the human perspective, and I am it. He is very knowledgeable, and spending time with him is very enjoyable, but there is nothing going on between us.*

She was such a liar, but if Kalugal was reading this, he might back off a little and give her some room to breathe.

> *Congrats on the new house. I'm so happy that you and Arwel are having a good time, resting and enjoying each other. Except, I keep wondering how you are going to solve the lifespans difference problem. I hope you don't mind me asking, and if you do, just tell me to bug off.*
>
> *Love,*
>
> *Jacki.*

She hit send and waited.

The return email came in a couple of minutes later.

> *Arwel and I have plenty of time to worry about that. My motto is; live today to the fullest and don't think about yesterday or tomorrow.*
>
> *My advice to you is to do the same.*
>
> *Have some fun, Jacki, enjoy the now and stop worrying about the future.*
>
> *Your bestie forever,*
>
> *Jin.*

Vlad

"Vlad, can you open the door?" his mother called from her craft room. "It's Vanessa. I'll be out in a moment."

His heart skipped a beat. As much as he didn't want to think about Wendy, he couldn't help wanting to hear what Vanessa had to say about her.

Was she sorry for hurting him?

Was she still crying?

Had she had an incredibly compelling reason to betray him?

Forcing an impassive expression, he opened the door. "Good evening, Vanessa."

"Hello, Vlad." She walked in. "How was your day?"

He shrugged. "The usual. I worked at the bakery from four in the morning until seven, did my school work, and then had a couple of classes."

"You're a busy guy."

"The busier, the better."

Everything was better than obsessing about Wendy, but the problem was that baking didn't engage his mind as well as schoolwork did, and he'd spent the entire three hours trying not to think about Wendy and failing.

"Hi." His mother walked into the living room. "You look like you had a long day."

Vanessa sighed. "I'm exhausted." She plopped down on the couch and put her purse on the coffee table.

"Can I get you something to drink?" Vlad asked.

"Do you have something bubbly?" She smiled. "Not champagne. It's too early to celebrate. But a soda would be lovely."

"Coming right up."

He walked into the kitchen and pulled several bottles of Perrier out of the fridge.

Despite looking tired, Vanessa seemed upbeat. Had she gone to visit Wendy and was she encouraged by what she'd learned?

A tiny spark of hope ignited in Vlad's heart, but he refused to let it spread. Unless Wendy had betrayed him to save someone's life, he couldn't forgive her, and the chances of that were slim because she'd been a planted mole from the very start.

"Are you excited about Saturday?" Vanessa asked as he handed her the bottle.

"I'm not." Vlad sat on an armchair facing her. "I'm still not sure that I want to go."

Frowning, Vanessa leaned toward him. "It's too late to back down now. Everything is set in motion." She grimaced. "Well, except for one thing. Ingrid bailed out. She has a backlog of work and can't get away."

"That's too bad." His mother reached for one of the other Perrier bottles. "What are you going to do? Leave that guy behind in the keep?"

Vlad shook his head. "I don't want to be alone with Wendy up there. You should cancel the whole thing."

Vanessa cast a sidelong glance at his mother. "I was hoping that you could take her place and keep an eye on the kids. The moral support would be good for Vlad."

The therapist's intentions were transparent, and his mother wasn't stupid.

"Come on, Vanessa. If you want to hook me up with the guy, just say so. I appreciate the offer, but I've never even met him. Don't you think I should at least get a look at the guy before committing to an entire week with him?"

"Look, I don't expect you to fall in love with him at first sight or anything like that, but I know that you can take your work with you, so it's not a problem in that respect, and who knows? You might like Richard. And if not, you're just going to enjoy a week in the mountains."

"What do you think about that, Vlad?" his mother asked. "What's your opinion on Richard?"

"He is okay. But I'm really not the one you should be asking. It's not like I want him as my stepdad." He cringed. "I really don't want to talk about it."

"Fair enough." His mother turned to Vanessa. "Are you offering this to me because I'm Vlad's mother, because I can work from anywhere, or because you think that Richard and I are a good match?"

"All of the above. I've talked with him today, and I think that you are going to like him."

As Vanessa and his mother continued discussing Richard and his attributes, Vlad tuned them out.

Thinking of Richard with his mother creeped him out, but it wasn't about him.

Vlad was an adult, and he shouldn't be living with his mother anyway. The only reason he'd done that was that he hadn't enjoyed living with his new roommates. After Gordon had moved away to college and Jackson moved in with Tessa, he'd been assigned housing with two older immortals, and when it hadn't worked out, he figured that he could be a good son and alleviate his mother's loneliness by coming back home.

Stella was like him, socially awkward and a little odd, and she didn't have many friends. Maybe a square dude like Richard was precisely the kind of guy she needed?

This was about his mother's happiness and not his ambivalence about Richard's worthiness. Besides, it had nothing to do with Richard. Vlad just couldn't imagine any guy as a partner for his mother. No male was good enough, and no one would understand or accept her eccentricities.

His mother was awesome, but she was also a handful.

She had mood swings that came out of nowhere, got emotional over nothing and everything, and threw tantrums over trivial things like misplacing a ribbon or forgetting to buy buttons for her costumes.

He never knew when she would fly off the handle.

"So, is it a yes?" Vanessa asked. "It's a rare opportunity. The Fates seem to favor the clan males for some reason, and most of the Dormants we've gotten so far were female. We don't get many potential male Dormants."

His mother let out a breath. "Fine, but I can't leave Saturday. I have a fitting scheduled at the theater. I can come up to the cabin on Sunday and stay the entire week. If that's okay with you, Vlad?" She looked at him. "I don't want to make you uncomfortable."

He shrugged. "You won't. Wendy will. I don't think I'm ready to forgive her yet, or ever. But I'll go so you can check Richard out." He couldn't believe that he'd actually said that.

"Then it's settled." Vanessa put her empty Perrier bottle on the coffee table. "Vlad, Wendy, Richard, and the two

Guardians will head to the cabin on Saturday, and you'll join them on Sunday."

"What about supplies, bedding, etc. Who is taking care of that?"

His mother's concern about practicalities was surprising. Usually, she was the opposite of pragmatic.

"Okidu, of course. He is going there tomorrow."

"Do I have to share a ride with Wendy?" Vlad asked. "Because I'd rather not."

"The Guardians will each take a car, so you can go with one of them, and Wendy and Richard can go with the other."

Vlad let out a breath. "That's good. I don't want to be stuck with her in a car for two hours."

Vanessa and his mother exchanged worried glances.

For some reason, they both seemed to believe that he and Wendy were fated for each other, but Vlad hoped that they were wrong.

Why would the Fates be so cruel to him? He didn't deserve to get hurt like that.

Except, life wasn't fair, and Vlad was well aware of that fact. He also knew that happy endings belonged in fairytales.

"Don't worry. I will be civil to Wendy. Just don't expect too much."

His mother turned to the therapist. "I think you should come with us, Vanessa. Vlad and Wendy could use some guidance."

The therapist nodded. "I'll see what I can do. I might join you there on Sunday."

Rufsur

Rufsur walked into the security office and stopped by Welgost's station. "You wanted to show me something?"

"Yes." Welgost switched from the live feed to a recording. "See this truck? It has made several passes by the house. I counted five so far today."

Rufsur leaned closer. "It could be one of Kian's men."

Welgost pulled up another screen. "Those are all their vehicles. I've listed the license numbers, and the truck is new. They might have decided to switch cars, but I doubt it. Why only one? Besides, they want us to know that they are watching."

"Right, and it's a major pain."

Welgost nodded. "I haven't been clubbing since before the lockdown."

"Me neither."

Kalugal had had to put all of his meetings with startup owners on ice, while the rest of them had to limit their outings to a minimum because Kalugal didn't want Kian to know how many men he had.

In Rufsur's opinion, that wasn't the best way to go about it, and the opposite should have been done. They should have made an effort to make it look like they had more men than they actually had. But it seemed that lately his opinion didn't count for much.

Kalugal was consumed by Jacki, and everyone else had gotten shoved aside, which was irritating on several fronts.

First of all, Rufsur had to concede defeat as far as his prospects for dating Jacki went. Kalugal had made it clear that she belonged to him and that Rufsur should back off.

If Jacki had given him the slightest indication that she was interested, Rufsur would have ignored his boss's elephant-sized hints.

He obeyed Kalugal's commands in everything but his personal life.

Kalugal owned his loyalty and his dedication, but he didn't own him. When competing for Jacki's favors, they were not a boss and his subordinate. They were equals. Regrettably, though, she seemed taken by Kalugal.

That in itself was a sour grape in Rufsur's mouth, but losing his position as Kalugal's best friend and confidant to Jacki was much worse.

He'd been with Kalugal since the guy had gotten his first command position, while Jacki had arrived only a few days ago.

Hopefully, things would change once Kalugal got her in his bed. As long as he was in hunting mode, he was funneling all his energy in that direction.

That he hadn't succeeded in seducing her yet was surprising. Usually, when the boss crooked his finger, females flocked to him, and it didn't matter what face he was wearing at the time. Even humans sensed his innate power, and females were drawn to that.

But Jacki was a hard nut to crack, which was why Kalugal had redoubled his efforts.

He'd already announced that tomorrow, Rufsur and Phinas wouldn't be joining him and Jacki for lunch or dinner. Today was probably the last time they were going to dine together.

"What do you want to do?" Welgost asked.

"Can you send me a still shot of the truck with the license number visible? I want to show it to Kalugal."

"Coming up."

As soon as he got the photo, Rufsur schooled his features into his usual nonchalant expression and walked over to Kalugal's office.

"Houston, we have a problem," he quoted the famous line.

"Another one? What is it now?"

Rufsur handed Kalugal his phone. "This truck has been making passes by the house all day, and as far as we know, it doesn't belong to Kian's force. You should check with him, and he should check with his men. Maybe one of them can follow the truck and check it out. Normally, I would have sent one of ours to investigate, but I figured if they are already here, they could at least be useful."

"It depends on who's behind it. If it's one of my business competitors, I don't want Kian butting his nose into it."

"It's unlikely that someone who lost an acquisition to you is snooping around. First of all because you always wear a shroud for meetings and we are extra careful making sure that no one is following us. And secondly, what would they gain by watching the house?"

"If Kian found me, others could as well. And as to what they want, I have no idea. Maybe they think to dig up some dirt on me, or maybe find out who else I'm meeting with and what other acquisitions I'm making. It's unlikely that someone deduced my long-term plan from the sort of technologies I invest in, but it's not impossible."

"What do you want me to do?"

"First, I'm going to check with Kian whether the truck belongs to one of his men. If it doesn't, we will take it from there."

Kalugal

After forwarding the photo of the truck to Kian, Kalugal waited patiently for the return text.

He wasn't overly concerned. There could be several perfectly logical explanations for the truck making rounds in the neighborhood. It could be as mundane as someone looking for a lost pet. Or maybe it was a paparazzo who wasn't necessarily looking to snap pictures of Kalugal, but rather of one of his neighbors. As far as he knew, none of his neighbors were movie stars, but many of them were tech moguls, and some of them attracted the media's attention.

When his phone rang, Kalugal was surprised to see his cousin's number on the display. Had Kian suddenly decided to trust him and talk to him instead of communicating via texts?

Leaning back in his chair, he clicked the green button. "I didn't expect a callback."

"My tech guy came up with an ingenious solution. It works similarly to the text messages that you can dictate and then have the computer read back to you. The way he programmed it, your voice gets translated into a text message, and then the automated voice reads it to me. You, on the other hand, get to hear me directly. There will be a very slight lag time in the communication coming from your side, so if I don't answer right away, that's the reason."

"It's barely noticeable. Can we use the same thing during our meeting?"

"Definitely. Instead of earplugs, we will wear earpieces."

"Excellent. Now, what about the truck? Is it one of yours?"

"It's not. Not only that, we have spotted suspicious activity near our community as well. It was just one pickup truck going back and forth on the road leading to our place, so I'd disregarded it until I got your text. I don't think it's a coincidence."

Kalugal swiveled his chair around. "Why pickup trucks?"

"The choice of vehicle might be a coincidence. Both the one we spotted and the one you had are old, light-duty models, which are very popular. And since they are used by construction workers, gardeners, and other people providing services, they are not particularly conspicuous even when seen making several rounds."

That made sense.

The last time Kalugal had hired a roofer for a repair job, the guy had gone several times to the building materials store to get miscellaneous items he'd needed. Kalugal had figured that it had been intentional, and not the result of disorganization. Every trip back and forth had taken an hour, stretching the guy's workday and making the job seem more complicated than it was.

The question was whether he was going to let Kian's men take care of that or send out his own. If both their bases were being watched, it might be somehow connected to the escapees from the government program.

Except, why only now? If the government knew where the recruits were all along, they would have already sent people to retrieve them.

"I suggest that we send out men to investigate. Do you want to handle the one making rounds next to my place as well, or should I?"

"I'm going to send out Guardians to thrall the driver and get information out of him. If it's just a construction guy working on a nearby house, then yours might be as well, and it's up to you if you want to investigate him. But if our guy is a snoop, then yours probably is too. If you want, my men can take care of him."

"Since yours are going to follow mine anyway, just have them do it."

"Very well."

When Kian terminated the call, Kalugal closed his eyes and played several possible scenarios in his head.

If the government was looking for its missing people, they must have been tracking them all along, but Kian had told him that the escapees had been thoroughly checked, so that wasn't it.

Perhaps the watchers had been sent by his father?

If Navuh's men had been monitoring Kalugal all along, they might have followed Kian's men back to their base.

Except, having a guy with a truck drive by Kian's place was not how his father would have done it. What was the point?

Once he knew the location, he would have sent out a large force and attacked it.

The other option was that there was more than one mole. What if Jacki had sent an email to someone in the government and let them know where she was?

He'd given her a tablet the day before to purchase whatever she was still missing; she might have used it to send out an email.

Maybe she'd even done it without any malicious intent, sending an email to a friend and telling her or him her whereabouts.

That could explain his place, but what about Kian's? Perhaps one of the other escapees had done the same thing?

Before he jumped to conclusions, though, he needed to ask Jacki whether she'd contacted anyone other than Jin. Or better yet, have Ruvon check her internet activity.

Kian

"Do you want me to do it?" Anandur asked.

Kian nodded. "Find out who he is and who sent him. The truck is registered to a dude named Joseph Portillo. Roni has done some digging on him, and the only interesting thing he found out was that the guy is a veteran. He works as a handyman for a property management firm, is married, has two kids, and a mortgage. An average Joe Schmo."

Anandur shrugged. "Joe might be the owner of the truck, but someone else might be driving it."

"That's why I want you to check him out. Take Brundar with you."

When the brothers left, Kian pulled out his phone, but then changed his mind and decided to walk over to Bridget's office instead of calling her.

As always, her door was open, but he rapped his knuckles on it before entering.

She lifted her head. "How can I help you, Kian?"

He pulled out a chair and sat down. "How good is your medical equipment at finding foreign objects in someone's body? Could you have missed very small trackers?"

"The CT scan can detect obstructions as small as a grain of sand. But if you want, I can go over the data again. Maybe I missed something."

"Please do. We've spotted suspicious activity on the road leading to the tunnel. The same truck has made several passes throughout the day, and Kalugal reported the same thing happening at his place."

"What about the keep?"

"I haven't heard anything from the security office, but I'll have them go over the footage from today. There is much more traffic there so it might have gone unnoticed."

Bridget pushed to her feet. "I'll go over the CT scans right now."

"Thank you."

After he left Bridget's office, Kian headed over to William's lab.

"Your phone gadget worked like a charm," he said as he walked in. "There was almost no delay. How is the modification of the earpieces going?"

William waved his hand over his messy worktable. "They will be ready for you by Saturday."

Kian clapped him on the back. "You are the best."

"What about me?" Roni turned his throne-like chair around.

Funny how the kid was still seeking approval. Roni was probably one of the top ten hackers in the States, and he knew it.

"You are the best at what you do, and William is the best at what he does."

"Good answer." Roni swiveled his chair back.

"I have another thing I need you to do, and I hope you can do that and finish the earpieces on time."

William pushed his glasses up his nose. "That depends on what it is."

"I suspect that the trainees we helped escape were implanted with trackers that our equipment can't detect. In case Jin is unknowingly sending out a signal, can you block it?"

William nodded. "I can modify one of the locator cuffs to cause interference. But she won't be able to use a cellphone while wearing it."

"What about emails?"

William shook his head. "Not with Wi-Fi. She would be able to use an Ethernet connection, though."

"Can you modify four of them? I want to put one on each of the ex-trainees."

"When do you need that done?"

"As soon as possible."

"What do you want me to finish first, the earpieces or the cuffs?"

"The cuffs. The earpieces are a convenience, the cuffs are necessary for security."

"I'll start working on the cuffs then. I can probably modify them by tomorrow."

"Thank you. The sooner you have them ready, the better. Let me know when the first is done so we can put it on Jin. If she is broadcasting, she is endangering the village."

"I will try to have at least one ready later tonight. But in any case, send Jin over, and I'll check if she is emitting transmissions."

Kian raked his fingers through his hair. "We did that when they arrived at the keep, and they were not emitting anything."

"The trackers might have been programmed for delayed activation. To do that is actually very clever. Those implanted with them pass the security check because the trackers are not broadcasting. But a day or two later, when it is ascertained that those implanted with them are safe, the trackers get activated."

That was both devious and ingenious. "I'll call Arwel and explain the situation."

Except, his call went straight to voicemail, but Kian didn't leave a message. Jin and Arwel were probably busy working on her transition, and he didn't want to interfere. Besides, the cuff wasn't ready yet, so there was no rush.

Passing by the café on his way back to the office, he spotted Syssi and Amanda at one of the tables and changed direction.

"Kian." Syssi's delighted expression made him doubly glad about deciding not to go back to the office.

He leaned down and kissed her softly. "How was your day?"

She shrugged. "Same as any other."

He turned to Amanda. "And yours?"

"Nothing new to report. We are still getting only mediocre test subjects."

He pulled out a chair and sat down. "It's been nearly three years since you found Syssi and Michael. Maybe it's time to call it quits."

"Not yet." Amanda crossed her arms over her chest. "Besides, this is only a small part of my research. There is still so much left to discover about how brains work. The neuroscience field is still in its infancy."

Jin

"I'm not in the mood for cooking." Jin stretched her arms and yawned.

"We can grab something at the café." Arwel turned on his side and pulled her against his chest. "But we should hurry. It's closing soon."

"I'll just hop into the shower."

He kissed her hard before letting go. "Get out of here before I change my mind. I'll shower in the other bathroom."

"You can join me." She jumped out of bed and wiggled her bare bottom at him.

"Then we will never get to the café on time."

"Fine. I'll be out in five minutes."

Life was good.

They had both fallen asleep after their afternoon sex, and the nap had been delicious.

There were no exams to study for, no spying missions to prepare for, and no job Jin had to return to. Jin's only mission was to enter transition, and since sex was necessary for that, she and Arwel could spend their days in bed guilt-free.

She wasn't even worried about it not happening yet. As Mey's sister, Jin was a Dormant for sure, and there was no doubt that she was going to transition. It would happen when it happened, and getting there involved lots of sex with the man she loved, so she wasn't complaining.

When she was done, she pulled on a pair of stretchy yoga pants, paired them with a cropped T-shirt, and pushed her feet into a pair of sneakers.

On second thought, she reached for a hoodie. It was a little cold outside, and after her bout with strep throat, she didn't want to catch something again. Immortals didn't get sick, but viruses could hitch a ride on them and jump on the only human host available for them in the village.

"Ready?" Arwel opened the door.

"Let's go."

"It's fifteen minutes to closing." He wrapped his arm around her waist.

"Do you want to jog?"

"Not really. A fast walk will do."

"Did I tell you already that Vanessa got Vlad's mom to agree to go with them to the mountains?"

"You mentioned something about that before pushing me on the bed and having your way with me."

"Right. I did. What do you think? Do you know Vlad's mom?"

"Stella is a bit odd, but who knows? Maybe she and Richard will hit it off. Opposites attract and all that."

"I wish we could go to the cabin as well. It's going to be really awkward for all of them, and we could help by providing a buffer. Vlad and Wendy are both in a bad place, Stella and Richard don't know each other, and the only other people going with them are a couple of Guardians. I'm not a therapist, but I don't know what Vanessa was thinking sending them out there alone."

He shrugged. "It's like teaching a kid to swim by throwing him into the pool. He either floats or drowns."

Jin stopped in her tracks. "That's awful. Promise me that you will never do it to our kids."

Grinning, Arwel pulled her into his arms. "Is that your way of proposing to me? Because if it is, the answer is yes."

She rolled her eyes. "Don't change the subject. I want you to promise."

"I promise to never throw any of our kids into the pool."

She rewarded him with a quick peck on his lips. "Now, was that so hard?"

He chuckled. "I would have never done it. I'm an empath, remember? I could never be so callous."

"True." She smiled up at him. "We really should go with Wendy and Vlad to the mountains, not only for them, but also for us. It would be fun to sleep in a motor home."

"I have no problem with that. But Kian still didn't get back to me about it. He's either forgotten or decided that he didn't want us there for whatever reason."

"You should remind him. And if you don't want to, I can."

"I'll do that right now." Arwel pulled his phone out of his pocket but then paused and lifted his head. "He is in the café. We can ask him in person."

"How do you know that he is there?"

"I can hear him. Syssi and Amanda are there as well, and so is Callie."

"Wonderful. I love that café. It makes meeting friends a breeze."

In fact, Jin loved everything about the village and about her new family. The only thing she regretted was not having her parents there. That would have made her life perfect as well as Mey's.

"Is there any chance Kian would ever allow humans in the village?"

"You are here."

"I mean humans that are not about to transition. I'm talking about my mother and father."

"I don't know." Arwel cast her a sad look. "But after your transition, we can go visit them in Israel. We could get you a fake passport."

"Are we also going to get married there? And what about Mey and Yamanu? Neither of us would agree to a wedding without our parents."

"That's not going to be a problem. They can come to the wedding, and after that their memories can be altered, so if they noticed anything peculiar, like a glowing goddess, they would not remember those oddities."

Jin sighed. "I would be honored to have the goddess marry us, but my parents are a different story. Whoever thralls them should implant in their heads a memory of a rabbi presiding over the ceremony. They really hoped for Mey and me to marry Jewish boys."

Kian

"Your phone is buzzing." Syssi pointed at the device.

Uncharacteristically, Kian had left it on the table when he'd gotten them coffees.

Putting the cardboard tray down, he glanced at the display and picked it up. "Did you get the guy?"

"We did," Anandur said. "He's a private eye, and the truck belongs to his brother-in-law. Anyway, he was hired to snoop around the set of coordinates he'd been given, and report what he'd seen. The troubling part is that the coordinates are right smack over the village. The good part is that the guy reported back that it must have been a mistake because he found nothing there. Naturally, I reinforced the conviction and sent him on his way. But the bottom line is that I think you were right about the undetected trackers."

"Fuck. We need to get Jin out of here until William modifies the cuff for her."

"The locator cuff?"

"He is going to make it so it will interfere with the broadcasting. It's like the one we had Dalhu wear before I trusted him enough to remove it."

"When will William have it ready?"

"I hope he will be done with at least one by tomorrow morning. I'll talk to you later. I have to call Magnus and tell him to find the guy snooping around Kalugal's place."

"What happened?" Syssi asked when he ended the call.

"Kalugal's men spotted a truck making several trips by his house, and our guys reported the same from the road leading to the tunnel. It's good that we have the cars programmed not to enter the tunnel if the sensors pick up any vehicles or people in the vicinity, otherwise the snoop would have discovered the entrance."

"Good thinking with that one," Amanda said.

"I need to make the call."

"Of course."

After he'd given Magnus instructions, Kian called Kalugal and told him what Anandur and Brundar had reported.

"What am I supposed to do, evacuate?" The computer transmitted Kalugal's speech in its monotone voice.

"My tech guy is working on a cuff that will interfere with any transmission Jacki might be emitting. As soon as it's ready, I'll get it to you. My men are going to find the guy snooping around your place and thrall him to forget what he saw and send him home, but your location is already compromised."

"Until you get the cuff to me, I'll move Jacki to the bunker. Whatever they put in her must be tiny and can't have a strong signal. The bunker will shield her."

"Sounds good. But I wonder if that's enough. Our location is secure because the guy couldn't even find the entrance, but your place is a different story. You might have to relocate."

"Are you offering me sanctuary in your village?"

"I can't do that, but I can find you a safe place to move into until you build your next fortress, and I can give you excellent advice on how to hide your new place better. I have a lot of experience in that."

"I appreciate the offer, and I will gladly accept your advice. But I'm not in a rush to move. I have nothing to fear from the government. They can try to come in to investigate me and my property, but they won't get past the gate."

"Right. I forgot about your special abilities."

"Nevertheless, when we meet, I would love to hear your advice on how to build a well-hidden and impenetrable fortress."

Kian chuckled. "I didn't say it's impenetrable, although it is. I only said that it is well-hidden. And if you think that my advice will help you locate my base, you are wrong."

"Oh, Kian, you are such a suspicious guy. Exploiting your show of goodwill to find your village hasn't even crossed my mind. Frankly, I don't care about your base and where your people are hiding. If we end up with a working partnership of some sort, that would be great, but if not, that's okay too. We can still be friends."

"I hope so. I don't consider you an enemy, Kalugal, and my suspiciousness is not personal in nature. I'm just very diligent when it comes to protecting my people. I can't afford to be any other way."

"I understand. I just wish I could prove to you that I'm not a threat to you or your people."

Jin

As Jin and Arwel reached the café, they found the group looking somber.

"What happened?" Jin asked.

"Take a seat." Kian motioned to the one next to him.

Arwel pulled it out for her and then grabbed another chair from the next table over for himself.

"You and your friends from the program might have trackers inside you that we have missed," Kian delivered his disturbing news. "Bridget is going over the test results to see if she missed something, but even if she finds nothing, that doesn't mean they don't exist. The circumstantial evidence says that they do. Suspicious activity was spotted on the road leading to the village and also next to Kalugal's place. I could've dismissed it if it happened only in one location, but the same thing happening simultaneously at both can't be a coincidence."

For a long moment, Jin processed the information. During her month-long stay in the program, there hadn't been any invasive procedures. There had been a thorough medical exam at the start of the training that included blood tests and immunizations, and later Doctor Roberts had injected them with various drugs to see if that enhanced their performance.

"Could I have been injected with a tracker? Because I didn't undergo anything other than blood tests, immunizations, and drug injections. And if Marisol compelled me to forget a procedure, I would have remembered it after Lokan removed the compulsion."

"Frankly, I don't know, and neither does William, who is on top of all the latest technological developments. It's possible that the military has come up with something new, and they are keeping it a secret from the public. It could be made from materials that don't show on scans, or it might be so tiny that it's not noticeable."

Jin glanced at Arwel. "I should leave the village. I'm endangering all of you."

"There is no need. William is working on a cuff that will interfere with any transmission you might be emitting, and until it is ready, you can stay in the underground facility. That was actually Kalugal's idea. He's moving Jacki into the bunker until we get a cuff to him."

"But what about the watchers? They must have reported to whoever sent them. Both locations are already compromised." As Jin's panic flared, her eyes started tearing. "I can't believe it. After all that we've gone through to prevent just that."

Kian put a hand on her arm. "Relax. We can handle this. I sent out Guardians to deal with them and find out what they know. Turns out that they were given the location and were instructed to snoop around. The one circling the road leading to the village thought that he'd been given the wrong coordinates because he couldn't find anything. My Guardians thralled him to stay away and go snooping somewhere else. He is going to provide the director or whoever else has sent him with bullshit information."

That was encouraging, but Jin couldn't help the tears prickling at her eyes. She loved the village, and she'd been having such a good time there, and now she was forced to live underground again.

"Should I go to the underground now?"

"William said that he will have the cuff ready by tomorrow, but knowing him, he will have it ready for you in a few hours. You can spend the time watching a movie in the theater or swimming in the pool. If he's not done today, Arwel will have to pack an overnight bag for you both and haul a bed down there."

Syssi waved a hand. "I wanted to prepare living quarters in the underground, but Ingrid didn't have time because of the new hotel you have her working on."

"We can do that," Amanda offered. "It doesn't need to be anything fancy. We can have Murphy beds installed in the classrooms. That would solve the space problem. It won't be private, and people would have to share rooms, but then most of the clan members don't have mates, so that's not a problem. The mated couples can use the smaller classrooms and the offices."

"That's a good idea, and it's not going to cost a fortune," Kian said. "Can I put you in charge of that?"

Amanda nodded. "Consider it done."

With the initial panic receding, Jin remembered what she'd wanted to ask Kian for.

"Are you making cuffs for Richard and Wendy too? They can't go to the mountains without them."

"Of course."

"Awesome. Can Arwel and I join them in the cabin? I know there aren't enough rooms, but as I suggested before, we can rent a motorhome. I think that us being there will make things easier for the others."

"I have no problem with that." Kian looked at Arwel. "Do you want to continue your vacation, or do you want to go as a Guardian?"

"I can be backup, but until Jin transitions, I'd rather not come back full time."

"Understood."

"What if Jin enters transition while you are there?" Syssi asked. "Is it wise for you to be far away from medical attention?"

Jin waved a dismissive hand. "It's only a couple of hours away. If I get a fever or any of the other signs, Arwel will drive me back."

"Then it's agreed." Kian tapped the table. "If the cuffs are ready in time, you and your friends can leave for the cabin tomorrow."

"I need to rent a motorhome first," Arwel said. "There might be none available on such short notice."

"Then buy one," Kian said. "We might have use for it in the future."

Jacki

As a knock on the door woke Jacki up, she opened her eyes and for a brief moment felt disoriented.

This wasn't her cozy little room adjacent to Kalugal's master suite. She was back in the bunker because she and the other escapees had trackers in them that had somehow been missed by Bridget's scans. Kalugal had confirmed the suspicion by checking her with a device that was designed to pick up transmissions, so there was no doubt that it was there, but she couldn't figure out how they'd gotten it inside her.

The others might have been compelled to forget a procedure, but that didn't apply to her. She also couldn't think of any timeline holes. Could they have used drugs?

She wasn't immune to those.

A second knock reminded her that there was someone outside her door waiting for her to acknowledge him.

Pushing up on the pillows, Jacki pulled the blanket up to her chin. "Come in."

"Good morning," Kalugal said as he opened the door and peeked in. "Good. You are decent." He motioned for Shamash to enter ahead of him with a breakfast tray.

"Good morning." Jacki pulled the blanket even higher, covering her mouth.

She hadn't brushed her teeth yet, and with the immortals' sensitive noses, they could probably smell her breath from across the room.

After Shamash put the tray down on the coffee table, he smiled at her and hurried out.

Kalugal closed the door behind him. "Did you sleep well?"

"Not really. I kept thinking about the tracker, and how the heck did they manage to put it in me without me noticing or remembering a thing."

"Why are you covering your mouth?"

"Morning breath. I need to use the bathroom. Would you mind turning around?"

The nightgown he'd gotten for her wasn't sheer, but the silk outlined every curve, and flaunting that in front of Kalugal would be like waving a red flag in front of a bull.

"Of course." He sat on the couch and turned sideways, so he was facing the door.

Ducking into the bathroom, Jacki was glad that she had left a change of clothes in there. Once she was done, she came out fully dressed.

Kalugal gave her an appreciative once-over. "You look very nice. I'm still waiting for those photos you promised me, though. Is there one of you wearing that beautiful blue nightgown?"

She sat down next to him. "I only modeled a few of the outfits. You gave me so many."

He pursed his lips. "That's a shame. Can I pour you coffee?"

"Yes, please. Did the cuff arrive?"

"It did. I have it in my pocket."

'Is it that small?"

"It's a compact design, but I wouldn't call it small." He handed her the coffee and then pulled a polished silver band out of his pocket. "I also have the key." He pulled it out from his other one. "Don't lose it."

"I won't." She took the cuff and put it on her wrist. "It's not so bad. It looks like jewelry. Is it activated?"

"Yes. You can come up to the house now, but first let's have breakfast." He removed the lids from the two plates.

She smiled. "Thank you for joining me here."

Kalugal took her hand, lifted it to his lips, and kissed the back of it. "I enjoy your company, and I've gotten so used to dining with you that it feels weird to eat without you."

When he said things like that, Kalugal stoked the flame in her heart and melted her resolve as if it was a wax candle.

How was she supposed to respond to that?

Jacki couldn't tell him that she felt the same. Sleeping in her old room in the bunker, she'd felt alone, and she'd missed knowing that he was near, just across the bathroom they shared.

Instead, she changed the subject. "As we are already here, you can show me the rest of your collection. You only showed me a fraction of it before I freaked out over your godly genealogy, and you took me to your office."

"I'd be delighted. But first, let's finish breakfast."

Kalugal

Kalugal stifled a smile.

When he'd told Jacki that he loved dining with her, her heartbeat had sped up. It was the honest truth, and maybe that was why she'd reacted to it so strongly.

Jacki had a healthy bullshit radar, probably developed from dealing with countless males who had tried to seduce her.

And that was why his slow approach was working so well. He was merely hinting at his interest in her, not coming on to her at all, and letting her dictate the pace.

She was softening toward him, and soon he would be able to move to the next stage and coax a kiss out of her.

Kalugal had never invested so much time and effort into seducing a female, but surprisingly, he was enjoying it. He was getting to know Jacki, which he'd never bothered to do with other women, and the more he discovered, the more he liked her.

If he'd had doubts before about her suitability for him, they were gone now. She was intelligent, eager to learn, and had a unique personality. Unlike most gorgeous women, Jacki wasn't stuck-up or full of herself, and she didn't expect every male around to drool over her. In fact, she'd seemed annoyed by Rufsur's flirting even though he'd been perfectly cordial.

Kalugal could actually see himself spending his life with her.

"I'm done." Jacki put her plate back on the tray. "Atzil seems to think that I can eat as much as you guys." She looked at the plate and shook her head. "This was enough to last me an entire day. Can I save it for later? I hate throwing food away."

Jacki sounded like someone who'd gone hungry before and had to ration her food, and just the thought of her living like that wrested a growl out of his throat.

She lifted her hands in the air. "It was just a suggestion. If it makes you so angry, you can throw it away."

Shaking his head, he took both of her hands in his. "I'm not angry at you. I'm furious about every day that you had to go without or with not enough."

"That's sweet. But you're jumping to conclusions. I was never hungry, I just had to be careful with my money and make sure that I had the necessities covered. Besides, I didn't want to get fat." She smiled and patted her flat belly.

It was a half-truth, but he wasn't going to press her. Jacki was a proud woman, and she didn't want to admit to having lived in poverty.

"I don't think there was any danger of that." Kalugal put his plate on top of hers and pushed to his feet. "Ready to continue the tour?" He offered her a hand up.

"Ready."

As she put her hand in his, he had a strong urge to tug harder and bring her against his chest and kiss the living daylights out of her. But this wasn't the right time. Jacki wasn't ready, and he didn't want to blow it by moving too fast.

In the display room, he walked over to the tablet with Inanna's hymn, which was where they had stopped the tour the day before, and then continued to the one next to it.

"This is a hymn to Ninkasi, the goddess of wine. As you can imagine, she was a very popular goddess." He moved to the next display. "This is an assortment of figurines. Some represent gods and goddesses, but several are just of regular people."

"How can you tell the difference?"

"Gods and goddesses have special headgear that symbolizes what they are in charge of. The others do not. So those without hats are just regular humans."

"Or maybe immortals." Jacki leaned over the glass display. "I'm surprised at the level of detail. I would have thought that figurines that old would be cruder. But these are really good."

"The Sumerian civilization was very advanced. Thanks to the gods, naturally. Those who came after didn't enjoy the benefits of having gods live among them and guide them. They inherited the symbolism and the stories, but with the passage of time, there was inevitable erosion, and the civilizations that came later were less and less advanced. It has taken humanity thousands of years to regain what it lost."

Jacki

As one figurine in particular caught Jacki's attention, she leaned even closer, her nose nearly touching the glass. "This one looks so familiar." She tapped her finger over the spot. "She looks a lot like Wonder. There are even traces of the blue-green color of her eyes. The resemblance is uncanny."

"Wonder. That's a peculiar name. Who is she?"

"I think that she's an immortal, but I'm not sure. Wonder was part of the group that came to snatch Jin away from the program."

"Is she a Guardian?"

Jacki shook her head. "Her boyfriend or husband is. She came along on the ski trip that was supposed to double as a reconnaissance mission and ended up with our escape."

Kalugal frowned. "Is her mate a tall, buff redhead?"

She turned to look at him. "How did you know?"

He chuckled. "That's one hell of a coincidence. I met them in Egypt, or rather saw them. They didn't see me because I shrouded myself. I suspected that they were part of Annani's clan. But the interesting part is that I noticed the woman because of her resemblance to the figurine."

"That's really weird. Maybe it's a statue of Wonder's ancestress?'

"Do you want to hold it?"

"Can I? I mean, it's an ancient artifact. I'm afraid to touch it."

Smiling, Kalugal opened a drawer under the display and pulled out two sets of surgical gloves.

"Put these on." He handed her one pair and then snapped the other over his hands. "Hold it gently," he warned while lifting the glass cover.

"That goes without saying."

"Here you go." He handed her the figurine. "Careful."

"I won't even breathe on it."

Except, as soon as Jacki's gloved fingers touched the statue, a vision started, so vivid that it was like watching a movie.

A horror movie.

A young man, who looked a lot like Wonder, was riding a wagon when a massive earthquake shook the desert. A chasm opened in the ground, and the wagons in front of him started toppling into it, people and donkeys tumbling to their deaths. The young man jumped, his speed and strength clearly that of an immortal. He caught one of the men and flung him to safety, and then reached for another, but the ground kept shaking and the wagon he'd been riding in rolled on top of him, sending him to his death.

Shaken up, Jacki thrust the figurine at Kalugal. "Take it!"

The entire thing lasted no more than a couple of seconds, but it was the worst thing Jacki had ever experienced.

"What happened?" He put the statue back and closed the glass lid.

"It was horrible." Jacki pulled the gloves off and flung them over the display. "They all died. The desert swallowed them."

"You are trembling." Kalugal wrapped his arms around her and pulled her against his chest.

Grateful for the warmth, Jacki let him rock her gently.

"Did you have a vision?"

"Yes. Terrible, terrible vision. The worst I've ever had."

"You can tell me about it in my office." He lifted her into his arms and started walking. "You look like you need a drink."

"Put me down. I can walk."

"You don't look like it. What would Kian think if you fell and broke something? I promised to take good care of you."

It was just an excuse to keep carrying her, but Jacki didn't mind. It felt good to be in Kalugal's arms. "I wouldn't want you to get in trouble with Kian."

He smiled down at her. "Thank you."

Out in the corridor, Shamash arched an eyebrow but said nothing. He opened the office door for Kalugal and then closed it behind them.

"I can't believe that I freaked out again. At this rate, I'm never going to see your entire collection."

"Maybe we should wait with the next tour." Kalugal deposited her gently on the couch. "Would you like me to make you the same drink as yesterday?"

"Yes, please." She chuckled nervously. "I feel weird about drinking so early in the day."

"This is not for fun. This is for medicinal purposes." He walked over to the bar and started on the drinks.

"I wonder who the guy in my vision was. It must have been Wonder's forefather. Given how strong he was and how fast he moved he was an immortal."

Kalugal handed her the drink and sat next to her. "You said something about the desert swallowing them all up."

She shook her head. "I thought that I told you what I saw. My head isn't working right."

"You had a scare. Can you tell me now?'

She nodded. "There was a long caravan, and a guy that looked like Wonder's twin brother was riding with an older man in one of the wagons. Then an earthquake started, and a big chasm opened in the desert floor. It started small but grew wider by the moment. The donkeys panicked and started running, and the wagons in front of Wonder's twin toppled into the chasm. He tried to save people, flinging them up and away, but then his own wagon slid forward, and he lost his hold. By the end of the vision, there was no one left." She started trembling again. "They all died, the people, the animals, everyone."

Wrapping his arm around her shoulders, Kalugal brought her against his solid form. She huddled closer to him, thankful for his warmth and his strength.

"Do you get visions like that often?"

"Never. My visions are always about the future. This was in the past. And they were never triggered before by touching an object either. Psychometry is not one of my talents."

Kalugal

As Kalugal held Jacki close, he tried to focus on what had just happened and not on how good it felt to just sit with her like that and comfort her.

The closeness was more than physical. The sense of intimacy and familiarity was surprising, given the short time they had spent together, and yet it felt incredibly right.

Still, there was a mystery to be solved. And to help Jacki, he needed to understand what had triggered the strange vision, and whether Jacki had witnessed actual events.

"I don't know much about psychometry, but what you've experienced doesn't make sense. If the guy who looked like Wonder died in the desert, he couldn't have imparted the memory to the figurine. The only way it would make sense is if someone who witnessed the events carved that figurine. But then why would he make it a female?"

"And what's the connection to Wonder? It's not like she and I became besties or even spent a lot of time together. I barely know her."

"The physical resemblance might be a coincidence. I'm just trying to understand how you could have gotten that vision from touching the object."

Jacki shrugged. "My other visions were about future events, and they were connected to people I knew. The director called them micro visions because they weren't about big events. They were always about something that was going to happen to a single person."

"Good or bad?"

"It was a mix. Some were about good things, like a girlfriend of mine falling in love with a guy she was going to meet on a trip. Or a bad one, like another friend of mine getting into a serious car accident. That was the only one that was kind of connected to an object. As soon as I saw that old clunker, I got a vision of it lying crumpled on its side in a ditch, and then of my friend going through rehab for her injuries. That vision kept coming back, and I kept warning her, but she wouldn't listen. I also had a vision about Jin's sister coming for her, and that one came true, but there was no object involved."

"We should ask Kian about Wonder's ancestry."

"That's a good idea." Jacki frowned. "You are right that it doesn't make sense for the figurine to have triggered the vision, though. First of all, because the statue is not of the guy I saw, and secondly because no one survived that earthquake to later sculpt it and imprint his memory on it. The vision I had might not have been triggered by my touching it. It just floated down from the ether at the same time for some reason."

Kalugal pulled his phone out. "Since Kian is expecting you to call with your daily report, we can call him together."

His call got answered right away. "Good morning, Kalugal. Is Jacki there?"

"Yes. She is here, and I have the phone on speaker."

"Hi, Jacki. Did you get the cuff?

"I'm wearing it. Thank you for sending it over so fast. But this is not about that. Something very weird just happened, and I hope you can shed some light on it."

"What is it?" Kian's tone turned gruffer than usual.

"I had a vision."

Kalugal listened as Jacki told Kian about the figurine that resembled Wonder, and about the guy who'd looked just like her, and the terrible tragedy that had befallen him and the rest of the caravan. It seemed that with each retelling, Jacki remembered more details from her vision, but it was also possible that her mind was filling in the blanks and embellishing on what she'd actually seen.

When she was done, it took Kian a long moment to respond. "What you have just told me is so unbelievable that it's shocking."

Frowning, Kalugal was about to tell Kian to mind his manners when his cousin continued.

"Once I tell you Wonder's story, you will understand why. You see, Wonder is ancient. She spent thousands of years in stasis and has woken up quite recently."

"Thousands of years? That's impossible." Kalugal had never heard of an immortal surviving so long. Warriors could go into stasis after sustaining grave injuries, but they usually revived in a few minutes, or hours, or at the most days.

"What's stasis?" Jacki asked.

"Kalugal can explain it later. But the fascinating part is that what caused her severe injury was exactly the earthquake you described, and the young man you saw in your vision was actually Wonder. She joined the caravan disguised as a man."

Jacki and Kalugal exchanged glances.

"Wow. That vision is even more bizarre than I thought. How long ago did that happen?"

"Five thousand years, more or less. It happened shortly before Mortdh dropped the bomb on the gods' assembly."

Jacki let out a breath. "Unbelievable is right."

Kalugal rubbed a hand over his jaw. "What I wonder is who made that figurine. It must have been someone who knew Wonder. I assume that she had a different name back then?"

"Her name was Gulan, and she was Annani's servant and best friend. She fell in love with a guy who didn't love her back, and when he got engaged to be married to someone else, she was broken-hearted and decided to run away. She joined a caravan heading toward Egypt. The earthquake must have hit when the caravan reached today's Alexandria, which was where she woke up from her stasis."

"Fascinating story. I didn't know immortals could survive so long in stasis."

"Neither did I," Kian admitted. "Now we know, though. Wonder is proof that it's possible."

Jacki

Throughout the call, Kalugal had his arm wrapped around Jacki's shoulders, but now that Kian was no longer on the line, it was time to pull away even though it was comforting, and she would have loved to stay.

"Wonder, aka Gulan, must have had a secret admirer." Jacki reached for her glass. "Someone must have carved it before the earthquake."

Kalugal shook his head. "I had the figurine tested, and it's not five thousand years old. Dating items is not a precise science, but the range I was given was half of that. Also, I found it in a dig in Egypt, not Iraq."

Jacki frowned. "So it's just a statue of a lookalike?"

"Not necessarily." Kalugal got up and walked over to the bar. "I like your theory of a secret admirer." He refilled his glass. "Someone who knew Gulan before she escaped Annani's court carved that lovely figurine of her, but since it was made only twenty-five centuries ago, that someone must have been an immortal who survived the bombing."

"So he might still be alive."

"Precisely." Kalugal sat next to her and unceremoniously wrapped his arm around her shoulders. "I've always suspected that some immortals survived the disaster. I found it inconceivable that Annani and her descendants and my father's people were the only ones left."

"How did they survive?"

"Annani left before the bombing. I don't have the details, but I assume that after her husband was murdered, she was heartbroken and wanted to get away from it all. My father's people were up north, in the area of today's Lebanon, and the nuclear wind blew east, so they were spared."

"How come there is no record of it?"

"There is. The Sumerians describe it perfectly, but historians interpret their writing as an allegory, not the reporting of what had actually happened. There is a lament talking about a poisonous wind blowing east and killing every living thing in its path but leaving the buildings and other inanimate objects intact."

"What about radioactivity? Can't they measure it even if the bomb was dropped five thousand years ago?"

"That's a very good question. If the bomb was detonated high in the sky, there would be no trace of radiation left.

Also, we don't know what kind of bomb it was. It might have been similar to the nuclear bombs we have today, or it might have been something completely alien."

"Ha, I knew it. I asked Arwel if his people were aliens, and he said that they were the descendants of gods, but he wasn't sure whether the gods were from somewhere else in the universe or the survivors of an ancient civilization that was wiped out during one of earth's extinction-level events."

Kalugal smiled. "I asked my father the same question. Usually, he gave me evasive answers, but on one occasion, he blurted something about the gods' home world."

"Why did they come to earth?"

"According to the Sumerian records, the official purpose was to mine for gold."

Jacki snorted. "That's silly. Why would the gods be interested in gold? Because it's pretty and shiny?"

"Not because it's pretty, but because it's crucial for space travel, among other things. In outer space, radiation from the sun transfers heat directly into objects, and gold-coated Mylar reflects heat without creating a glare. Gold is also one of the best natural conductors of electricity, it is resistant to rust and corrosion, and that's why it is used in computer chips, cellphones, and other electronic devices."

That made much more sense.

"You said that gold mining was the official reason given in the Sumerian records. Was there an unofficial one?"

"When I was growing up, I tried to get as much information out of my father as I could. He wasn't very forthcoming, but here and there he would blurt something out, and I collected those puzzle pieces like gold nuggets. I might be completely off, but from what I managed to piece together, things weren't always peaceful on the gods' home world, and there was a revolt in which some of the ruler's children were involved. It was quashed, but since executing a god was not allowed, the ruler exiled them to earth."

"He wouldn't have killed his own children."

Kalugal arched a brow. "You need to read up on history, Jacki. Things like that happened a lot. Besides, you can't apply human standards to an alien race. That being said though, human morality and just laws originated with the gods. They established the code of law in Sumer, and later it got incorporated into the Bible. But as I mentioned before, once the gods were gone, everything kept deteriorating for thousands of years, and that included their code of law."

Jacki lifted a hand to her forehead. "I'm flabbergasted. It all sounds so logical but at the same time fantastic. How much of it is speculation and how much is fact?"

"Everything except for the alien planet can be substantiated. For most humans, the gods would fall into the category of myths and legends, but immortals are proof of their existence."

Kalugal

"Do Kian and his clan know anything about it?" Jacki asked.

"I'm not sure," Kalugal admitted. "It depends on how much Annani knows, and what she shared with her descendants. As I said, my father wasn't forthcoming with the information, and what I've learned was from bits and pieces interwoven in casual remarks that he made. I'm a good listener, and I'm also curious by nature, so I was on the lookout for those. Still, he might have been untruthful, or he might have exaggerated some of it. But it makes sense given what we know about how valuable gold is for technology and space travel. Also, in many cultures, gold was considered the property of the gods."

"You make me want to dive into books and learn as much as I can about all this. It's like you've opened a whole new window on the world to me." She looked at him with admiration in her beautiful eyes. "Thank you for sharing all that."

"You're welcome." He rubbed his hand over her arm. "It's my pleasure. I don't get to talk about this so openly with anyone. Humans are a no-no for obvious reasons, and my men are not interested. They treat my preoccupation with the past as an eccentricity, and they find the subject boring. It's refreshing to have someone listening so attentively and getting excited about a subject that fascinates me."

Suddenly looking uncomfortable, Jacki pulled away from his embrace. "I should start on lunch. Is it okay for me to go back to the house?" She got up.

"Sure. Let me escort you back. Do you need to pack your things first?"

"Yes. I almost forgot about that. But it will only take me a minute. I don't have much. Just the nightgown, the robe, and the toiletries."

"Take your time. I'll wait for you."

She was talking fast again, a sure indicator that he'd made her nervous. Was it the arm rubbing? Or maybe his admission of how much he enjoyed talking to her?

He had to find a way to overcome her skittishness. Why was she fighting her attraction to him so hard? Was it because he was the son of a goddess? Or maybe it was just because he was immortal, and Jacki thought that she was human.

From her perspective, a long-term relationship between them was not possible. But then, contemporary women, especially young ones like Jacki, weren't overly concerned with the future. Most were content with one-night stands as long as the guy met with their approval.

Jacki was acting like a maiden from a bygone era, when young women had been expected to be virgins on their wedding nights. Surely that couldn't be the reason for her odd reluctance to let him get close to her?

Could it be that she was still resentful because of his fake attack?

Maybe he could ask her in a roundabout way.

"I'm ready." Jacki stepped out of the room.

He took the overnight bag from her and slung it over his shoulder. "I was wondering about something, and if my inquiry is too personal, you can tell me to mind my own business."

"What is it?"

"Rufsur is a fine male, and he made it very obvious that he's interested in you. What do you find objectionable about my second-in-command?"

She narrowed her eyes at him. "Did he put you up to this?"

"He didn't. I'm just curious about what's your type. If you had to describe your ideal man, who would he be?"

For a long moment, Jacki stared at him as if he'd asked the stupidest question possible. "What do you want me to say? That I like tall guys? Or guys with blue eyes? Physical attributes are not the most important thing."

That was a good start. Kalugal was tall, and his eyes were blue.

Jacki shook her head. "Wipe that smirk off your face. I wasn't describing you."

Liar.

"Of course not. So, what's important?"

"Love, respect, devotion, and loyalty."

"Those are all feelings, not attributes."

"Precisely."

Jacki

"How are you today?" Atzil asked as Jacki walked into the kitchen.

"I have a new bracelet." She showed him her cuff.

"Pretty."

The guy looked unimpressed. Perhaps Kalugal hadn't told anyone about the tracker?

"You know what it's for, right?"

He nodded. "I heard that you were implanted with an undetectable tracker. Sucks."

She let out a breath. "It does. I don't know how they did that without me noticing anything. The only way I can think of is through the immunization shots or the blood tests. But those were just small needles and the shots were quick. How the hell did they manage to put a tracker through that?"

Atzil shrugged. "The technology of tomorrow is here today. It's like living in a sci-fi movie."

"Absolutely." Jacki rolled her sleeves up and tied an apron around her middle. "I'd better start cooking if I want to make it in time for lunch."

"You don't have to. Kalugal has been eating my cooking for years, and he never complained. I can serve you lunch in the library the way he likes."

"You are already serving us dinner. Lunch is all that's left for me to do."

He cast her a sidelong glance. "You know that this is not what the boss wants from you."

Jacki grimaced. "I know. But since he's not going to get that, I feel obligated to compensate him in other ways."

"Why not, if I may ask?"

Men. Were they all in cahoots to find out what made her tick?

"You may not," she spat.

Atzil lifted his hands in mock surrender. "Okay, okay. No need to get antsy. I was just curious. But I'll keep my mouth shut from now on."

"Thank you. I appreciate that."

She needed to think and doing that while Atzil was prattling on would have been impossible.

What was she going to do about Kalugal?

He was taking more liberties with her, but none that she could object to without looking like a damn prude or a stuck-up bitch. Besides, she liked it when he put his arm around her and pulled her against his body. He made her feel safe when she felt like the walls were closing in on her, but that safety was an illusion.

Right now, Kalugal was more dangerous to her than the director and his damn tracker or even the disturbing vision. The worst that could happen if the director found her was that she would go back to the program, and the worst thing that the damn vision could do was a few nightmares and bouts of bad mood. Watching people die a horrific death was going to haunt her for a long while.

Kalugal, on the other hand, could break her heart.

Except, she was tired of fighting the attraction, and Jin's words still echoed in her mind.

Live for today, Jacki. Don't think about tomorrow or yesterday.

There was wisdom in that approach too.

With a sigh, Jacki immersed herself in preparing a light lunch. The chickpea spinach salad looked fancy and was flavorful but took only ten minutes to make, and since Atzil had gotten fresh shrimp, she also made shrimp-stuffed avocados. The best part was that both were served cold, so nothing needed heating up, and she had time to go freshen up.

"Looks good," Atzil commented. "A little on the girly side, though. It's not a hearty meal."

Jacki took the apron off. "If Kalugal is still hungry after eating my lunch, he can have some of your stew."

"Good deal."

Heading upstairs, Jacki planned on brushing her hair and spraying a little perfume on, but when she walked into the bathroom and looked at herself in the mirror, she grimaced.

Kalugal was always so elegant, wearing slacks and fitted button-down shirts, with or without a cashmere sweater over them. She didn't want to look like the hired help while sitting next to him.

It was a silly thought. First of all, the jeans and the soft sweater she had on were both top designer label, and secondly, it had been her idea to cook for Kalugal. He'd never asked her to do that.

Still, after putting on a skirt, a nice blouse, and low-heeled pumps, Jacki felt much better. She even pinned her hair up, making herself look a little bit more sophisticated.

What for, though?

It wasn't as if she wanted to encourage Kalugal.

Or maybe subconsciously she did? Maybe this was about her wanting to feel worthy of him?

Her entire life Jacki had been staving off advances and planning to have sex only with her husband. It wasn't that she wanted to be a virgin on her wedding night, she just wanted her first to be her last. Was that too much to ask for?

Kalugal

At one o'clock in the afternoon, Kalugal left his office and headed to the library, wondering what kind of mood he would find Jacki in.

The morning had been full of excitement for her, and he hadn't made it any easier by putting gentle pressure on her with his well-placed comments.

First, he'd told Jacki that having her sleep in the room next to him made him feel as if they were a couple, and then he had told her how much he enjoyed talking to her.

Both comments had been sincere, and he hoped that they'd conveyed his feelings for her without making her think that all he wanted was to get her in his bed.

And yet, she was still skittish like a Victorian-era virgin.

Kalugal had a feeling that if he waited for Jacki to initiate their first real kiss, it was never going to happen.

When he opened the library doors, she wasn't there, so he walked over to the bar and poured himself a drink. Should he make one for Jacki as well?

She'd already had an old-fashioned this morning, so maybe that wasn't a good idea. Kalugal remembered reading somewhere that women shouldn't have more than one alcoholic beverage a day, and since Jacki was still human, that warning applied to her.

Perhaps a bottle of Perrier would be better.

He took one out of the bar's fridge and put it on the games table, which had been used exclusively for dining lately.

Ever since he'd set his sights on Jacki, Kalugal hadn't played even one chess game with Rufsur or Phinas, or Shesh Besh with Atzil or Shamash.

He was neglecting his men, but it was necessary.

Finding out whether Jacki was the one for him was more important. He needed to seduce her, and then make her fall in love with him. Or the other way around. The most important part was her falling in love with him. Until that happened, he couldn't tell her about the possibility of her turning immortal, and he was getting impatient to do that.

Except, his progress was too slow. He needed to get the first step out of the way so they would officially become a couple. So far, he'd managed to foster friendship, which was a good start, but it was time to move to the next step and encourage romance.

Perhaps soft background music would contribute to the right atmosphere. Frank Sinatra or maybe Bing Crosby. But what if she'd never heard of them?

Jacki wasn't like other women her age, and it was easy to forget how young she was when she appeared so much more mature.

Still, good music was good music.

Kalugal pulled his phone out and scrolled down his playlists. Choosing the one he had in mind, he patched it through to the library's sound system.

As the first song started playing, the door opened, and Jacki came in, looking absolutely gorgeous in a knee-length skirt, pumps, and a hairdo that accentuated her high cheekbones.

Pushing to his feet, Kalugal walked up to her. "You look stunning." He leaned and kissed her cheek, then took her hand and led her to the games table. "My lady." He pulled out a chair for her.

"I need to get back to the kitchen and bring the food. I just came to see if you were here."

"Nonsense. You are going to sit down, and I am going to serve you."

Jacki shook her head. "You wouldn't know what to bring."

"I'm sure Atzil can help me with that."

"Maybe Shamash can do it?"

Jacki seemed uncomfortable with him serving her, but that was precisely what he wanted to do. Perhaps the role reversal would finally convince her that he was serious about her.

Lifting her hand, he kissed the back of it. "It will be my pleasure to serve you."

A blush painting her cheeks a deeper shade of peach, Jacki nodded. "I see that there is no arguing with you."

"Not about this. I'll be right back."

Jacki

It felt so weird to be served by Kalugal. If he was any other guy, Jacki would have had no problem with it, but he was a freaking demigod, or half a god, or whatever term having one parent who was a goddess qualified him for.

And it wasn't only that.

Kalugal was regal, sophisticated, and well-educated, even though he was basically self-taught. Heck, that only made him even more impressive.

Her fancy outfit was just a sham, a cover-up for the fact that she was a nobody in comparison, and that she was the one who should be serving Kalugal and not the other way around.

The only reason he had done it was to make her feel good, but it had the opposite effect. It only amplified the vast difference between them.

Why was he trying so hard, though?

Kalugal could have any woman he wanted. Why her?

So yeah, she was pretty, but so what? She wasn't gorgeous, and there were thousands of girls more beautiful, smarter, and more sophisticated than her. Was he chasing her because she was the only one who hadn't fallen into his bed right away?

Some guys liked the challenge of the chase. Was that Kalugal's thing? Would he lose interest the moment he had sex with her?

Probably.

She just needed to stay strong and keep saying no.

Straightening her back, Jacki reached for the bottle of Perrier, unscrewed the cap, and took a long sip. The bubbles induced a small burp, which made her chuckle.

If Kalugal were there to witness it, he would no longer think that she was such a lady.

Note to self. Don't drink carbonated beverages on a date.

Right. As if she was ever going on one. Did immortals even date? Jin and Arwel had just hopped into bed on the second day after they met and had become a couple.

A loving couple who had just moved into a new house together and were having the time of their lives.

Maybe she should follow Jin's example and take a chance. Could she possibly have the same with Kalugal?

As the doors opened, Kalugal walked in with a large tray, and then someone closed the door behind him.

Probably Shamash. The guy was like Kalugal's shadow.

"Do you like the soundtrack I put on?" He put the tray down on the table and sat across from her.

She hadn't even noticed it. "Yes. It's lovely."

Leaning closer, Kalugal reached for her hand. "What's the matter? You look perturbed."

She chuckled. "I love the way you talk."

"And how is that?"

"You always sound so sophisticated. You look young, but you sound old."

"I guess that's because I don't spend enough time talking with young people."

"And when you do, they are usually the well-educated types who talk like you."

He nodded. "True." Lifting one of the plates off the tray, he put it in front of her. "I can't wait to taste those stuffed avocado halves. What an original recipe."

That was a smooth change of subject, but Jacki was glad of it. She would rather steer away from the topic of what had made her look perturbed.

"Not really. I found it online."

Taking a bite, Kalugal made a satisfied sound. "Delicious."

"I'm glad that you like it."

"The salad is excellent too."

She wondered whether he was really enjoying the meal so much or just pretending, and when he finished his portion and then waited until she was done and finished hers as well, Jacki still wasn't convinced. Maybe Atzil was right, and this wasn't a hearty enough meal for an immortal?

"Are you still hungry? Atzil made a stew. I can get it for you." She started to get up.

He put a hand on her arm. "I don't want stew. I want you to stay right here and talk to me."

She let out a breath. "As you wish."

His lips lifted in that signature panty-melting smirk. "There are a lot of things I wish for. Are you willing to fulfill all of them?"

Crap. She'd walked right into that trap. "That depends on the wishes."

"I wish for a kiss."

"I can do that." She leaned and pecked him on the cheek.

He caught her hand and pulled her onto his lap. "I want a real kiss."

Crap and double crap. "I can't."

"Why? Am I so repulsive?"

Jacki snorted. "I wish. You are too damn sexy for your own good." She shook her head. "Let me rephrase. For my good."

"Maybe you are just shy." He cupped the back of her neck.

With the most perfect lips on the planet a mere inch away from hers, it was a mighty battle to keep from closing that small distance and kissing them for all they were worth.

Kalugal's patience lasted for about thirty seconds, and then he did it for her.

His kiss was soft as a feather, just a brush of those perfect lips of his over hers, and then he pulled back and smiled at her. "Was that so terrible?"

She shook her head.

"Can I do it again?"

All coherent thought gone from her head, Jacki nodded.

With permission granted, Kalugal's amused expression turned into a ravenous one. His fingers on her neck tightened, and when he took her mouth, it was like no other kiss she'd had before.

He devoured her, and she loved it. Moaning into his mouth, she wrapped her arms around his neck and tried to kiss him back, but he refused to let her tongue past his lips. He was in total control, and it only added fuel to her mounting desire.

That was precisely how she wanted to be kissed, made love to, possessed...

No. She didn't want any of that. Not without the love and the commitment and devotion.

Her moans of passion turning into desperate whimpers, she pushed on his chest.

He let go right away. "What's wrong?" He frowned. "Why are you crying?"

Kalugal

Something was very wrong, while a moment ago, it had been perfection.

Jacki had been so into the kiss, so passionate and responsive, and then she suddenly wasn't. Her sweet scent of desire was replaced by the terrible scent of despair, and Kalugal's arousal had deflated as fast as a balloon that had been stabbed with a sharp knife.

"Talk to me, Jacki. I need to know what's happened."

Tears still streaming down her cheeks, she shook her head. "I can't do it. I can't be the new toy that you play with until you get bored with it. I wouldn't survive that."

"What the hell are you talking about? Do you think that this is a game for me?"

She nodded. "What else could it be? You are you, and I am me, and we are not in the same league on any level. There could never be something long-lasting between us, and I don't do hookups or flings or whatever you want to call them. It's all or nothing for me."

She looked so distraught, and what she was saying was such utter nonsense, but it wouldn't do him any good to say that. He needed to tread lightly and gently, or she would just shut down completely.

"This is not a casual fling for me, Jacki. I have feelings for you, and I think we could have something beautiful together. But it's not going to happen unless we take the first step." He started rubbing small circles on her back. "What are you so afraid of?"

"I just spelled it out for you. You are an intelligent guy. It shouldn't be so hard for you to understand."

"You think that we are too different to make it work?"

She nodded. "You are the immortal son of a goddess. I'm a human. I could never be more than a plaything for you, and I refuse to be anyone's toy. Even yours."

"What can I do to prove to you that I am serious?"

"You can't be." She lifted a pair of teary eyes at him. "What I want is love, respect, devotion, and loyalty. Nothing less will do. Can you give me that?"

"You have my respect, and as long as we are together, you have my loyalty as well. Love and devotion will take more time, but they need a starting point. They can't happen if you are not willing to take the first step."

"And what is that? Having sex with you?"

"To be frank, yes. I'm not an expert on relationships, but I believe that intimacy and sexual compatibility are vitally important. Those are the building blocks of love."

"Well, I'm not an expert on any of that, but for me, love and commitment are vitally important, and without them, there will be no intimacy and no sex."

Suddenly the pieces of the puzzle started to align into a pattern that he should have figured out much sooner.

"Have you ever been in love, Jacki?"

She shook her head.

"Have you ever had sex?"

She shook her head again.

"That explains it."

Jacki was not going to have sex with him unless she was convinced that he was in love with her, and he couldn't allow himself to love her before he knew that she could transition.

They were at an impasse.

"Have you ever been in love?" she asked.

"No, but I've had plenty of sex."

She chuckled. "I believe that."

"I don't know if I can fall in love without experiencing intimacy first."

"And I can't allow myself the intimacy without having the love first."

He sighed. "Then we have a problem. Any idea how we can solve this?"

She shrugged. "You could marry me. That would at least fulfill the commitment and devotion requirements, and you wouldn't even have to lie and tell me that you love me."

"I will never lie to you, Jacki. I might keep things from you, things I can't reveal before I have your love and loyalty, but I promise never to deceive you."

There was hope in her eyes when she looked at him. "It seems that we are not that different after all. You can't tell me your secrets before you are sure of my love and loyalty, and I can't be intimate with you before I'm sure of your love and devotion. Perhaps marriage is not such a crazy idea. It might be the best solution for both of us."

JACKI & KALUGAL'S STORY CONTINUES
The Children of the Gods Book 39
Dark Overlord's Wife

Turn the page to read the excerpt—>

Join the VIP Club

To find out what's included in your free membership,
flip to the last page.

DARK OVERLORD'S WIFE

Jacki is still clinging to her all-or-nothing policy, but Kalugal is chipping away at her resistance. Perhaps it's time to ease up on her convictions. A little less than all is still much better than nothing, and a couple of decades with a demigod is probably worth more than a lifetime with a mere mortal.

Jacki

Previously.

"What's wrong?" Kalugal frowned. "Why are you crying? Talk to me, Jacki. I need to know what's happened."

It was the damn kiss's fault.

One passionate moment shouldn't have affected her like that, clouding her judgment and weakening her convictions. She was supposed to be stronger and smarter than that.

"I can't do it. I can't be the new toy that you play with until you get bored with it. I wouldn't survive that."

She should have left when she'd had the chance. Agreeing to stay in Kalugal's home had been a colossal mistake, and now she was freaking out because she wasn't sure she could survive it.

But how could she have said no?

For every day she stayed with him, Kalugal made a twenty-five-grand contribution to Kian's charity. At that rate, in just thirty days, the sanctuary for rescued trafficking victims would have received three quarters of a million in donations.

Except, lasting a month without succumbing to temptation or falling for Kalugal was impossible.

In fact, it was already too late.

She hadn't lasted even a week.

Jacki had tried to deny it, refusing to let herself admit how much she wanted him, but the incredible kiss they'd shared just a few moments ago had blasted that thin layer of denial into oblivion.

He was perfect, the kiss had been better than anything she could've imagined, and Jacki realized that forgetting Kalugal would be impossible, and that was after spending only five days with him.

An entire month would destroy her.

She needed to run, find a cave to crawl into, and lick her wounds for a decade or two.

Instead, she was sitting on Kalugal's lap and crying her eyes out while he was still waiting for an explanation. He must be thinking that she was having a nervous breakdown, and he wasn't far wrong.

Except, he wasn't looking at her as if she was crazy. Frowning, he seemed offended. "What the hell are you talking about? Do you think that this is a game for me?"

Why was he playing dumb? Did he enjoy hurting her? Or maybe he just didn't understand?

By his own admission, Kalugal had very little contact with humans, and his hookups didn't count as relationships. He probably knew less about women's emotions, fears, and insecurities than the average teenage boy, and she had no choice but to spell it out for him.

"What else could it be? You are you, and I am me, and we are not in the same league on any level. There could never be something long-lasting between us, and I don't do hookups or flings or whatever you want to call them. It's all or nothing for me."

He shook his head. "This is not a casual fling for me, Jacki. I have feelings for you, and I think we could have something beautiful together. But it's not going to happen unless we take the first step." He started rubbing small circles on her back. "What are you so afraid of?"

"I've just spelled it out for you. You are an intelligent guy. It shouldn't be so hard for you to understand."

"You think that we are too different to make it work?"

She nodded. "You are the immortal son of a goddess. I'm a human. I could never be more than a plaything for you, and I refuse to be anyone's toy. Even yours."

"What can I do to prove to you that I am serious?"

Evidently, she hadn't been clear enough. "You can't be. What I want is love, respect, devotion, and loyalty. Nothing less will do. Can you give me that?"

"You have my respect, and as long as we are together, you have my loyalty as well. Love and devotion will take more time, but they need a starting point. They can't happen if you are not willing to take the first step."

Smooth.

All that talk about respect and loyalty and the supposed feelings Kalugal had for her had been a prelude to convincing her to have sex with him.

Why was it so important to him, though? Was he one of those guys who couldn't tolerate losing or accept no for an answer?

Except, that was usually a sign of insecurity, which wasn't something that Kalugal suffered from. He was full of himself and for a good reason. Not only was he a freaking demigod, but he was also smart, incredibly handsome, and charming. Nevertheless, even if he meant what he said, he'd said it with one motive in mind.

"And what is that? Having sex with you?"

"To be frank, yes. I'm not an expert on relationships, but I believe that intimacy and sexual compatibility are vitally important. Those are the building blocks of love."

Jacki had heard a similar speech from most of the guys she'd dated and refused to have sex with.

Her answer to that was well-rehearsed. "Well, I'm not an expert on any of that, but for me, love and commitment are vitally important, and without them, there will be no intimacy and no sex."

That should have been the end of that, but Kalugal persisted. "Have you ever been in love, Jacki?"

She shook her head.

"Have you ever had sex?"

For some reason, that was more difficult to admit than never having been in love. People assumed that there was something wrong with her, and Jacki had learned that it was best to give evasive answers and leave them guessing.

Except, Kalugal had asked a direct question, and the only way she could answer it was with a yes or no.

Jacki shook her head again.

"That explains it."

Finally, he was getting it. Maybe she should have opened with that. "Have you ever been in love?"

"No, but I've had plenty of sex."

She chuckled. "I believe that."

"I don't know if I can fall in love without experiencing intimacy first."

The guy was relentless, but it wasn't going to work. "And I can't allow myself the intimacy without having the love first."

He sighed. "Then we have a problem. Any idea how we can solve this?"

Yeah, he could fall in love with her, propose to her, and then she might consider it for about five seconds before saying no. There was no future for them.

Perhaps she should suggest marriage.

In her experience, when every other argument failed, mentioning that scared off even the most persistent guys.

"You could marry me. That would at least fulfill the commitment and devotion requirements, and you wouldn't even have to lie and tell me that you love me."

Holding her breath, Jacki waited to hear Kalugal back out gracefully. He would probably do a better job than other guys who'd just told her to have a nice life and left. And those were the polite ones. Those who hadn't believed her, thinking that she'd used marriage as a way to reject them, had been much worse.

"I will never lie to you, Jacki. I might keep things from you, things I can't reveal before I have your love and loyalty, but I promise never to deceive you."

He seemed sincere.

Was he just an incredible actor, or had he meant everything he'd said?

There was only one way to find out. Her previous marriage proposal had been intended as a jibe, but if she could convince Kalugal that she was serious, he might realize how much he was hurting her by playing games with her feelings, and if he had a heart, he would stop.

"It seems that we are not that different after all. You can't tell me your secrets before you are sure of my love and loyalty, and I can't be intimate with you before I'm sure of your love and devotion. Perhaps marriage is not such a crazy idea. It might be the best solution for both of us."

Kalugal

Marriage could be a solution. A human ceremony that would mean nothing to Kalugal.

They could get a license and be married three days later. If things didn't work out, and Jacki didn't transition, they could get a divorce.

Naturally, he would have her sign a prenup so she wouldn't walk away with half of his fortune, but he would take care of her. The agreement would provide Jacki with enough money to live comfortably for the rest of her natural life, but it would be a reasonable amount. A couple of million should suffice.

The only downside he could foresee was the emotional impact a divorce would have on Jacki, and probably on him as well.

Despite his best efforts to keep an emotional detachment, he was getting used to her company, and losing it would have a significant impact on him. But that would have happened with or without a marriage ceremony, so why not humor Jacki and give her what she wanted?

Should he go down on one knee and propose?

Given that she was sitting on his lap, it would be difficult to do.

Besides, if he was going to do it properly, he needed a ring. Or maybe not? Damn, he should have paid better attention to human customs.

Perhaps it was better to wait until he had everything ready. Also, he should at least pretend that he'd given it some thought. If he popped the question right now, Jacki might not take him seriously.

"I didn't think for a moment that marrying you was a crazy idea. In fact, I was excited about your proposal. But I know that you weren't serious. Besides, you seem to value old-fashioned traditions, and I want to propose to you properly."

Jacki arched a brow. "Are you serious?"

"Very. But since this is all very sudden, I suggest that both of us sleep on it."

Jacki narrowed her eyes. "Not in the same bed."

"Of course not." He stifled a chuckle. "You must have encountered very persistent suitors to be so cautious. Or is it still about my pretend attack on you?"

He'd thought that Jacki had forgiven him, but maybe some residual resentment lingered, and that was why she didn't trust him.

Jacki might think that he was tricking her once again, which in a way he was. Their marriage would be real, but it would be short-lived if Jacki didn't transition, a fact that he was still keeping from her.

"It didn't feel fake when you forced a kiss on me, or when you pushed me down on the couch and got on top of me."

"I know, and I'm sorry. But I explained why it was necessary."

She waved a hand. "I get it, and I even understand that you had no other way of proving that Jin's tethers to you and me were gone, but it wasn't a pleasant experience."

He smiled. "It was for a little bit. You were excited when I started kissing you."

Jacki blushed and looked away. "I'm attracted to you. There, I admitted it. And I was semi-okay with a kiss. But when you pushed me down, I got scared."

He arched a brow. "Only semi-okay?"

"Fine. I liked the kiss. But I knew that there could be nothing between us, which, by the way, hasn't changed. There is nothing really for us to sleep on. We can't get married."

"Because of my immortality?"

She nodded. "Even if you eventually fall in love with me, I only have two or three decades until I get too old to still be attractive to you."

"First of all, I'm already half in love with you. You have your reasons for holding back, and I have mine. But just so you know, I like everything about you. I love spending time with you, and when I don't see you for more than a couple of hours, I miss you." He rubbed his chest. "An ache starts right here, and the only way to alleviate it is to go to you."

"Oh, Kalugal." Her eyes softening, she lifted her hand to his cheek. "That's so sweet, and I feel the same. But all it means is that we are setting ourselves up for a major heartache. There is no solution to the disparity in our lifespans."

"I'll take whatever time I can have with you. Let's enjoy each other one day at a time while it lasts."

It wasn't a lie, but it wasn't the whole truth either. If Jacki didn't transition, he would have to let her go to prevent precisely the heartache she was talking about.

The longer they stayed together, the more difficult the separation would be.

In fact, he was already in trouble.

Since Jacki had moved into his old office, the first thought that entered his mind upon waking up each morning was that she was right there, and it made him happier and more excited to start his day than anything in recent or distant memory.

Waking up with Jacki in his bed would be a hundred times better and losing that would be a thousand times worse.

She shifted and leaned her head against his shoulder. "I asked Jin how she's dealing with Arwel being an immortal, and she said the same thing. Her motto is live for today and don't think about yesterday or tomorrow."

"Smart advice."

Jacki shrugged. "For some. I'm not like Jin."

"In what way?"

She chuckled. "It took her no time at all to get intimate with Arwel. She saw something she liked, and she took it. Case closed. She wasn't thinking about forever, or about love and devotion."

"Good for her."

"I bet you wish that I was more like Jin."

It was a trick question, and despite his limited relationship experience, even he knew not to fall for it.

"I don't want to change anything about you. You are perfect the way you are."

Except for her mortality, the statement was true.

"Are you referring to my looks or to my personality?"

"Everything."

He liked that Jacki was reserved, and that she didn't flirt with every eligible male, and he also liked that she was honest about her feelings. He loved that she was brave, loyal, and devoted to her friends, and he loved her curiosity and her eagerness to learn.

"Are you saying that I'm perfect?" she asked mockingly.

"Absolutely."

"No way. There must be something that I'm missing."

Smirking, he looked at her bare earlobe. "Diamond earrings. You are definitely missing those." He lifted her hand and examined her fingers. "A diamond engagement ring and a professional manicure. You're missing those as well."

Simmons

"Jin and Jacki's signals disappeared again." Elijah walked into the Director's office.

With his sparse hair sticking out in odd directions and his dress shirt unbuttoned at the neck, the esteemed Doctor Roberts looked frazzled. Had he fallen asleep on his office couch again?

"I know." Simmons lifted a finger, signaling for his friend to remain quiet until he activated the loud fan that functioned as a noise machine to keep their conversation private.

His office was clear of surveillance, he had enough clout for that, but the adjoining offices were not, and the walls had ears.

With that done, he sat across from Roberts and braced his elbows on his knees. "They must have returned to the underground facility they've been hiding in."

The signal from the trackers was weak, and it came and went. Nine days ago, Jacki and Jin had started broadcasting, then Jacki's signal winked out for a couple of days before coming back up. Wendy and Richard had started broadcasting only about a week ago, and after Wendy's phone call, they had stopped again.

Simmons figured that Richard and Wendy had been hiding in an underground facility for some reason. Then they had been taken to a cabin in Big Bear, and after Wendy's call, they had been returned to the underground.

But Jacki and Jin hadn't been with them. Last night, Jin's signal had disappeared, and this morning Jacki's had as well. But unlike Wendy and Richard's, their signals had snuffed out of existence abruptly without them changing locations first, which was more troublesome.

There was no way for their hosts, or rather captors as he suspected, to locate the trackers and remove them, so that left only two other possibilities.

The first and more probable cause was interference, but then why had it been absent before?

Also, it was not likely to happen in two separate locations only several hours apart.

Jacki's signal had been coming from an affluent town in the Bay Area, and Jin's had been transmitting from somewhere in the Malibu mountains, but his operative had reported that there was nothing there. Jin must have been camping in the outdoors, but the operative had been too lazy to go searching on foot, saying that the area was too large and too inaccessible for one man to cover.

The other possibility was death. The nanos needed a live host to form the grid and broadcast. But that didn't make sense. Why help the group escape and then get rid of them?

Except, it might have been done in retaliation for Wendy's call. Their captors might have concluded that the trainees were not worth the risk of keeping. Which, with the exception of Jin, was true. Her talent was priceless.

"They could be dead," Roberts echoed his thoughts. "Perhaps the people who helped them escape realized that they'd let a Trojan horse into their community, and they decided to destroy it before it did that to them."

"I doubt it. Jin is too valuable. They might have gotten rid of the other three, but not her."

She was the only one he actually wanted to get back. The others had interesting talents, but they were all pretty useless. Wendy's empathic ability had limited applications, Richard's object telepathy was weak, and Jacki's visions were unpredictable and of little importance. The girl was a knockout, but she was either a lesbian or asexual, so she was of no use to him as a plaything either.

The three were good for only one thing, and that was combining their genetic material to produce more talented offspring.

"I need to make the damn trackers transmit a stronger signal." Roberts smoothed a hand over his sparse hair, trying to force it to behave. "When we send the trainees on missions overseas, they will be useless."

"Can you do that and still keep the trackers undetectable?"

Elijah shook his head. "That's the problem. But science is advancing at breakneck speed, and miniaturization is at the forefront of that. In a year, I might be able to do that."

"That's too far off. Our current group of trainees will be ready for deployment beforehand, and we might need to send some of the graduates overseas." Simmons crossed his arms over his chest. "What about the miniature drones that you've been working on? The drones would follow the weak signal closely, and they could broadcast a much stronger one that we can pick up from anywhere."

"The problem with the small ones is their limited flight range. I'm trying to work out a solution where they attach themselves to moving vehicles, but that's not going to work with aircraft."

Simmons nodded. "We would have to send another operative with each of them to handle the drone and monitor them closely."

Roberts snorted. "As if that's going to prevent them from running away."

Simmons leaned back in his chair. "Our four escapees are a special case that I don't expect to encounter again in the future. To run, they must have had the help of someone with the ability to remove Marisol's compulsion. Not only is it an incredibly rare talent, but to bring him or her along on the mission, their abductors also had to know about the compulsion beforehand."

"The organization captured Marisol. That's how they knew about it."

"That's not going to happen again. After the incident, Marisol agreed to report in every couple of hours and to be implanted with a proper tracker. If she gets abducted again, we will know about it much sooner and retrieve her before she reveals what she knows."

"My trackers are proper. They are just not strong enough." Roberts crossed his arms over his chest. "I wish we could compel our recruiter to keep her mouth shut about the program the way she compels the trainees."

"That would be great, but unfortunately, we don't have another compeller. Besides, Marisol is probably immune to compulsion like she is to every other kind of mind manipulation."

Roberts grimaced. "I really don't like that woman. But that's neither here nor there. Now that we've lost their signals, what are we going to do about our missing trainees?"

"I think they moved all four into an underground facility, where they are probably incarcerated. Except, Jacki and Jin's signal just stopped without first moving to another location, and since one was in the Bay Area and the other in Malibu, I have to assume that the organization has several underground facilities. When they move them again, the trackers will resume broadcasting."

"And if they don't?"

"We only have Jacki's precise location, but my guy reported that the place was an impenetrable fortress with security cameras all over the place. He later changed his report saying that the first address he'd given me was the wrong one, but I suspect that he's been compromised, and that someone either paid him to lie or got into his head. In any case, we could check out both addresses."

"How are you going to pull that off? It's not like we have a massive backup."

Simmons chuckled. "I came up with a good cover story. While collecting information on paranormally talented people, we stumbled upon a suspected terrorist organization that plans to use paranormal abilities to sabotage our government. I'll just forward it to Homeland Security and let them take care of the problem for us."

"I like it. But then what?"

"Then I'll offer to use those damn paranormally talented terrorists in our program. Naturally, they will enjoy none of the privileges our regular trainees do because they are dangerous, and we have to keep them locked up. We can't send them out on missions, but we can use them as test subjects."

Roberts smirked. "In our breeding experiment."

"Bingo."

Vlad

As Vlad drove into the parking garage of the building across the street from the keep, he had the urge to turn around and go home.

He wasn't ready to face Wendy. What was he supposed to say to her? How should he act around her?

Why the hell had he agreed to spend an entire week with her in the remote mountain cabin?

Because he still had feelings for the traitor. That's why. And because he was a fool.

Except, it was too late to chicken out.

So instead of turning around, he navigated the narrow lane spiraling down through the building's many parking levels until he reached the lowest one, which was reserved for the clan.

Bowen and Richard were meeting him there, and he was going to hitch a ride with them to the cabin. That way, he wouldn't have to see Wendy before or during the drive.

Perhaps inspiration would come on the way.

Vanessa should have given him some pointers, but apparently therapists were only good at talking the big talk but useless at giving actionable advice.

"Be patient," she'd said. "Don't keep your anger bottled up inside you," she'd advised. "Be a good listener."

How was he supposed to be patient and at the same time not keep the lid on his anger? It was either one or the other. And what did she mean by being patient? Should he say nothing and just listen?

What if Wendy didn't say anything either?

He could have called Bhathian, who was much better at giving useful advice, but Vlad was sick of everyone butting into his personal life.

Besides, he needed to figure things out for himself, and if things got really awkward between him and Wendy he could just spend his days hiking and not come back until nightfall.

The problem with that was his mother, who was joining them on Sunday. In case things didn't work out between her and Richard either, she might need him there as a buffer.

Watching his mother with the guy, or any man for that matter, would be difficult and would add an additional layer of discomfort. If the jerk misbehaved or wasn't taken with her right away, Vlad was going to blow.

There was a limit to how much he could keep boiling inside of him.

He had suggested that they introduce Stella as his sister, but she and Vanessa had come up with a different story to explain his mom's youthful looks. She was thirty-five years old, had Vlad at sixteen, and looked young because she took good care of her skin.

It was a lame story, but it wasn't up to him.

As the door marked storage opened, Bowen came out with Richard in tow, and Vlad popped the trunk. After taking his duffel bag and guitar case out, he walked over to the two.

"Vlad, my man." Richard pulled him into a bro hug. "I'm glad that you're coming with us, but I'm surprised that you're willing to give Wendy another chance. If it were me, I doubt I would be able to forgive her after the stunt she pulled. You are a better man than me."

Bowen nodded in agreement. "Vanessa must have forced your hand."

Ignoring their remarks, Vlad walked over to Bowen's car. "Can you open the trunk?"

The Guardian clicked the remote, the thing opened, and Vlad dropped his things inside.

Once the three of them were seated, Richard turned around and lifted his arm. "I got a shiny new bracelet. Apparently, my friends and I are emitting transmissions. Bridget thinks that we were implanted with miniature trackers that didn't activate until recently. That's why she didn't detect them."

"I didn't know that was even possible." Vlad pushed his hair out of his face. "When and how was it discovered?"

Backing out from the parking spot, Bowen glanced at him. "The security guys noticed a truck making rounds near our community, and Kalugal's men noticed the same thing next to his place. William tested Jin again, and this time she was emitting a signal, so he made cuffs for all of them to disrupt it."

"Why not just remove the trackers?"

"Because Bridget doesn't know where they are in our bodies, and she doesn't want to cut us up." Richard put his arm down and turned to face the front.

Bowen pulled up to the gate and waited for it to retract. "What it means, though, is that Wendy took a risk for nothing. They knew where she and the others were the entire time."

"But she didn't know that." Vlad crossed his arms over his chest. "So, it doesn't lessen her betrayal."

"I'm with you on that," Richard said. "I don't understand why she would do such a thing, though. Maybe they were holding something over her?"

"Perhaps she didn't like being a fugitive," Bowen suggested. "It's not an easy life, and she is just a young girl. Not everyone is brave."

Richard cast the guardian an incredulous look. "Don't tell me that you are softening toward her."

Bowen shrugged. "Following Vanessa's advice, I'm choosing to reserve judgment."

ORDER DARK OVERLORD'S WIFE TODAY!

JOIN THE VIP CLUB
To find out what's included in your free membership, flip to the last page.

The Children of the Gods Series

Reading Order

THE CHILDREN OF THE GODS ORIGINS

1: Goddess's Choice

When gods and immortals still ruled the ancient world, one young goddess risked everything for love.

2: Goddess's Hope

Hungry for power and infatuated with the beautiful Areana, Navuh plots his father's demise. After all, by getting rid of the insane god he would be doing the world a favor. Except, when gods and immortals conspire against each other, humanity pays the price.

But things are not what they seem, and prophecies should not to be trusted...

THE CHILDREN OF THE GODS

Dark Stranger

1: Dark Stranger The Dream

2: Dark Stranger Revealed

3: Dark Stranger Immortal

Dark Enemy

4: Dark Enemy Taken

5: Dark Enemy Captive

6: Dark Enemy Redeemed

Kri & Michael's Story

6.5: My Dark Amazon

Dark Warrior

7: Dark Warrior Mine

8: Dark Warrior's Promise

9: Dark Warrior's Destiny

10: Dark Warrior's Legacy

Dark Guardian

11: Dark Guardian Found

12: Dark Guardian Craved

13: Dark Guardian's Mate

Dark Angel

14: Dark Angel's Obsession

15: Dark Angel's Seduction

16: Dark Angel's Surrender

Dark Operative

17: Dark Operative: A Shadow of Death

18: Dark Operative: A Glimmer of Hope

19: Dark Operative: The Dawn of Love

Dark Survivor

20: Dark Survivor Awakened

21: Dark Survivor Echoes of Love

22: Dark Survivor Reunited

Dark Widow

23: Dark Widow's Secret

24: Dark Widow's Curse

25: Dark Widow's Blessing

Dark Dream

26: Dark Dream's Temptation

27: Dark Dream's Unraveling

28: Dark Dream's Trap

Dark Prince

29: Dark Prince's Enigma

30: Dark Prince's Dilemma

31: Dark Prince's Agenda

Dark Queen

32: Dark Queen's Quest

33: Dark Queen's Knight

34: Dark Queen's Army

Dark Spy

35: Dark Spy Conscripted

36: Dark Spy's Mission

37: Dark Spy's Resolution

Dark Overlord

38: Dark Overlord New Horizon

39: Dark Overlord's Wife

40: Dark Overlord's Clan

As Jacki and Kalugal prepare to celebrate their union, Kian takes every precaution to safeguard his people. Except, Kalugal and his men are not his only potential adversaries, and compulsion is not the only power he should fear.

Dark Choices

41: Dark Choices The Quandary

When Rufsur and Edna meet, the attraction is as unexpected as it is undeniable. Except, she's the clan's judge and councilwoman, and he's Kalugal's second-in-command. Will loyalty and duty to their people keep them apart?

42: Dark Choices Paradigm Shift

Edna and Rufsur are miserable without each other, and their two-week separation seems like an eternity. Long-distance relationships are difficult, but for immortal couples they are impossible. Unless one of them is willing to leave everything behind for the other, things are just going to get worse. Except, the cost of compromise is far greater than giving up their comfortable lives and hard-earned positions. The future of their people is on the line.

43: Dark Choices The Accord

The winds of change blowing over the village demand hard choices. For better or worse, Kian's decisions will alter the trajectory of the clan's future, and he is not ready to take the plunge. But as Edna and Rufsur's plight gains widespread support, his resistance slowly begins to erode.

Dark Secrets

44: Dark Secrets Resurgence

On a sabbatical from his Stanford teaching position, Professor David Levinson finally has time to write the sci-fi novel he's been thinking about for years.

The phenomena of past life memories and near-death experiences are too controversial to include in his formal psychiatric research, while fiction is the perfect outlet for his esoteric ideas.

Hoping that a change of pace will provide the inspiration he needs, David accepts a friend's invitation to an old Scottish castle.

45: Dark Secrets Unveiled

When Professor David Levinson accepts a friend's invitation to an old Scottish castle, what he finds there is more fantastical than his most outlandish theories. The castle is home to a clan of immortals, their leader is a stunning demigoddess, and even more shockingly, it might be precisely where he belongs.

Except, the clan founder is hiding a secret that might cast a dark shadow on David's relationship with her daughter.

Nevertheless, when offered a chance at immortality, he agrees to undergo the dangerous induction process.

Will David survive his transition into immortality? And if he does, will his relationship with Sari survive the unveiling of her mother's secret?

46: Dark Secrets Absolved

Absolution.

David had given and received it.

The few short hours since he'd emerged from the coma had felt incredible. He'd finally been free of the guilt and pain, and for the first time since Jonah's death, he had felt truly happy and optimistic about the future.

He'd survived the transition into immortality, had been accepted into the clan, and was about to marry the best woman on the face of the planet, his true love mate, his salvation, his everything.

What could have possibly gone wrong?

Just about everything.

Dark Haven

47: Dark Haven Illusion

Welcome to Safe Haven, where not everything is what it seems.

On a quest to process personal pain, Anastasia joins the Safe Haven Spiritual Retreat.

Through meditation, self-reflection, and hard work, she hopes to make peace with the voices in her head.

This is where she belongs.

Except, membership comes with a hefty price, doubts are sacrilege, and leaving is not as easy as walking out the front gate.

Is living in utopia worth the sacrifice?

Anastasia believes so until the arrival of a new acolyte changes everything.

Apparently, the gods of old were not a myth, their immortal descendants share the planet with humans, and she might be a carrier of their genes.

48: Dark Haven Unmasked

As Anastasia leaves Safe Haven for a week-long romantic vacation with Leon, she hopes to explore her newly discovered passionate side, their budding relationship, and perhaps also solve the mystery of the voices in her head. What she discovers exceeds her wildest expectations.

In the meantime, Eleanor and Peter hope to solve another mystery. Who is Emmett Haderech, and what is he up to?

49: Dark Haven Found

Anastasia is growing suspicious, and Leon is running out of excuses.

Risking death for a chance at immortality should've been her choice to make. Will she ever forgive him for taking it away from her?

Dark Power

50: Dark Power Untamed

Attending a charity gala as the clan's figurehead, Onegus is ready for the pesky socialites he'll have a hard time keeping away. Instead, he encounters an intriguing beauty who won't give him the time of day.

Bad things happen when Cassandra gets all worked up, and given her fiery temper, the destructive power is difficult to tame. When she meets a gorgeous, cocky billionaire at a charity event, things just might start blowing up again.

51: Dark Power Unleashed

Cassandra's power is unpredictable, uncontrollable, and destructive. If she doesn't learn to harness it, people might get hurt.

Onegus's self-control is legendary. Even his fangs and venom glands obey his commands.

They say that opposites attract, and perhaps it's true, but are they any good for each other?

52: Dark Power Convergence

The threads of fate converge, mysteries unfold, and the clan's future is forever altered in the least expected way.

Dark Memories

53: Dark Memories Submerged

54: Dark Memories Emerge

55: Dark Memories Restored

Dark Hunter

56: Dark Hunter's Query

57: Dark Hunter's Prey

58: Dark Hunter's Boon

Dark God

59: Dark God's Avatar

60: Dark God's Reviviscence

61: Dark God Destinies Converge

Dark Whispers

62: Dark Whispers From The Past

63: Dark Whispers From Afar

64: Dark Whispers From Beyond

Dark Gambit

65: Dark Gambit The Pawn

66: Dark Gambit The Play

67: Dark Gambit Reliance

Dark Alliance

68: Dark Alliance Kindred Souls

69: Dark Alliance Turbulent Waters

70: Dark Alliance Perfect Storm

Dark Healing

71: Dark Healing Blind Justice

72: Dark Healing Blind Trust

73: Dark healing Blind Curve

Dark Encounters

74: Dark Encounters of the Close Kind

75: Dark Encounters of the Unexpected Kind

76: Dark Encounters of the Fated Kind

The Children of the Gods Series Sets

Books 1-3: Dark Stranger trilogy—Includes a bonus short story: **The Fates take a Vacation**

Books 4-6: Dark Enemy Trilogy —Includes a bonus short story—**The Fates' Post-Wedding Celebration**

Books 7-10: Dark Warrior Tetralogy

Books 11-13: Dark Guardian Trilogy

Books 14-16: Dark Angel Trilogy

Books 17-19: Dark Operative Trilogy

Books 20-22: Dark Survivor Trilogy
Books 23-25: Dark Widow Trilogy
Books 26-28: Dark Dream Trilogy
Books 29-31: Dark Prince Trilogy
Books 32-34: Dark Queen Trilogy
Books 35-37: Dark Spy Trilogy
Books 38-40: Dark Overlord Trilogy
Books 41-43: Dark Choices Trilogy
Books 44-46: Dark Secrets Trilogy
Books 47-49: Dark Haven Trilogy
Books 50-52: Dark Power Trilogy
Books 53-55: Dark Memories Trilogy
Books 56-58: Dark Hunter Trilogy
Books 59-61: Dark God Trilogy
Books 62-64: Dark Whispers Trilogy
Books 65-67: Dark Gambit Trilogy
Books 68-70: Dark Alliance Trilogy
Books 71-73: Dark healing Trilogy

MEGA SETS
INCLUDE CHARACTER LISTS

The Children of the Gods: Books 1-6
The Children of the Gods: Books 6.5-10

TRY THE SERIES ON

AUDIBLE

2 FREE audiobooks with your new Audible subscription!

PERFECT MATCH SERIES

Vampire's Consort

When Gabriel's company is ready to start beta testing, he invites his old crush to inspect its medical safety protocol.

Curious about the revolutionary technology of the *Perfect Match Virtual Fantasy-Fulfillment studios*, Brenna agrees.

Neither expects to end up partnering for its first fully immersive test run.

King's Chosen

When Lisa's nutty friends get her a gift certificate to *Perfect Match Virtual Fantasy Studios*, she has no intentions of using it. But since the only way to get a refund is if no partner can be found for her, she makes sure to request a fantasy so girly and over the top that no sane guy will pick it up.

Except, someone does.

> **Warning:** This fantasy contains a hot, domineering crown prince, sweet insta-love, steamy love scenes painted with light shades of gray, a wedding, and a HEA in both the virtual and real worlds.
>
> Intended for mature audience.

Captain's Conquest

Working as a Starbucks barista, Alicia fends off flirting all day long, but none of the guys are as charming and sexy as Gregg. His frequent visits are the highlight of her day, but since he's never asked her out, she assumes he's taken. Besides, between a day job and a budding music career, she has no time to start a new relationship.

That is until Gregg makes her an offer she can't refuse—a gift certificate to the virtual fantasy fulfillment service everyone is talking about. As a huge Star Trek fan, Alicia has a perfect match in mind—the captain of the Starship Enterprise.

The Thief Who Loved Me

When Marian splurges on a Perfect Match Virtual adventure as a world infamous jewel thief, she expects high-wire fun with a hot partner who she will never have to see again in real life.

A virtual encounter seems like the perfect answer to Marcus's string of dating disasters. No strings attached, no drama, and definitely no love. As a die-hard James Bond fan, he chooses as his avatar a dashing MI6 operative, and to complement his adventure, a dangerously seductive partner.

Neither expects to find their forever Perfect Match.

My Merman Prince

The beautiful architect working late on the twelfth floor of my building thinks that I'm just the maintenance guy. She's also under the impression that I'm not interested.

Nothing could be further from the truth.

I want her like I've never wanted a woman before, but I don't play where I work.

I don't need the complications.

When she tells me about living out her mermaid fantasy with a stranger in a Perfect Match virtual adventure, I decide to do everything possible to ensure that the stranger is me.

THE DRAGON KING

To save his beloved kingdom from a devastating war, the Crown Prince of Trieste makes a deal with a witch that costs him half of his humanity and dooms him to an eternity of loneliness.

Now king, he's a fearsome cobalt-winged dragon by day and a short-tempered monarch by night. Not many are brave enough to serve in the palace of the brooding and volatile ruler, but Charlotte ignores the rumors and accepts a scribe position in court.

As the young scribe reawakens Bruce's frozen heart, all that stands in the way of their happiness is the witch's bargain. Outsmarting the evil hag will take cunning and courage, and Charlotte is just the right woman for the job.

My Werewolf Romeo

The father of my star student is a big-shot screenwriter and the patron of the drama department who thinks he can dictate what production I should put on. The principal makes it very clear that I need to cooperate with the opinionated asshat or walk away from my dream job at the exclusive private high school.

It doesn't help matters that the guy is single, hot, charming, creative, and seems to like me despite my thinly-veiled hostility.

When he invites me to a custom-tailored Perfect Match virtual adventure to prove that his screenplay is perfect for my production, I accept, intending to have fun while proving that messing with the classics is a foolish idea.

I don't expect to be wowed by his werewolf adaptation of Red Riding Hood mesh-up with Romeo and Juliet, and I certainly don't expect to fall in love with the virtual fantasy's leading man.

The Channeler's Companion

A treat for fans of *The Wheel of Time*.

When Erika hires Rand to assist in her pediatric clinic, she does so despite his good looks and irresistible charm, not because of them.

He's empathic, adores children, and has the patience of a saint.

He's also all she can think about, but he's off limits.

What's a doctor to do to scratch that irresistible itch without risking workplace complications?

A shared adventure in the Perfect Match Virtual Studios seems like the solution, but instead of letting the algorithm choose a partner for her, Erika can try to influence it to select the one she wants. Awarding Rand a gift certificate to the service will get him into their database, but unless Erika can tip the odds in her favor, getting paired with him is a long shot.

Hopefully, a virtual adventure based on her and Rand's favorite series will do the trick.

Note

Dear reader,

I hope my stories have added a little joy to your day. If you have a moment to add some to mine, you can help spread the word about the Children Of The Gods series by telling your friends and penning a review. Your recommendations are the most powerful way to inspire new readers to explore the series.

Thank you,

Isabell

FOR EXCLUSIVE PEEKS AT UPCOMING RELEASES &
A FREE COMPANION BOOK

Join my *VIP Club* and gain access to the VIP portal at itlucas.com
To Join, go to:
http://eepurl.com/blMTpD

INCLUDED IN YOUR FREE MEMBERSHIP:

YOUR VIP PORTAL

- Read preview chapters of upcoming releases.
- Listen to Goddess's Choice narration by Charles Lawrence
- Exclusive content offered only to my VIPs.

FREE I.T. LUCAS COMPANION INCLUDES:

- Goddess's Choice Part 1
- Perfect Match: Vampire's Consort (A standalone Novella)
- Interview Q & A
- Character Charts

If you're already a subscriber, and you are not getting my emails, your provider is

SENDING THEM TO YOUR JUNK FOLDER, AND YOU ARE MISSING OUT ON **IMPORTANT UPDATES, SIDE CHARACTERS' PORTRAITS, ADDITIONAL CONTENT, AND OTHER GOODIES.** TO FIX THAT, ADD isabell@itlucas.com TO YOUR EMAIL CONTACTS OR YOUR EMAIL VIP LIST.

**Check out the specials at
https://www.itlucas.com/specials**

Printed in Great Britain
by Amazon